"A NOVEL T]
REALISTIC AND HOPEFUL
—*Maine P.*

"Monica Wood's *Secret Language* is beautifully done—*her* language is gorgeous. She's one of the few writers I know who can take a long, serious journey through a dark place and come out—convincingly—on the side of redemption."
—DAWN RAFFEL

"Unforgettable . . . A graceful and insightful literary debut, brimming with emotion and depth. With simple and subtle language, Wood captures the complex relationship between two sisters."
—*The Boston Phoenix*

"Deft and delicate . . . I can think of no more impressive recent debut of a novelistic voice, one that speaks not to our minds, but to our hearts."
—*Ft. Lauderdale Sun-Sentinel*

"Powerful . . . Wood tells the story of Faith and Connie Spaulding with such compelling honesty, this reader was lifted out of her seat and into the hearts of these sisters. I believed it all."
—*Maine in Print*

"The prose is crisp and not a word is wasted. Wood has taken a long, deep look at life in cur time and provided fresh insight into human nature."
—*Maine Sunday Telegram*

"[Wood] has written pitch-perfect dialogue, rendered the sustaining rhythms and tones of family life, and demonstrated with understated wisdom and beautiful language some of the rules that govern the human heart."
—*Casco Bay Weekly*

"Fiercely lyrical . . . [Wood] writes with sensitivity and intuitive insight about relationships coming apart and the walls people erect to keep others out."
—*Publishers Weekly*

Praise for Monica Wood
and *My Only Story*

"Luminous . . . Monica Wood has brilliantly captured the human
need to love, the heart's desire to nurture, and the soul's urge to
sacrifice."
—ANDRE DUBUS III
Author of *House of Sand and Fog*

"[An] accomplished new novel . . . Wood's command of voice
holds a reader all the way through to the last page, where . . . she
holds up a mirror and encourages us to recognize ourselves."
—*San Francisco Chronicle*

"A thoroughly captivating book: warm and wise and beautifully
written."
—RICHARD RUSSO
Author of *Straight Man*

"One of the best novels I've read in the past year . . . A slender
book that unfolds as gracefully as the petals of a rose . . . A small
gem to be read, reread, and, yes, treasured."
—*The Roanoke Times*

"Engaging . . . Wood skillfully works the competing threads of
motivation into a tight, surprising knot of a story. . . . Wood's generous vision is uplifting as well as entertaining. . . . Full of the best
human longings."
—*The Maine Times*

"A compelling and unusual tale that combines humor with
tragedy, heartbreak with promise."
—*Booklist*

"Recommended . . . At once bittersweet, funny, and moving."
—*Library Journal*

Also by Monica Wood

My Only Story
Ernie's Ark

SECRET LANGUAGE

a novel

Monica Wood

Ballantine Books • New York

A Ballantine Book
Published by The Ballantine Publishing Group

Copyright © 1993 by Monica Wood
Reader's Guide copyright © 2002 by Monica Wood and The Ballantine Publishing
Group, a division of Random House, Inc.

Originally published by Faber and Faber, Inc., in 1993.

www.randomhouse.com/BRC/

Library of Congress Catalog Card Number 2002090619

ISBN-10: 0-345-44907-X
ISBN-13: 978-0-345-44907-8

Cover design by Min Choi
Cover art based on photos © Hulton/Archive by Getty Images

Manufactured in the United States of America

Ballantine Books Edition

for Anne Wood,
my guardian angel

Acknowledgments

For the time and space to write this book,
I am happily indebted to the staff and crew at
the Virginia Center for the Creative Arts, and
especially to my husband, Dan Abbott,
who built me a room of my own.

Contents

SECRET LANGUAGE

I

CONSTANCE

FOR THE LONGEST TIME, Connie thinks the house in Connecticut is two houses. The one they used to live in with Grammy Spaulding had a pretty yard with giant white flowers growing next to the door, and window boxes with smaller flowers, pink, spilling over the lip. It had a shiny wooden floor in the upstairs bedroom where she and Faith used to skate in their socks. It had places to hide: big closets that smelled like cotton, and an open shape behind the stairs, not the cramped, creepy places of the house they're in now. Connie hasn't seen that other house since Grammy went away, and she longs for it, the snow filling in the windowsills, Grammy's crooked finger tracing their names on the cold pane.

"What happened to that other house?" she asks Faith.

Connie is three. Faith is big; she's five.

"What house?" Faith says. She is sitting on the dull floor, her legs splayed in front of her, reading a book with butterflies on the cover.

"That house where it snowed and had pink flowers."

"We didn't have a house like that. Flowers don't grow in snow."

"Oh," Connie says. She waits a minute. "Where's Grammy?"

Faith looks at her book, hard. "In heaven," she says. "I told you."

Connie knows Faith won't talk to her anymore now that she has mentioned Grammy.

"Grammy took care of us when I was one," Connie says, but Faith won't answer. "I was one years old."

The house is silent and too small. The other house was big.

"Fix my pants?" she asks Faith.

Faith puts down her book with the butterflies. Connie trails her

3

to the bathroom, yanking her rubber pants and wet panties down to her knees, walking bent over her bare feet.

"Did you go number one or number two?" Faith asks, stepping onto the toilet to reach the sink.

"Number one."

Connie lies on the bathroom floor—her ruined pants next to her in a shameful heap—and watches Faith wet a washcloth. Faith's hair has a snag in the back, but the rest of it is combed just right. Faith knows how to do everything. She steps off the toilet, one hand on the sink for balance. "Go like this," she says, wiping Connie's bottom. Connie does, then Faith wipes her again and dries her with a towel.

Connie stays on the floor while Faith gets clean panties. "Can I have powder?" she asks, hoping she doesn't sound too much like a baby. Faith shakes some on. She puts Connie's feet through the legs of the clean panties and pulls them up, then follows with the same pair of rubber pants. "All done," she says, and goes out to find her book.

Connie's rubber pants smell funny but she doesn't care. She follows Faith, remembering that other house, the one Faith says they never lived in. But they did. Connie remembers everything, even the flower smell of Grammy's lap, and the stories Grammy used to read over and over from grown-ups' books, and her songs about animals. Billy says Grammy used to sing like a rusty hinge, but she didn't. Billy and Delle sing all the time in bird voices, tall, mean, beautiful birds. Sometimes they sing their own names—Billy and Delle, Billy and Delle—up and down the scale. Connie wonders if everybody's mother and father sing like that.

"Faith?"

"What."

"Faith?"

Faith tips her head up. "*What.*"

"Look at me."

"I'm looking."

But she isn't really, and her head tips down again into her book. Connie wishes she could read. She stares out the window over the

4

bumpy lawn. That other house had pink flowers, and snow. She knows it did.

CONNIE HAS TROUBLE with time. She always has to stop and think a minute: how old is she now? Is that smell in the air winter coming, or spring? Faith always seems to know, though her life is the same as Connie's: back and forth to theater towns all over. The same dingy food, the same noisy sidewalks, the same cramped suites in the same hotels, too cold or too hot. Nothing moves forward. Sometimes they go to school, sometimes not, though they always have books to read: big packets of books that Armand sends to them in every city. Armand is Billy and Delle's lawyer, the only person they know who likes children.

The hotel they're in now, where they are watching Billy and Delle run lines, is hot. Not because of the weather, which is cold, but because of the steam heat they can't control. This is Cleveland, or Columbus—Connie keeps forgetting. Next comes New York, Broadway, weeks and weeks in the worst hotel of all, the noise of the city battering the windows and walls.

Connie can remember being here in Columbus or Cleveland once before, with a different show, when she was seven, or five. She remembers the lady downstairs who does nothing all day but suck on lollipops and smile politely and check people in. She likes Connie and Faith, brings them sandwiches when Billy and Delle don't, tells them all about her romantic husband. Connie also remembers this sofa, its lurid orange flowers. Today it feels like wet sweaters. Faith is shifting next to her, lifting her sticky legs.

"Charmed," Billy says from the exact center of the room, extending his hand. He is a count who can't remember where he hid some important papers; Delle is the countess. Her amber eyes slide over.

"Enchanted," she says. She rises from a chrome chair she retrieved from the kitchenette. In the play it's a red velvet divan.

Billy filches a pitch pipe from his pocket, blows one note, and they begin to sing. They sing two verses and a chorus, then break to perform a complicated two-step, counting softly as the imaginary orchestra plays. Connie thinks she can hear it. The song picks up again, then fades off the ends of their voices, the harmony lingering.

Connie doesn't clap until Faith does. Billy and Delle bow deeply, showing the hard gleam of their teeth. For an instant Connie is flattered by this extravagance, but she senses their looking beyond, sees their eyes sweep past her and her sister into the imaginary second balcony.

"You balled up that same line, Delle," Billy says. Connie hears the huff of the couch as Faith drops back against it. Billy and Delle are nervous and high-strung because the tour is going badly. They are the same way, only more, when a tour goes well.

"Well, listen to you," Delle says. "You haven't had a new line in three weeks." Connie watches her mother's neck redden, blushing up into her cheekbones. She is beautiful.

"Don't start, Delle."

"How many times can they rewrite this part?" Delle says. "My God, Garrett can pick some losers. What does he care, he gets his cut." She gathers up the script in a messy heap and shakes it at him. "You think the Lunts would take a dog like this? You think Helen Hayes would look once at this thing?"

"So Garrett's a bastard." Billy ticks the edge of Delle's script with his thumb. "Tell me something I don't know."

Delle sighs theatrically, her chest heaving with the effort. "We won't last a week in New York."

Billy smiles the thin smile that means trouble. "Not unless you get top billing, Countess?"

Delle holds up her finger as if it could shoot a bullet. "Don't give me that. Don't you give me that."

Connie is invisible, silent on the sofa, next to her invisible sister. Her parents begin to fire words back and forth. Their voices pick up, their faces pulse blood, the words they use sound whipped and snapped and dirty.

A flutter of paper explodes from Delle's hands, and now they're screaming at each other amidst a tornado of pages. Connie freezes. The speed with which these storms start and stop always shocks her. She thinks her parents might have some secret mechanical parts, so that when they talk of pushing each other's buttons they mean real buttons.

Faith is on the floor, gathering the spilled script one page at a time. Connie slips off the sofa and crouches next to her, imitating her precise movements. At the toe of her mother's white pumps, cold, black, typed lines of dialogue stare up at her, their composure marred by smeared crossouts and writeovers in different colors of ink. She takes the sheets between her hands and taps them against the clammy carpet, listening hard.

Everything goes quiet, except for another burst of steam from the radiators. Delle is at the window, seething, her jaw tilted out toward the street; but her carriage, the subtle turn of her shoulder, shows her to be fully tuned, wholly there. She's wearing a navy blue dress with a boat neck and fitted waist and tapered skirt. Her ears are dotted by white button earrings. Billy goes to her, his stride effortless, as if the horrible air weighed nothing at all. They murmur to each other, then kiss deeply, for an embarrassingly long time. He touches her shoulder near the neck and she lists into his hand, a tableau they're known for on the stage.

Finished, they cross to the sofa, where Connie sits with Faith, the rescued script between them in a stack so even it might have been run through a paper cutter.

"We're going to the Stardust for a bite," Billy says. Connie's cheek is warm where he holds it.

"Can't we come, Billy?" she asks. She is hoping so hard it feels like a little animal in her stomach.

"It's a bar," Delle says. "They don't allow children." She smiles hugely, as if to make up for not inviting them. Her hair is chestnut red, piled up on her head. Her mouth is also red, but deeper, bloodier.

Billy runs a hand over his forehead. "Jesus, I have to get out of this heat. It feels like goddamned Cuba in here."

"We'll be quiet," Connie says. She turns to Faith. "Won't we, Faith?" She can almost hear the turn in Faith's stomach. Faith hates to beg.

Faith moves to the window and sits on the wide, low sill. She isn't going to help.

"Please, Billy," Connie whines. "Please please please pleeease." She contorts her face, tucks her fists up under her chin. Though it never gets her anywhere she does this almost every single time.

7

"Don't whine, Connie, for God's sake," Billy says. "It makes your face look ugly."

Delle slips into the white and navy topper that goes with the dress. She stops in mid-sleeve, frowning. "We've got to get them into a school," she says, as if she's just now thought of it. She looks toward the window. "Remind me tomorrow, Faith."

Connie trails her to the door, still begging, but it's no use.

"Back soon," Billy says. He stops at the mirror to pat his hair close to the sides of his head, then they're gone.

Connie turns to Faith, forgetting that Faith is disgusted with her. "Is my face ugly?" she asks.

"How should I know?" Faith says darkly. She's still looking out the window.

"He always says that."

"Then don't listen."

Connie never understands Faith's directions. How do you not listen? "He never says it to you," she says.

"I don't beg."

Connie moves to the window next to Faith to watch for Billy and Delle on the street below. They're always easy to spot, and there they are, Billy's bright yellow hair appearing like a streetlamp on the sidewalk.

"Do you wish you were that lady downstairs, Faith?" Connie asks. "That lollipop lady?"

"No."

"She's not very pretty."

Faith doesn't answer.

"She has that romantic husband."

Faith doesn't answer.

"Are you going to get married someday, Faith?"

"No."

"Why not?"

Faith sighs. "First you have to find somebody who wants to marry you, that's why not."

"Oh." Connie hadn't thought of that. "Do you think somebody will want to marry me?"

"If you stop asking a million questions about everything."

8

"Are you sure?"

Faith gets up and pulls the drape hard, hiding the grimy city. "Your face isn't ugly," she says.

"He said it was."

Faith points to the mirror next to the door. "Look for yourself."

Connie does. To her surprise her face looks just the way it did the last time she looked in a mirror. It looks a lot like Faith's.

"See?" Faith says.

"See what?"

"How pretty your face is." She has moved to the sofa and picked up a book. "No matter what he says."

Faith is reading now, their conversation is over. Connie wanders around the room, flips the TV on and turns the dial, but nothing good is on. She returns to the window, opens the drape, and looks out at the big, sad city. She'd like to ask Faith how you're supposed to know if somebody is lying, but Faith is done talking, Connie can tell. It's getting dark, and the evening will be long, and Billy and Delle won't come back soon even though they said they would. In the wavy reflection of the window she can see Faith hunched over her book, a world away, solid and focused. She runs her hand over her face, over her nose and mouth, and decides not to believe Billy, to believe Faith instead.

CONNIE'S FIRST DAY at the school in Columbus, or Cleveland, is her fifth, maybe sixth, first day this year. It's way past Christmas and the kids are too far friends to let Connie in, even a little. But the teacher is nice, the nicest one so far.

A girl approaches Connie out of the den of coats in the coatroom. "What's your lucky number?" she asks. She has shiny, pinkish skin and fuzzy hair buckled with a pink barrette. All the other girls have pink barrettes, too, Connie notices. Everyone except her: her head feels big and bald. In every school it's something different. Last time it was shoes with straps; the time before that, cigar-wrapper rings and saying *Oh right*.

"What's your lucky number?" the girl repeats. She waits, her eyes round and judging.

"Eighty-five," Connie says, knowing she's wrong, way wrong, but it's the only number that comes to her.

The girl wrinkles her forehead. "What kind of lucky number is that? Eighty-five? That's not lucky."

"Yes it is," Connie says. "It's the luckiest number there is."

The girl's expression disintegrates like a punctured balloon, and Connie's life takes a little turn. This is her first victory.

"Not only that," she says, "it's the same lucky number as Kathy on 'Father Knows Best.' "

By this time two other girls are watching, their pink barrettes beaming back at the heavy overhead lights. The fuzzy-hair girl's eyes narrow, mean blue slits. She's the leader. "How do you know that?"

Connie gives her hair a shake. "I live in a hotel."

The fuzzy-hair girl withdraws, the others inch nearer.

If Faith were here she would be angry, but Faith is back at the hotel, faking sick on the fold-out couch in the too-hot room, faking a fever so she doesn't have to do another first day. At first Connie was frightened to be coming here alone, but now she's glad. She can say anything she wants. Faith would tell her not to say where they live, not to say anything about Billy and Delle. When other kids ask Faith what her father is, she says a fireman. It's the only lie she ever tells; usually she just won't answer.

At science time the teacher brings a small cage to the front of the room. "Let's see how our friends are today," she says. "Connie, these little creatures belong to our class."

"We're raising them," the fuzzy-hair girl says, as if to say We saw them first.

The teacher places the cage on Connie's desk and lets her peer through the wires. Two taffy-colored hamsters sit at opposite ends of the cage, each peeping out from a fortress of wood chips. Their beady eyes are trained on her and their faces quiver. For some reason they make Connie think of her and Faith.

"Are they girls?" she asks the teacher.

The fuzzy-hair girl laughs, then everybody else.

The teacher smiles. "One's a girl, one's a boy. We're waiting for them to have babies."

10

Mortified by the laughter, Connie doesn't hear much else. She watches the hamsters in their metal cage and thinks of them poised there, forever and ever, banking the wood chips against themselves.

At lunchtime a tall woman comes in to speak to the teacher. Connie knows they're speaking about her, that once again she's in the wrong grade, the wrong group; something is wrong.

The tall woman—the principal—beckons with her long nail. "Come with me, honey," she says, smiling too hard, leading Connie into the hall. A dozen pink barrettes move at the same time.

The hall is tall and dark, the principal tall and dark, the world tall and dark.

The principal bends down. "Is Faith Spaulding your sister, honey?"

Connie shakes her head yes. Whatever the principal says Connie will believe. No matter how bad it is, she will believe it.

"Are you living at the Grandview?"

Connie shakes her head yes, her eyes smarting.

"Do you happen to know where your mom and dad are today, honey?"

Connie shakes her head no.

"Well." She places a hand soft on Connie's shoulder. Connie falls instantly in love with the face that goes with the hand. "Faith had a little accident today and had to go to the hospital, but she's just fine, you don't need to worry one bit." Her voice is low and reassuring. "Would you like me to take you to see her?"

Connie shakes her head yes, her voice nothing but a heap of feathers.

On the way to the hospital Connie continues to shake her head no as the principal asks in her rosy voice, Maybe they went to visit a friend? Maybe you have an uncle or aunt in town? Maybe they went out for lunch somewhere, do you know where they go out for lunch?

The hospital is too bright, too steely, too white. The long, polished corridor is quiet but desperate; it's like the wasps buzzing underneath their nest in the field across from the Connecticut house, a distant, dangerous teeming. With the principal Connie walks down this corridor until they get to a door near a counter where

11

nurses pad back and forth on hard rubber soles. "Wait just a minute, honey," the principal says, and goes over to speak to one of the nurses.

In the corridor is a chair. One chair all by itself, and Connie sits in it. She doesn't care if it is wrong to sit in this chair, this chair is hers now, her lucky chair, she claims it. The wasps sound a little thicker now, and cutting through their dull whine comes a whimper—just one, in the buzzy quiet—that she recognizes as Faith's.

The bed on which Faith lies stretched out, face up, her hands clasped loosely over her stomach, is made of steel, its sheets white, almost fluorescent, almost hard to look at. On a chair by the window lies her coat, the red one, its arms opened up. It's hard to believe a girl once moved in it.

Faith stares at the ceiling. Her eyes are green and heavily flecked, like Connie's, her eyelashes still. Her chin is extravagantly bandaged, starting just under the lip. Connie watches, horrified, convinced she is staring at the face of death. She moves to the bedside so that if her sister is alive she will know someone is there.

The green eyes slide over, the face does not move. The front of Faith's blouse is blood-spattered, dried into puckers.

"Fell in tub," Faith says, barely moving her mouth. At least that's what it sounds like. "Hit faucet bad."

Connie can't talk—her voice seems to have permanently left her. Her own chin begins to tingle; she imagines her wet foot slipping and her hands flying out, then the cold smack of the faucet and the horrid warmth of drawn blood. She knows how ashamed Faith is to be here, to have strangers looking at her.

From the hall outside comes a shriek, and behind it a low and jumpy carping. Connie recognizes these sounds as Billy and Delle, and watches Faith's eyes slide back, fix themselves again on the ceiling.

"Take me to her, take me to my baby!" Delle commands. And Billy: "We demand to see the doctor! Where in bloody hell is the doctor?" They sound like the count and countess: imperious, peevish, and English. Connie knows exactly what they look like: Delle's red mouth drawn tight in judgment, Billy's squared shoulders.

12

Their voices are rising now, drunken and shrill. Why weren't they notified sooner? Bloody hell, their poor, precious girl in the hands of strangers!

"She would have *bloody* bled to death if the chambermaid hadn't found her," says a voice that sounds like an angry nurse's.

When Connie hears them all thundering down the hall, she shrinks from the bedside and grabs the red coat, clutching it so hard her fingernails hurt, repeating *eighty-five eighty-five eighty-five* as fervently as she can. She sinks to the chair and drops her head, crushing Faith's red coat into the bend of her body.

AFTER CONNIE HAS SPENT a lot of days in the classroom with the hamsters—a month, maybe, or a week, she simply can't measure time—the play moves to New York.

It is a cool, starlit, energetic night, the marquee like a dozen tiny moons drizzling light on her head. She feels a little like a princess in her white dress, its lacy frill falling just below her knees. She's dressed exactly like Faith, her hair winched into the same yellow braids. She can still feel the afterbite of Delle's nails as she raked the hair back, complaining.

"Smile, honey," somebody says. They have posed like this in every city in the country, it seems, but New York is different: the light, the air, the nervous click of spike heels on the sidewalk, the timbre of her parents' voices—these things carry the dread and exhilaration of arrival. And something else—Delle's prediction, smuggled in somehow with the joyful tones that rain down like confetti: *The play won't last a week.* They'll have to go back to Connecticut for a while, to a school Connie hates. Sundays Armand will come out from the city to take them to lunch and a long walk, with ice cream at the end; other than that, nothing will move. She and Faith will stare out the windows, or hang around in the weedy yard, while Billy and Delle drink brandy or rum in their musky bedroom, waiting for Garrett to call with another show.

For now, though, everyone is smiling, talking faster than squirrels, their faces clear in the circle of light. The women wear red lipstick, their dresses shimmer with color: red, pink, green, violet. Connie likes pink, but Delle makes them wear white, this way they

13

stand out, they make a fine picture. Billy looks handsome in his tuxedo, Delle beautiful, a fur thrown over her thin sequined dress.

The cameras sound a little like insects, their flashes far too bright. Connie stands perfectly still inside her prickly white dress, thinking of her posture, her mother's hand on her neck, her father's hand cupping her shoulder. "Smile!" someone calls, and again: "Smile!" She does. Behind her she hears the crack of Billy and Delle's smiles, too.

Next to her Faith is a stiff, unyielding presence. She won't smile, not until the last possible minute. Faith hates this, hates having all these people looking at them. Connie feels a stab of guilt, but she can't help liking this, in fact she loves it. Though Billy and Delle's hands on her are no warmer than claws she can make herself feel them as the hands of love. She imagines they do indeed make a fine picture, the four of them all dressed up and standing in front of the poster for Billy and Delle's show. She smiles again. She smiles until her cheeks hurt, pretending it is like this all the time. This is opening night.

II

FAITH

ONE

FAITH HARBORS FEW WISHES. What she wishes today, with unaccustomed passion, is to have a new school to go to. Instead this is Maine, again, the school Long Point High, where everybody knows your business. They know, for example, that Billy Spaulding died drunk in a car crash back in July, about four hours after the Long Point Summer Theater had closed its doors for the night. She can feel the sidelong stares of the other kids in the cafeteria, warm and thin and musing.

With her lunch tray balanced in one hand, she drags a chair to the reject table and sits with a couple of pock-faced boys from the marching band and a new girl, Marjory. They let her eat in merciful silence, the thrum of voices from surrounding tables a halo of space between her and the virulent world.

Faith doesn't have to sit at the reject table; she's pretty, for one thing, and she's in College Prep. But the College Prep table comes with questions. In Long Point Billy and Delle are—were—celebrities; the kids grill her every chance they get, about actors and acting and Broadway and backstage, as if she should know a thing about it. Now that Billy's dead it's even worse. Sometimes she thinks everyone on earth was put there to ask questions she doesn't know the answers to.

The new girl, Marjory, looks up from her shepherd's pie. "Yucky food," she says, lifting her roll, wet with string bean juice, as if to prove it.

Faith nods, smiling faintly. She's already given up on this meal. Usually she can catch the food in time, keeping the portions inside

17

the tray dividers, but today the cafeteria lady slopped the food every which way; pale juices are draining into all the wrong pockets.

"In Missouri it's just as bad," Marjory says. "That's where I'm from."

Faith steals a look at Marjory's books; for some reason all the General Course books are brown. Marjory's notebooks are pink, though, with *Marjory loves Kevin* scrawled over the covers in a bold, happy hand.

Faith is an A student, a fact that her guidance counselor says is a shock considering her scholastic history. The words *scholastic history* sound like a disease. Connie's in Commercial Course, passing her classes by just enough to keep the school from calling Delle in to discuss things.

"Are you from here?" Marjory asks.

"Yes," Faith says, because it's easier. She remembers living in Missouri once for a couple of months, on the tour for *Count Your Change*, and again, though not as long, during *Mister Mistake*.

"I saw you walking to school this morning," Marjory says. "Was that your sister?"

Faith nods. At the far end of the cafeteria, under a bank of windows, Connie is sitting at the burnouts' table with a bunch of boys, her face animated with some fib she's telling, probably the one about sitting on Marlon Brando's lap when she was five, or meeting James Dean. Her hair is long, parted straight down the middle. It's naturally blonde but she dyes it blonder. At night she rolls it up with empty orange juice cans. She has to keep waving it out of her eyes in a way boys like; they show off for her, punching each other on the arm and laughing loud enough to get the eye from the assistant principal. Faith can hardly remember the time when Connie used to follow her around at new schools, afraid of peeing her pants. Her makeup—blue eye shadow and blue eyeliner and blue mascara that Faith can see all the way across the room—makes her look older than she is. She's a freshman, only one grade behind Faith. Faith is sixteen, almost a year older than everybody else in her class because Billy and Delle put her in the wrong grade once in Connecticut. She will be nineteen years old when she graduates from high school, a humiliation she feels in advance.

"Maybe we could walk home together," Marjory says.

Faith doesn't say no, and finds Marjory waiting for her in the lobby at the end of the day. They walk down the long hill from the high school, Marjory chitchatting happily, not seeming to mind that Faith doesn't say much. At the ball field, where the road divides, they stop.

"Which way do you go?" Marjory asks.

Faith points the way, ashamed. This road divides the town in more ways than one.

"I go the other way," Marjory says, reaching below the plaid hem of her jumper to yank up her tights. In Long Point this year white tights are out, but Marjory has no way of knowing. "Why don't you come to my house for a while?"

"I don't think so," Faith says. If she goes to Marjory's house then wouldn't Marjory expect to see the trailer sometime?

"My mother makes something sweet every day," Marjory says. "Today's blond brownies."

Marjory must be lying. "I've got to get home," Faith says. "But thanks."

At the end of the gravel drive that leads up to the trailer, the mailbox glints on top of a splintery post. The flag is still up, the mail and newspaper sticking out the end of the box. Faith sinks at the shoulders; this is not a good sign.

Connie is already there, sitting on the bottom step, waiting. Behind her the dingy trailer hunkers like some sleepy monster: the frosted, slatted windows, designed for a hotter climate, look like half-closed eyes. It's only September but already the yard has gone yellow, the result of a killing frost come early. A few marigolds linger along the edge of the step. Faith scans the trailer, the crooked trees, the last of the flowers she and Connie planted. The plastic ducks they found once at a rummage sale are set into a family unit on the grass.

"She's on the floor," Connie says. "She's been writing to Garrett."

Garrett quit being Billy and Delle's agent years ago, when they got fired from *Silver Moon*, but now that Delle's a widow she thinks he owes her something. She's blown up too many bridges, Garrett

19

says; he couldn't get her a job canning tuna. Every once in a while Delle writes him pages and pages of illegible rage.

Connie moves over enough to let Faith sit down.

"I picked up the mail," Faith says. "Didn't you see it?"

"It's never for me."

They wait for a few minutes, looking out at the soon-to-be-forsaken yard. The air snaps of winter; already dusk falls too early.

"There's a letter from Armand," Faith says. Armand's letters, which come once a week, include a check for each of them. He says it's money from Billy's life insurance, but they don't believe it, and neither one of them has ever told Delle. Delle thinks they buy their clothes from the piddly allowance she gives them.

"Why did you sit with the rejects today?" Connie says. "It's embarrassing."

"They're not rejects."

"Says you."

"That new girl is nice."

Connie smirks in a way that infuriates Faith. "If you like white tights."

"She can't help it if she's from Missouri. Nobody asked her opinion to move here."

Faith opens Armand's note and hands Connie her check. She reads the note, which is handwritten on the stiff, beige stationery of his New York law office. It reads like most of his notes—did they need anything, how's their mother, how's school. She gives that over as well.

"I've heard some things about that guy you've been sitting with," she says to Connie.

"Who?"

"That guy."

"Danny?"

"You know which one."

This is a lot of talking, for them.

"Don't believe everything you hear," Connie says.

Faith shrugs. "It's your life."

They sit a while longer. Finally Connie lets go the sigh of an old woman. "Should we go in?"

20

They go in. Faith hates this trailer more than any place she has ever lived. The Connecticut house seems blurry and far away, a place she might have seen from the window of a bus. When Billy and Delle left *Silver Moon*, banished to summer stock in Maine, they all lived in a candy-striped motel just outside of Long Point, the first time Faith and Connie had their own room to share on the road. Even with Connie in the next bed, Faith felt a blessed sense of privacy, for when Billy and Delle fought or ran lines, their voices were no more than an urgent hum on the other side of the wall. They stayed there for three years. In summer Billy and Delle delighted tourists with their faultless harmonies, their genteel dancing, their gift for comic timing. In winter they retreated to the Connecticut house for days or sometimes weeks at a time, vainly looking for a director still willing to work with them. For Faith, left behind with her sister in the striped motel, Maine became a steady landscape, something like a home. After Billy died, Delle sold the Connecticut house and bought this place—on purpose, she says, a message to all the flapjaws in town who thought Billy might have left her well provided for.

"You take her feet," Faith says.

Delle is lying on her side in front of the couch. It looks as if she's been chewing tobacco, but the dribble of brown is coffee brandy. A few petals of notepaper drift around her, scarred by outraged indentations from a pen that skips. Her clothes, a sweatshirt and a pair of stretch pants, are streaked with coffee-colored stains. She's thin but puffy-looking, her hair mashed against one cheek.

"Up," Faith says, prying her mother's shoulders from the floor. Delle is mumbling something, her voice dark and petulant.

"Bastard ruined us," she says, her words slurry and wet.

Faith meets Connie's eyes, the same as her own, glazed from knowing exactly what's coming.

"Bastard bastard," Delle says. " 'Work ethic' my ass, we *made* that show." Now she's laughing, an eerie, disconnected cackle. "Didn't last long without us, now did it?" Her eyes roll, the amber irises set into an unhealthy yellow gleam.

Faith looks away.

21

"Two years we did that show. Hah! Eight days they lasted without us. Eight pissy little days."

Her fists threaded through her mother's armpits and clamped together over her chest, Faith bends her knees and lifts. She waits until Connie hefts Delle's feet, then begins to back down the hall. Once or twice she has to pause as Connie, her blue makeup clinging to her face like an illness, struggles with her part of their mother's trifling weight. Faith is stronger than her sister, has always been. To her, Delle is no heavier than a sack of dry laundry.

They bring Delle into her bedroom and lower her to the bed. Faith pulls a clean nightgown from the laundry basket while Connie swabs Delle's face with a washcloth. "Oww," Delle mutters as Faith works the stained sweatshirt over her head. Delle starts to whimper —small, self-pitying whinnies. Faith ignores her, as she always does, flashing Connie a look of complicity. Then Delle gets serious. Her cries become gummy and harsh, thick with phlegm; they permeate the fetid air of this bedroom, until Faith can hardly breathe. "Stop it, Delle," she hears Connie say. "It doesn't do any good."

Delle stops. Faith pulls off her mother's shoes, socks, pants. A soft bruise wells on Delle's hip where she has fallen. Her belly is veiny and a little swollen, though her legs, taut from years of dancing, would still be pretty if she shaved them. Her hands are dry, with starry cracks over the knuckles. It no longer embarrasses Faith to see her mother's body. She regards it shamelessly, reminding herself to never look this way. Her mother is no longer beautiful.

"Get the bucket," Faith tells Connie, but Connie has it already and places it next to the bed.

Faith shimmies the nightgown down over her mother's head and shoulders, guides her arms through the sleeves, reaches underneath her to shake it down under her bottom. She snaps on a lamp so Delle won't scream when she wakes. As she adjusts the lampshade away from Delle's eyes, the light shivers onto the framed photograph of Billy and Delle in *Silver Moon*.

Faith closes the door and follows Connie into the trailer's tiny kitchenette. They eat at the same time every day. They get up at the same time, too, even on weekends. No matter what Delle is doing, these rituals do not change. It's something they've never discussed, just one of their silent pacts, like not telling Delle about the checks from Armand.

Connie rummages in the cupboard and extracts a box of macaroni. "You want this?" she says.

"Okay." Faith runs some water in a pot and sets it on the stove.

"I'll be out tonight," Connie says. Her hair looks greenish under the kitchen light from whatever she's been putting in it.

"You don't have to lighten your hair," Faith says. "You're blonde enough."

Connie shrugs. "You can't be blonde enough."

Faith watches the pot boil. Connie used to be nothing but questions, and now she is nothing but answers. "Are you going out alone?"

"Nope."

"With Danny?"

"Uh-huh."

"Will you ask him to pick you up at the road?"

Connie looks up.

Faith's eyes slide toward Delle's room. "The motorcycle might wake her up."

Connie goes to the phone while Faith drops half a box of macaroni into the pot. The water settles down, then foams up. She hears Connie murmur a few words into the phone, then hang up and open the fridge.

"You want Pepsi or 7-Up?" Connie says.

"I don't care."

"Danny's not coming." Connie gets two glasses down from the cupboard and pours two 7-Ups.

"Why not?"

"I'd rather stay in, that's all."

"You don't have to."

Connie sits at the table and shakes her hair, green light zigzagging through it. "I'm sick of him anyway."

"Why?" Faith really wants to know. She's only gone out with one boy: Thomas, from her English class. But not for long; his way of not being shy was to ask a million questions.

23

Connie sighs. "Danny's just like every other guy I know. Stupid and pushy." She stops to help Faith pour the macaroni into a colander. "Besides, I think he's getting sick of me, too, if you want the truth. Rule number one: Dump them before they dump you."

It shames Faith to be getting this kind of advice from her younger sister, but she listens to every word, not knowing the first thing about boys. Or anything else, if you got right down to it. So she listens, seizing the opportunity. Usually they eat in silence, Connie twisting the ends of her hair, Faith reading a book.

"That new girl Marjory has a boyfriend back in Missouri," Faith says. "He sends her a card every day."

"It's easy to be in love if you don't have to talk to each other," Connie says, mashing the macaroni with butter in a way that makes Faith sick.

"She says her bedroom is pink. Pink carpet, pink everything. She has a bunch of posters of the Beatles, especially Paul."

"John's the best one," Connie says. "He's the talent."

"She says her mother bakes her a sweet every day."

Connie pauses, a forkful of smashed macaroni caught in midair. "She's lying."

Faith nods. "That's what I thought."

"She probably just wishes that."

"Probably."

A deep moan floats down the hall. Faith puts down her fork. "Delle's awake."

Connie stares straight ahead as if she hasn't heard. She gets up and puts her half-eaten meal in the sink. Faith does the same, then follows Connie out the door into the chill of the early evening. They sit on the ground, their knees drawn up, looking out at the marigolds, the lawn ducks, the grass.

"The flowers are still pretty," Faith says.

"They are."

From inside the trailer comes the muffled thump of Delle falling out of bed and scrambling to get up. Faith hugs herself against the chilly air, waiting for the first star of the evening.

TWO

When Faith meets Joseph Fuller Junior, she is out of high school, a working girl, and for the first time her life feels like a real life. Even the trailer seems like a place where real people live: she and Connie have painted the walls the whitest white they could find, and replaced the mishmash that hung there—black-and-whites of Billy and Delle in their plays—with peaceful dime-store paintings of rivers and streams. Tabletops no longer suffocate under magazines and popcorn bags and sticky bottles, dishes no longer fester in the sink. After Delle died, they packed her things into her room and shut the door.

Armand paid off the mortgage on the trailer, and still pays the monthly bills: the heat, the lights, the telephone; he also pays for Faith to take a medical secretary course at night, in Portland, and will pay for Connie to go away to become a stewardess, which she swears to do the second the Long Point High School diploma crosses her palm. First she must repeat her senior year.

Faith isn't sure where all this money is coming from. Armand says Delle saved more than he thought. Faith draws some comfort from this knowledge, as if her mother—who in the space of two years dried up on the couch like a vegetable peeling—is more fluid in death, has learned, under the pale, rangy grass of her grave, how to give a gift.

The first thing she notices about Joseph Fuller Junior is his eyes, a blue so dark they seem another color altogether. Except for his eyes, and black, black hair, he is colorless, his face drained of blood.

25

He has mononucleosis, and is here to see Dr. Howe. Even sick he's good-looking.

"Ooh," says Dr. Howe's nurse, Marion, just under her breath. "Go for it." A few years older than Faith, and married, Marion always has plenty to say.

As usual, Faith has no idea what she means. How do you go for it? Not the way Connie does, going out to drive-ins with guitar players or guys just back from Vietnam. Faith doesn't like any of the things Connie does, they have less to say to each other than ever, and yet they live contented in the trailer, cleaning it before it gets dirty, taking the lawn ducks in at night so they won't get ruined. They are inseparable, and separate, like parallel lines, defined by the distance between them. Still, the thought of a year from now, with Connie gone, chokes Faith a little. She doesn't think she knows how to live without her.

"I've got an appointment," Joseph Fuller says. He leans against the counter as if he were too weak to hold himself up. Faith will later discover this as a habit of his, leaning into people.

"Name?" Faith asks, feeling the flush on her cheeks.

"Joseph Fuller, Junior." He leans clear across the counter on his elbows—his long, shiny hair falling forward over his collar—and taps his name in the appointment book. "Right there. Three-fifteen."

Faith straightens up, hoping to get him to do the same. "New patient?" she asks officiously. Her duties in this office so far are slight and she tries to make the most of them.

"Nah," he says. "There must be a file on me somewhere. My family's been coming here for a thousand years."

"Oh?" Faith looks down at the appointment book as if checking for something, but in fact her mind is backtracking through the day, all the way to this morning when she pulled the files. There is no file for Joseph Fuller Junior, she is sure. Dr. Howe is kind to her and she hates to do things wrong.

"One moment, please," Faith says, then turns on her heel and steps into the file closet, trying to appear brisk. She thumbs once again through the F's: Fuller, Joseph, Sr.; Fuller, Phoebe; Fuller, Gregory; Fuller, Brian; Fuller, William; Fuller, Peter (deceased).

After another inch or so of Fuller files—wives and children—there it is: Fuller, Joseph, Jr. It's so thin she missed it. She plucks it from the stack and opens it. Normal childhood diseases, inoculations, and a broken ankle playing basketball when he was ten. Last visit, age fifteen.

"You'll have to fill out one of these," she tells him when she gets back to the front desk. He's still leaning. She snaps a history form to a clipboard and hands him a pen. "Dr. Howe requires new information if it's been over six years."

He grins at her. "It's only been seven."

"It's required."

Instead of sitting down, he dawdles at the counter, then stays to fill out the sheet. He is lean but very big and takes up a lot of space. Faith stands there, not quite knowing how to ask him to move, keenly aware of Marion's amused eyes on her.

"You might be more comfortable sitting down," Faith suggests.

He hunches over the sheet, and his shiny hair moves. Faith gets a whiff of some new herbal shampoo, the same one Connie's been using. His hands are large, nicked, black under the nails—a boy who does real work.

"You live around here?" he asks, not looking up from the sheet, which he completes at a maddeningly slow pace.

"Long Point," she says. She wishes the phone would ring. She's very good on the phone.

"What's that, a twenty-minute drive?"

"Fifteen."

"Close enough." He smiles grandly and finally sits down.

HE COMES IN once a week after that for a spot test, waiting for the go-ahead to get back to work. He looks healthy enough now, Faith thinks, but his parents won't let him work till he's officially cured.

"You know how parents get about stuff like that," he says, leaning.

"Yeah," Faith agrees, though she doesn't know. She has no idea.

"So. Whereabouts on Long Point are you?"

"Just outside town."

"With your folks?"

"My sister. We have a trailer."

"Huh," he says. "I've been looking for an apartment. I love my folks but they're driving me nuts."

Faith tries to smile knowingly. "I bet."

They talk for five or ten minutes each time he comes in. He's been to college; his brother Peter was killed in Vietnam; he works as a machinist in his father's shop with the remaining brothers, all older, married, with three or four kids apiece. Faith tries to envision the whole family, spreading like tree roots; as far as she can gather, Joseph Junior fits in like the right color button sewn on with the wrong color thread. They must all love him very much.

On the day his spot test reads negative he comes out of the examining room smiling. She smiles back, pleased that she knows why he's so happy. He fills up the tiny hall in a way that makes her want to laugh out loud.

"Will you go out with me?" he asks her.

She says yes.

JOE IS THE FIRST BOY Faith has ever gone out with who is not shy, also the first with whom she has a good time. She's fascinated by the way he walks and moves: to Faith, who secretly believes that some of her internal organs are misplaced—some notable but not life-threatening alteration she was born with—Joe moves as if he knows exactly where everything is. She finds him so cheerful and easy to be near that her skewed parts seem to be listing toward their proper places.

He says something to tease her, something about how much ice cream she can put away. She laughs and knocks him on the arm, feeling—happily—like an ordinary girl. She let a boy put his hand under her bra once, at the end of senior year, and once she made out in the back seat of a car. But she has never before knocked a boy on the arm in play.

On the ride back to Long Point he tells her all about his friends, his family. He seems to be surrounded by people who love him. The car is a falling-apart red Corvair with a broken heater, and when it stalls on a hill he has to get out twice to investigate the engine. Faith stays in the front seat, looking out, dusk failing into dark by seconds.

When it's her turn to talk, she tells the truth: her parents were actors, she says, and now they're dead.

"My father died first," she says, watching Joe's profile change with the lights from oncoming cars. "And then a couple of years later, my mother."

"How?" His eyebrows are heavy and dark where he furrows them.

"Um, they both drank quite a bit. My father crashed his car, and my mother overdosed on alcohol."

"You and your sister stayed here by yourselves?"

"Our lawyer wanted us to come to New York to live with him, but we hate New York."

"You have your own lawyer?"

"He's more like a friend, really." A pleasant thought dawns on her. "I guess he's always looked out for us."

For a while neither of them speaks. The road unrolls in front of them, the beam of Joe's headlights flickering over the jagged shadow of pine trees that rises over each hill.

"That must have been weird, being left alone," Joe says finally.

"Not really," she tells him. "We were used to it."

"Huh." His frown returns.

She tells him a little bit about her life.

"You hear stuff like that about actors," he says.

Faith shakes her head. "It has nothing to do with being actors. It was just them." This is a revelation to her, for she herself has blamed the theater from time to time. "My parents were never very, well, mature." The word, *mature*, is meager, a pinprick of a word, compared to all she means it to describe.

He says nothing more, and the stutter of the Corvair's ailing engine fills their silence. She pictures the generations of folders stacked up in Dr. Howe's file closet and imagines what Joe must think of her.

At the mailbox they turn onto the gravel and roll to a stop in front of the trailer door. The living room light is on, and Connie has taken the ducks in.

"Well, thanks," she tells him. "I had a wonderful time."
She is sure she will never see him again.

"I've never met anybody like you," he says, leaning over to kiss her warm on the mouth.

She draws away, watching him. "What do you mean?"

"I mean I like you," he says. "I mean we should go out again."

They do go out again, and again, to Faith's continual surprise. Every time she watches the red Corvair bump over the pitted drive, then turn down the road to Portland, she is sure it's her last sight of Joseph Fuller Junior.

But he always comes back, and before long Faith and Joe are a couple. Sometimes they go out with his friends, who think it's a howl that Joe Fuller picked a quiet girlfriend. They drive their cars around and sing along with the radio and drink beer and philosophize about life, the war, the meaning of music. Faith doesn't say much and doesn't drink any beer. They are all twenty-two, Joe's age, and talk a lot about their futures. Faith is twenty and has never in her life thought about the future except what she doesn't want it to be.

He takes her to his family for Sunday dinner. "Call me Phoebe," his mother says. She is tall and wiry, with magnificent black and silver hair. His father, a shy, large man, smiles at her from the calm of his brown Naugahyde chair. Bald and brown-eyed, Joe Senior looks nothing like Joe, but his height and bulk mark him as his son's father. He rises to enfold her one proffered hand in both of his. He has the biggest hands Faith has ever seen. They are warm, wide, ground smooth with calluses, dyed in places with machine oil. It is not just the breadth of his hands that she finds overwhelming; it is the breadth of his family, all the sons but Joe trailing tentacles of wives and children.

All the brothers are big, too: Will and Greg and Brian, broad and solid, real workers. Their wives are graceful and wise and talkative, all perfect, perfect. There are some babies, and some middle-sized children, and one or two who might even be in high school. Even the house is big, though Phoebe and Joe Senior and Joe are the only ones left. It's filled with well-worn rugs, stray jackets, dense, permanent furniture that makes the furniture in the trailer look like a

30

bunch of sticks. Knickknacks and photographs litter every surface, Fullers smiling wherever she looks. On the mantle is a picture of the lost brother, Peter, not in uniform but in a gray sweatshirt, standing in front of a jeep.

"He let me drive his car once," Joe says. "I was nine. Actually he drove, I just steered, sort of. It hooked me on cars for life."

Faith laughs. They'd had to stop the Corvair on the drive over here. To put in oil, or take some out, or something. She moves closer into the shelter of his arm while the family bustles around them, noisy and intimidating, exactly the type of people who could begin bombarding her with questions at any moment. "He looks like you, Joe."

Joe picks up the photograph. "You think so?" He seems pleased.

"He does. Especially the eyes."

One of the sisters-in-law, Amy, breaks in to take Faith's hand. "You're in Long Point?"

"Yes."

"You live with your sister?"

"Yes." She moves closer to Joe. Sarah, another sister-in-law, joins them.

"Faith lives with her older sister, isn't that sweet?" Amy tells Sarah.

"It's her younger sister," Joe explains.

Will and Brian and Greg have drifted over now, with Maggie, Brian's wife, and two of the smallest children. They're all staring at her, smiling, except for the littlest boy, who looks suspicious.

"Younger?" Amy says, puzzled. "How much younger?"

"She's in high school," Faith says. "A senior." She doesn't add, *for the second time.* She feels suddenly protective not only of herself, but of her sister, too, and thinks of Connie back at the trailer, eating alone. She'd dearly like to be there herself.

"My goodness," Amy says. "Mom, come here. Did you know Faith's been fending for herself?"

Phoebe looks at Faith, then back at Amy. "She has an older sister."

Faith is beginning to get nervous, for she has no way of knowing whether or not this is a normal conversation. Joe seems comfortable

31

enough as his older brothers and their wives explain to Phoebe that Faith is the older one, Faith is the one in charge. They have it all wrong—no one's in charge—but she doesn't dare say a word. She's hoping the conversation will magically stop.

"Do you mean to tell me this child is on her *own?*" Phoebe says to Joe.

Joe gives Faith's shoulder a squeeze. "For years," he says. "She's something."

Her cheeks burning, Faith looks away from the horror on Phoebe's face. She feels like a duck in a sparrow's nest.

"How on earth did I get that wrong?" Phoebe says. Her feathery hands light on Faith's cheeks. "You dear thing," she says. "Welcome to the family."

"Where's your sister now?" Brian asks. He's even bigger than Joe, but quieter.

"Um," Faith stammers, "she's home."

Phoebe looks sternly at Joe. Abashed, he turns to Faith. "We should have invited her."

"You certainly should have," Phoebe says. She raps on the chair where Joe Senior sits, barely visible for the three children moving on his lap. "Are you hearing this, Joe? The thought of that poor child . . . "

Faith agrees to fetch Connie just to get out of the house. Joe starts up the car, which shimmies for a few blocks until it gets warmed up. "They love you," he says. "I knew they would."

They're on the Long Point–Portland road now, the trees flying by, bringing her closer to the quiet of the trailer. "Are they always this friendly?" she asks.

Joe laughs, tapping his knuckles on the dashboard. "This is nothing. This is *shy*. They don't know what to make of you."

Faith leans back, exhausted. When they arrive at the trailer, Connie is just coming out the door, followed by a skinny guy with a braid down his back. His jacket reads PEACE, but he looks anything but peaceful.

"That was quick," Connie says. She's wearing a peasant blouse and a cotton skirt that make her look like a girl in a shampoo commercial. The guy looks evil by comparison.

32

"My mother ordered us to come get you," Joe says.

Connie frowns, not comprehending.

"For dinner," Faith says. "Sunday dinner. They want you to come."

"You're kidding."

"I warn you, they're a noisy bunch," Joe says. "I think Faith was a little taken aback." He looks to her for confirmation and she smiles politely. She still feels short of breath from the Fullers' suffocating welcome.

"Well . . . " Connie says. She glances at her boyfriend, or whatever he is. "Duane and I were going to go out for pizza." But she continues to stand there, folding and unfolding her arms.

"You're welcome to come, too," Joe says to Duane.

Connie is chewing thoughtfully on her lower lip. She seems to be trying to figure out how a sweet guy like Joe Fuller ever turned up on their doorstep. Faith is wondering the same thing.

Duane laughs. "Sunday dinner?" He purses his thin lips and looks at Connie. "I don't do Sunday dinner."

He heads toward his car, a GTO with flames painted on the doors. He's parked it on the grass, the right front tire crushing one row of marigolds. Connie follows him to the car, then stops.

"You coming?" Duane says. Connie doesn't answer. Duane gets in the car. "Later," he says, and backs down the gravel drive.

Connie squints down the drive after him. "He's a jerk anyway," she says. She stoops to right the flowers. Faith helps her.

"Do you really want to come?" she whispers.

"Sure," Connie says. "I'm curious, to tell you the truth." She bears down on the marigolds, her long fingers twined around their stems, pushing them securely into the ground.

Faith imagines returning to the Fullers' enormous house, to Joe's swarming family. It might not be so bad with Connie there to absorb some of the shock. She pushes a marigold toward its roots, her fingers bone-white on the black ground. Next to hers, Connie's fingers work and work. Their fingers are exactly the same, they could belong to the same hand. She remembers how pleased Joe was to resemble his brother.

"We're missing the salad," Joe says from the car.

Faith gets up and swishes her hands together. She moves toward the car, Connie just behind her. Her heart calms a little, even with the thought of more introductions and a new round of questions. She understands that Connie means to help her.

FAITH IS AFRAID of sex, but not of Joe. She's afraid sex will hurt, so afraid that she tells him. He pulls her close and whispers, and they go slow, so slow it feels like dreaming, like the dreams she has had about Joe. It does not hurt; it feels like yellow butterflies scuttling through her body, even her fingers and toes, even her eyelashes. In the dark she is not afraid to hold him tight, wrap her legs all the way around. She is laughing, watching the ceiling, imagining a crowd of angels smiling down.

On the first day after they claim in her narrow bed to be in love, they go to a miniature golf course tucked behind some trees on the Long Point–Portland road. Faith laughs at the hulk of Joe among brightly painted windmills, neat blue pools. They are near real water, the green ocean, but the view is lost on her.

He watches her smallest movements, an audience unto himself, and it makes her feel conspicuous, a little foolish. He cheers when her ball skitters across the water and makes it through a lime-green tunnel; he teases her about the way she bears down on each shot, the mini club snugged into her hands. After she gets a hole in one, he grabs her by the waist and twirls her around: she is dizzy, mortified, the candy-colored landscape veering past her eyes.

When he puts her down her face goes scarlet. An elderly couple beams all over them; another couple, their own age, regard each other knowingly. It reminds her of the way Billy and Delle used to fawn over her and Connie in public, how Connie used to beg to go with them for exactly that reason, how it diminished her to beg.

Joe is standing close to her, waiting for her to laugh. She looks up at him. "I hate that," she says. "I'm sorry." She can see he is stricken. He tells her all the time that he's in love with her and yet she can't bear to believe it. She thinks of him every minute, seeks out his warm physical presence as if she had lived a lifetime underground, but she has no way of knowing that what she feels is love. About love she has no notions.

34

Her hands hang at her sides, defenseless. "I can't help it," she says. "I'm not very spontaneous."

He gets used to her ways. They settle in. Her reserve becomes part of their shape together; he stops taking it personally.

Sunday dinners notwithstanding, they spend most of their time together at the trailer, which Joe says is nice and homey. They sit on the couch in front of a blank TV, listening to music on the stereo. Faith's taste runs to soft guitars, women's voices: Judy Collins, Joni Mitchell, Joan Baez, anything peaceful. Joe likes the Rolling Stones, so they compromise: odd nights are Faith's pick, even nights Joe's. When Connie is there she picks: Bob Dylan mostly; she likes songs with a lot of words. Her lips move, but, like Faith, she doesn't sing. Joe sings them all, loud, unembarrassed by his ordinary voice.

Faith rides to work with Marion as she always has, but it is Joe who picks her up at the end of the day and drives her home. She wonders if this is like being married; her happiness is immense, monster-shaped, terrifying.

Connie is going out less, Faith notices; she might even be doing her homework. She seems to like staying in with Faith and Joe, where they listen to their music or play board games or cards. They don't talk much, and Joe claims to have gotten used to it. One night he teaches them to play poker and they play seven nights running, the three of them gathered at the spindly, ill-lit table of the kitchenette, Connie beating the pants off them all, looking gleeful, like a little girl.

"So this is a quiet evening at home," Joe says, shuffling the cards. "I always wondered."

Faith smiles, believing she might after all have something to give him. A lesson about quiet, the wisdom in hesitation. He begins to read into her silence all kinds of magnificence, taking her every gesture and turning it, while she enters his imaginings willingly, filling herself with borrowed grace.

THREE

"HAVE YOU ASKED Connie to be your maid of honor?" Phoebe asks Faith. Faith blushes. She hasn't even told Connie about the wedding.

Phoebe has done everything, thought of everything. Faith, who has never been to a wedding, follows her around like a feeble dog. Phoebe knows things without being told, and for this Faith is deeply grateful. Joe has enough friends and family to fill three church halls, yet Phoebe suggests a small wedding, right in the Fuller front room. She sits Faith down at the dining room table and asks her things: What are your favorite flowers? What songs? Will our family minister be all right? Who would you like to invite?

Except for Connie and Armand and Marion and Dr. Howe, Faith can't think of anyone. She lost touch with her friend Marjory from high school, who moved back to Missouri. Faith doesn't know how to tell Phoebe—how do you tell someone like Phoebe you have no friends? Phoebe, unblinking, says: "Well, I have an idea. What if your uncle Armand performed the ceremony?"

"He's not my uncle," Faith says, looking down. It feels like a personal failing.

Phoebe shakes her head, the black and silver hair moving. "Close enough. He'll do a heck of a job."

"But he's a lawyer," Faith says, another apology.

Phoebe waves it off. "In Maine the family dog can do a wedding." She smiles, her bright lips parting over her teeth. "Don't worry, you'll really be married."

The thought of Armand, who has known her since she was born,

36

performing her wedding, reminds Faith of greeting cards, camera commercials, the ending of a good movie. She is painfully happy.

Phoebe taps Faith twice on the hand. "Another brainstorm! Since Armand's doing the wedding, why don't we just keep the whole thing inside the family?" She slaps her palms together. "That's just the ticket: family only. Won't that be fun?"

Faith nods, unable to speak. She leaves her hands on the table for Phoebe to touch again.

FOR SIX DAYS Faith has been wondering how to say it, how to ask. Because she tries to find exactly the right time, every moment seems important: passing each other in the skinny hall on the way in or out of the bathroom, pouring cereal into shallow bowls before Faith leaves for work, Connie for school. She's hoping for one of life's indelible moments — lately she is filled with hope — but she doesn't expect to recognize one even if it comes.

"I'm getting married," she murmurs one morning as Connie starts out the door.

Connie turns; her blonde eyebrows go up. "Wow."

"You want to be my maid of honor? Phoebe said she'd buy you a dress."

Connie shifts on her flat red shoes, the frayed hem of her jeans brushing the cotton strap. A month from the end of her second senior year, she looks poised for flight. She glances around the trailer, at the white walls, the clean tabletops, the new scatter rugs.

"Where are you guys going to live?" she asks. Her eyes, made up in the palest green, seem furtive, scared.

"In a house," Faith says. "It's in Portland, and the man says we can rent as long as we want, till we have a down payment." She feels terribly sad, watching Connie's high-boned face, remembering herself as a nineteen-year-old senior.

Connie is half in, half out of the trailer, not moving. "Oh."

"You can live with us if you want. I mean, if you don't go to stewardess school right off." Connie has been working at Long Point Variety all year and hasn't mentioned stewardess school once. "It's a nice house," Faith says. "It has an upstairs."

"Does it have a yard?"

"Yes."

"A fence?"

Faith thinks. "I don't remember."

"How many rooms?"

"More than you can imagine." Faith looks away. "Enough for all of us."

Connie lingers at the door; Faith has no idea what she's thinking. It occurs to her that moving into her first real home with a new husband would be easier if Connie came along. At times Faith is enchanted with the idea of marrying Joe—she dreams of a home with windows thrown open, a big dog asleep on the porch—but at other times she feels like a foundling left on a mountainside to die.

"I suppose we could sell this place," Connie says, looking around.

"Do you want to?"

Connie makes a sound between a cough and a laugh. "Why wouldn't I?"

Faith can't think of any reason, but the idea is troubling. "So, will you?" she says.

"Will I what? Live with you or be the maid of honor?"

Faith shrugs. "Both."

"Okay," Connie says, and is gone from the door.

FAITH STANDS in the archway of the Fuller front room, the family assembled, their eyes on her. Connie stands just ahead of her, dressed in pink silk, her arms held close to her sides. Faith might as well be looking at herself, a column of stone set into the watery motion of Joe's family. The satin of Faith's ivory dress brushes her cold skin all the way down to her ankles. She holds the flowers a few inches from her middle, half expecting them to explode.

The front room burgeons with peonies from Phoebe's garden, grand bursts of white and pink. One of Joe's sisters-in-law is playing something momentous on the family piano, a monstrous thing, resoundingly stolid under the considerable weight of framed photographs of various stages of boys.

Faith looks at nothing but the pink, lacy hem in front of her as Connie leads the way in a graduation-style march to the mantel, where Armand stands, round as a preacher, on the scuffed brick.

Heat bears down on her from all sides but she cannot warm herself. She's gone cold with the fear of love and the knowledge of her unbelonging, so cold she can barely stand, and so she removes herself from this joyful gathering, steps secretly away from them all while her chilled body stays.

She watches Joe slip the ring over her knuckle. She watches herself murmur "I do," all the faces tensing forward because they cannot hear her.

She will remember this moment many, many times. Remembering, she will believe that if she had only been able to warm herself, if she had only stayed inside her body as she pledged forever and true, she might have learned to live with a man like Joe, a man who loved her.

FOUR

WHEN FAITH AND CONNIE come to clean out the trailer, they are accompanied by a flock of Fullers darting in and out like birds: Joe; his brothers, Will and Brian and Greg; the sisters-in-law, Sarah and Maggie and Amy; most of the nephews and the lone niece; Joe Senior; and Phoebe, in a strictly supervisory role. In all, nineteen people, two cars, four trucks. Far too many people, more than the trailer has ever seen. They cheerfully step out of each other's way as they carry out the sofa, the kitchen table, the box of knickknacks, the lawn ducks, the TV, the beds. They talk a lot, a vigorous chittering all around Faith's head.

Without a word, Faith and Connie assign themselves to Delle's room, which is suddenly Billy's room too when they discover his clothes in the closet, bunched at the end of the rod. Faith grabs them in musky hunks and rolls them into the pile of Delle's clothes. She drops the heap into a carton the size of a trash can which Phoebe has marked SALVATION ARMY—DO NOT LOAD. The room, long closed, smells of must, illness, secrets. Faith takes Delle's things from the top of the dresser—a decorative marble box that was given to her by Helen Hayes; the framed glossy from *Silver Moon*; a pillbox of polished stone; a doily made by Grammy Spaulding—and places them on top of the mound of junk in Billy and Delle's traveling trunk, a great gilded thing with a rounded top that looks like something from a pirate ship. Then Will and his oldest boy heft the emptied dresser, moving slow as bears in the narrow hall.

"Do you mind if I take the doily?" Connie says.

Faith looks at the doily, a delicate, lacy square, mottled with white shapes where Delle's things lay untouched for years. "Go ahead." Connie plucks the doily from the trunk, folds it daintily, and tucks it into the back pocket of her jeans.

Faith pushes the lid of the trunk and it groans shut with the finality of a closed coffin. Faith and Connie grab it by the handles, but it is far too heavy for them, so they drag it across the floor and all the way down the hall to the front door. As Faith backs out into the dazzling sunlight, a blur of faces and hands appears at her side, waiting to help. In the midst of this breathtaking abundance she is seized with a timorous gratitude—not for her new family, but for the sight of her sister at the other end of the trunk, for the knowledge that she will not have to bear alone the burden of ordinary love she has married into.

She offers the last look and wanders through the small, stripped rooms. Her footsteps echo behind her, and then she hears another set of feet.

"It looks like no one ever lived here," Connie says. Faith nods, taking in the naked windows, the swept corners. She watches Connie run her hand over the bare kitchen counter. "It looks like *we* never lived here," Connie says.

Faith doesn't answer. She looks around, for some sign of herself, her sister. On the back wall where the sofa used to be is a cruel scar that still shows through the white, white paint, where Delle once tried to gouge her name with a fork.

"Let's just go," Faith says. But Connie stays put. Her eyes move over the cramped rooms inch by inch, as if she's imagining what used to be there. Then she turns her back and marches outside, into the flurry of Joe's family.

Faith checks the rooms one last time. Finding nothing left, she shuts the trailer's tinny door on what she hopes is her old life.

IF JOE MINDS being a threesome he doesn't say. The arrangement suits Faith even better than she expected. When she arrives for Sunday dinner on Joe's arm, the house swallows her instantly into the stampede of Joe's family and the rituals of food, family stories, and tedious, off-key sing-alongs around the piano. But when Connie joins them, as she often does, the stampede slows to a purposeful

41

walk, and the cloud of family presses on her less urgently, it seems, as if giving room to these two sisters and the shelf of silence they carry between them, their unarticulated sorrows.

Connie has chosen the smallest bedroom in Faith and Joe's house, at one end of the upstairs hall. At the other end Faith fusses over the bedroom she shares with Joe, papering the walls with tiny flowers. Joe Senior comes over to help her, lugging a utility table and oddly shaped instruments for hanging wallpaper. There is nothing the Fullers can't do.

Little by little the house fills with furniture—big, heavy things, gifts from Joe's parents and brothers that are almost impossible to move. Their immutability thrills Faith, fills her with the notion that she has landed somewhere permanent. Though she thinks of it as Joe's house—Joe is the one who checked it from top to bottom, Joe's family furnished it, Joe's humor and grace now fill it—she loves it already; she wants to die here.

Connie's new job, at New England Bonding & Casualty, makes for little conversation. She calls it New England Bondage & Slavery. After six months she's still a file girl, running files from floor to floor, but she doesn't seem to mind. She has plenty of friends, and plenty of plans: every week a brochure comes from a different airline.

Faith is usually the first one home from work, and Connie arrives soon after. They cook something together from Phoebe's store of recipes, working in silence, following Phoebe's carefully printed directions. The recipes aren't simple—Phoebe gives them a lot of credit—and there have been disasters. Joe comes in later, stopping at the sink to wash his hands in a mixture of dish soap and sugar that grinds away the grease from his father's shop. Then he puts his hands on Faith's cheeks, looking at her till she blushes, and kisses her long on the lips. His attentions still disarm her; every time he comes back to her at the end of the day, her heart registers a subtle surprise.

"We sold a machine today," he says. He's beating cake batter in a huge bowl tucked under his arm like a football. Joe always makes dessert, evil, thick things that smolder under mounds of Redi-Whip, while Connie and Faith, dinner made, sit at the table and watch him. "I thought Dad was going to cry."

Faith smiles. Joe Senior keeps saying he's going to retire and thinks every machine they ship out is his last.

"Well," Joe says. "That was *my* day. Did anybody else around here have a day?" They laugh. He goes through this every night; he tells them he feels like a stand-up comedian held captive by Trappist monks.

Sometimes Connie goes out at night, with one of her boyfriends or a girl from work, leaving Faith and Joe together. But more often she stays in. Evenings in the new house are much like the evenings in the trailer, except for the husk of permanence that encases them: the immobile furniture, the thicket of hydrangea bushes hemming in the yard. They play cards at night, like old people. The family stops over not in bunches, but in manageable ones and twos. With Connie as an unwitting ally, Faith steeps her home in a comforting quiet, the only thing left in her life that is truly hers.

THE RESULTS ARE POSITIVE. Dr. Howe places a fatherly kiss on her cheek. "Go tell that nice husband of yours," he says, but she doesn't. She waits until the twelfth week, when, lying in bed, Joe runs his hand over the hard curve of her belly. His hand stops.

"Faith?" His eyes are impossibly blue and tender. "Could you be pregnant?" She covers his hand, holding it against her stomach, until he yelps with joy, hoisting himself up on one elbow. "Why didn't you *tell* me?"

She simply laughs, relieved that he knows on his own. She doesn't know what to do with life's magical moments; she never expected these ordinary miracles. She couldn't utter "I'm pregnant" any better than she had uttered "I do."

"Twelve weeks?" he says. He looks at her the way he does so often, as if he's just figured out what he has on his hands. "You didn't tell me for twelve weeks?"

"I was embarrassed," she whispers, pulling the covers over them. She feels safe in this bed, its rose-pink quilt shielding them from the world. "I didn't want to turn it into a ceremony."

He shakes his head, smiling. She believes her lack of ceremony is

43

what continues to draw him toward her; perhaps his choosing her was in part a respectful rebellion against his ceremonial family.

She peels his hands from her belly and brings them to her face, hands a heady mix of sweat and soap and sugar. "I love you, Joe." These are words he likes, and he seems satisfied, fitting himself around her like a coat.

In the morning he's ready to call his mother and father, his brothers, his friends, the newspaper, the president.

"Please let's wait," Faith tells him.

"But Faith," he says, grabbing her hands and dancing her around the bedroom, "we're going to have a baaay-yay-beee!"

She smiles. "I don't think I'm ready for the brass band." Surely the Fullers have some automatic program for First Baby news: a party, a blizzard of presents, special teas, advice handed down like heirlooms.

He laughs. "Okay."

"Besides, I think we should tell Connie first."

"Great. Let's tell her now."

"Right this minute?"

"Faith," Joe says, still dancing, "you have to learn how to *move*." He waltzes her out of their room and down the hall.

"Joe . . . "

He bangs on Connie's door. "Open up! Big news!" he calls.

He flings the door open. Connie lifts her head, her hair a yellow tangle. "What's going on?"

Joe tugs at her covers. "Time to get up, time to make plans."

"Joe . . . " Faith says.

Connie is looking at her, half smiling. She sits up.

"Prepare yourself," Joe says. "The news is amazing."

Connie's eyes are barely open. "What are you talking about?"

Joe raises his hand with a flourish and brings it down gently on Faith's stomach. "Connie Spaulding, your sister is going to be a mother."

Faith tightens her robe and looks at the floor. She can feel herself separating from her sister, a slow ache. This rending confuses her, for haven't they always been separate?

"Wow," Connie says. "You must be happy." It comes out woodenly, as if she's reading a greeting card out loud. Her eyes are wide open now, looking into the chasm that divides them. "A mother. I can't believe it."

Joe doesn't see it; he's grinning like a child, looking into his imagined future. He doesn't see Connie's decision. But Faith sees it; Connie is going to leave. "You can still live with us," she says softly.

Connie nods. "Thanks."

How big is a heart? Faith wonders. The baby inside her is already carving out room. How can she hold all the things she never dared wish for?

Connie's eyes are resolute, fixed on the hard knot of Faith's stomach. *There's room for you,* Faith wants to say, but she is not at all sure.

FIVE

IT IS A SPRING-YELLOW DAY. The three of them stand in the yard, Faith big as a walrus, Joe waiting by the car to drive Connie to the airport. Faith claims to be ill, vague pregnancy complaints, but in fact she cannot bear the thought of watching her sister's plane recede into a silver dot of sky.

"This is it," she says, her voice catching. She lifts her arms to Connie, takes one awkward step. Their goodbye is tearless, quick, a clumsy hug in which their cheeks accidentally bump together, hard. Faith retreats into the house before the car moves, confounded by physical pain.

Before Faith has time to see it coming, before she can maneuver herself to the window to watch the red Corvair disappear down the street, Connie's stunning absence rains down on her. Connie is gone, gone; this is Faith's first day, ever, without her sister. In the empty hall she sits heavily on a deacon's bench, a gift from Brian and Maggie. She spreads her palm out on her chest, drags it over her massive stomach. Filled though she is with this fidgety baby, she feels empty.

When Joe returns, Faith is wild to see him, meeting him on the porch steps with her arms out. His face goes white. "Is it time?" he says. He's looking at her stomach, guarding it.

"Oh," Faith says. "No, no. I'm just glad to see you."

"I waited till the plane took off." He helps her into the house. "Look, you want to cry or something?"

She smiles wanly. "No."

"You want to just sit here a while, maybe take a stroll down memory lane?"

"What?"

"You know, the good times you had together, stuff like that."

Faith shakes her head The baby is thumping against her back. "I can't think of any right now." Why is her heart breaking?

"It's okay to be sad, sweetie," Joe says. He coaxes her into his arms and holds her there. "I would be. I am, in fact." Faith drops her head on his shoulder. She waits there until her sadness passes.

With Connie gone, the house seems like an echo with walls. She fills it, for the first time, with the sound of her own voice. She begins to talk about the baby, the baby's room, the baby's name, the baby's prospects. Joe's face, always close to hers, is a sheen of love and longing. They seem to have a lot to say to each other; they have a wealth of good intentions, not for themselves but for their child, their future children. Faith is grateful for this common ground, for with Connie gone she is back to puzzling over Joe, his capacity for joy, his choosing her for a mate.

The family churns around them, with plans and alternative plans and contingency plans for getting her to the hospital in case the baby comes early, or late, or in the morning, or at night. Faith freezes in their midst, continues to work for Dr. Howe just to get away from their overwhelming competence. When her time approaches and the phone rings every night for a progress report to be passed down the Fuller telephone chain, she is paralyzed, she might as well be looking for the bathroom in a new school or listening to sinister voices in a hotel hallway. She is the only person on earth who doesn't know where things are.

Chris is born exactly on time. When she sees her son, no bigger than an eggplant crooked into his father's arms, she is felled by love, and by an insidious fear that her heart is indeed a finite thing that has run out of room in a day.

He's a noisy baby, with long, stringy hands that waggle out of his blanket. When she and Joe bear him home, they are greeted in the front yard by a band of Fullers who move toward her like a parade float, ponderous and colorful, unfurling a baby blue banner.

"Here he is!" Joe says, leaving her side and working his family like a politician, pushing cheap cigars into his brothers' pockets.

Joe Senior peers into the blanket, then gives Faith a shy smile. "He's a champ, all right." Though Faith loves Phoebe, Joe Senior is her favorite Fuller, for, like her, he is a person of few words who prefers to watch the family dance from a chair pushed against the wall.

"Come here, darling," Phoebe says, and shepherds Faith over the steps and into her own house. "Oh, what a *baby*!" she squeals, lifting baby Chris out of Faith's arms. "My goodness, Faith, he looks more like you than he did yesterday. Look at those eyes!"

The baby's eyes are already green. Faith almost feels she should apologize. The baby looks exactly like her.

Joe is laughing, idiotic with delight, yet he's tuned to her discomfort, her exhaustion. He swoops her into his arms, heading for the stairs. "New mothers need rest," he announces. The sisters-in-law gather around baby Chris, whose hands are again poking out of his blanket. "Don't drop him," Joe calls. His happiness is palpable, dear as the skin on a peach. She closes her eyes and lets him carry her up, jostling against his chest.

In the blessed quiet of their bedroom, he tucks her under their quilt and kisses her hard on the cheek.

"You beautiful, beautiful thing," he says. "Thank you for our little boy."

She smiles, her eyes closed, already drifting away from him. She will never catch up to his version of the world.

Not until she is teetering on the very edge of sleep does she stop to wonder if anyone in the family machine has thought to call Connie. She would be on her Rome layover now, or perhaps Frankfurt. Faith can't seem to remember what day it is.

She surrenders, finally, to sleep, dimly aware of the good-natured noise below, hoping Connie knows already that a new person has arrived in the world, a little boy, a blood relative.

BY THE TIME Ben is born, over three years later, Faith knows how the family wheels turn. She gives in to the Fullers' celebration and awe: Ben might as well be the first baby they have ever seen.

They surge into her house and she does not retreat. She shows off baby Ben, puts on some coffee, listens to their endless talking, passes herself off as family—because Joe is watching. He believes he has finally made her into family, that he has taken her all the way in, but he has not. Giving in is not the same as giving.

Even with Joe and her sons she becomes more and more a stranger: their world, too, is unfathomable, often alarming. She listens to Ben—a flourishing, black-haired Fuller—jabbering in his crib, making eerie, high-pitched squeaks that Joe reminds her are the sounds of joy. And Chris—she holds her breath many times, as his tiny grip tightens on the outside world. He runs through the house with his head pitched forward as if trying to ram himself into the nearest wall. The stakes increase with time: he falls from a bike, swings from a tree, rolls down the porch steps while trying to dance. His father is happy to contribute to the peril, twirling his son round and round into unbridled, hiccupping laughter. Even with the baby Joe shows no fear, dramatically jiggling Ben on his knee, singing to him in a loud, ecstatic voice. Faith prefers the quiet tasks: she reads Chris to sleep, takes Ben for long walks in the stroller, listens to Chris's convoluted stories. She watches Joe with both sons—his crazy faces and slam-bang play—with a stupefied awe, convinced that the child he once was still exists, dancing just under his skin.

"How can you just let him go like that?" she asks him.

"Higher! Higher, Daddy!" Chris calls from the swing. Joe pushes him higher, pitching him into a scuff of clouds.

"Joe," Faith says. "That's too high."

He stops for her sake, ignores the complaints from the boy on the slowing swing. "He's big enough to hang on, Faith," he tells her. "Kids love to go high."

She believes him, but can't watch. Joe bends down to kiss the top of Chris's yellow head. "Your mother's nervous, pal," he says, and Chris looks up, resigned. They stop their game and swing primly for her benefit. God knows what they do behind her back.

They hear from Connie, regular but short notes, a few lines on a postcard. She has called four or five times in the last couple of years, but they don't talk well on the phone. Once she came for a week's visit, but without the habit of day-to-day living between them, the time was awkward, full of holes.

Lately Connie has been talking about getting an apartment nearby, using Portland instead of Boston as her home base. Faith hopes so. Without Connie she feels more and more caught in the wrong life, as if she found the right door but tripped over the threshold. She doesn't know anybody like herself; even her own children are mysteries.

When both boys get old enough to play at danger, Joe insists that Faith experiment with them: two-wheelers, toboggans, hockey skates. "Go, Mom!" they yell down the street. It is her first ride on a bicycle, the sun beating a yellow melting puddle on the street, Joe chuffing beside her, his sneakers slapping the pavement like a metronome, anchoring the wild beating in her heart.

"Keep pedaling!" Joe yells, and she does, furiously, knowing he has let go, and for a moment she knows what it is to be a child, hurtling into the sun.

When she finds her feet again, the feeling is gone, her wits and suspicion of the world returned, and her husband, running toward her ruddy with triumph, looks like a stranger.

"Yes! Yes!" he hollers, laughing, grabbing her hands and shaking them so hard as to send ripples up her arm. He says he loves her calm, yet he is always trying to move her.

"Oh," she says, catching her breath, laying one hand over her chest. "Oh boy." Her children are running down the shallow hill of their street.

"All right, Mom!" Chris hollers.

"She did it, guys," Joe says. He squeezes her hands hard. "It's in your bones now, lady. Once you learn you don't forget."

She falls against him. "Can you hear my heart?"

"Yes," he says, clutching her with one arm and steadying the bike with the other, his arms awkwardly spread. He manages to make even this look natural. She watches him watching her, trying to see what he sees. He's enchanted by her monstrous need for him, not understanding the nature of this need, how it mutes her, how cold it has become, how separate it makes them.

SIX

FRIDAY NIGHT, and Faith is alone. The boys are with Phoebe and Joe Senior for one of their weekends: they'll go to the Fryeburg fair and eat until they get sick. Ben usually likes the ox pull, Chris the spotted pigs. This year it's hard to tell what they'll like, for they're changing before her eyes. Chris is eleven, still a child in many ways, but already there are signs: he takes a shower every day; he likes salad.

She waits for Joe but he doesn't come home. The house is tomb-like and sad, and she doesn't know how to break the spell. She considers putting on a record but can't think of anything she wants to hear.

Joe calls, his voice strained. "I'll be late," he says.

"Where are you?"

"At the shop." She waits, but he doesn't say anything. Does he want her to tell him to come home? "So, I'll be late," he says again. He is warning her and doesn't yet know it.

"Okay," she says. She sounds fine. She always sounds fine; it's an old skill.

She heads upstairs, each footfall like a slap against bare skin. She perches on the edge of their bed, careful not to wrinkle the rose-colored quilt, the wedding present from Phoebe in which they'd wrapped themselves on their wedding night twelve years ago.

Twelve years. Faith tries to back her way through them, but the years arrive in a clump: a rush of love, a baby, another baby, work, family celebrations, a whirl of days. And Joe: his open arms, his endless gifts, his eternal competence. He could fix anything: his

51

father's machines, his friends' cars, his sons' bicycles and toy trucks and hurt feelings. He had visited his gifts on Faith, too, again and again, but whatever needed fixing had been too long broken.

She must have turned away by inches, for the days refuse to separate in her head. Sitting here now she can't imagine that they ever laughed together, or shared an inside joke, or reached for each other in the night. Yet she knows they did these things, these married things. How long ago? It has been a languid drifting, and here they are, washed up on different shores.

She hears his truck pull up, the thump on the porch, the quick opening of the front door. These sounds are more familiar than anything else in her life. In a few minutes he stands before her, leaning against the door of their bedroom. She looks at her watch, amazed that she has sat here, in this one spot, for three hours.

"Boys get off all right?" he asks.

His face is taut, the corners of his mouth turned down. Though physically he fills up the doorway, he appears to be shrinking. This is what he must have looked like at thirteen, being told that his big brother was lying dead in a blackened rice paddy on the other side of the world.

"I have something to tell you," he says.

She looks beyond him. "You slept with someone." Her voice seems to be coming from someplace else in the room. He slips down, watching her, his back against the doorjamb, until he is sitting on the floor, looking up. He says nothing, struggling against the muscles in his face.

She knows who it is, though he has mentioned her only once. Her name is Judy—the woman Joe Senior hired to do the taxes.

He's gasping for breath. "We were just friends." Minutes tick by. "Oh, God. Faith, I don't know how this happened."

Faith stands up. "I see." She smoothes the quilt. It is faded where the sun has lain upon it for years of mornings. Turning to him, she sees his face buckle, hears the unseemly croak of a man's crying.

"Oh, Faith," he says. "I'm sorry. God, I'm sorry."

"How long has it been?"

He is crumpled by the door. Terrible sounds escape him, the echoey bottom of love.

"Please move out of my way." She feels like a bundle of twigs, snapped into pieces and tied back together.

"Faith, where are you going?"

"I don't know. Please move."

He catches her by the leg as she tries to pass.

"Stop it, Joe."

He holds her fast by the ankle.

"Let me by."

"Talk to me!"

She turns on him, her voice thick with shame. "Why? So you can ease your guilty conscience about fucking that woman?"

For Faith, who doesn't swear, these words are a shock, to her ears loud as an explosion. She glances around—at the flowery walls, the mirror, the shelf of porcelain birds, the glass-shaded lamps on either side of the bed—to make sure nothing has moved. Joe scrambles to his feet and grips her by the arms, his moist, scarlet face inches from hers, smelling of somebody else. She tries to shake him off but his hands tighten around her.

"Talk to me, damn it!"

"No."

He shakes her, once. "Yes!"

"*Stop* it, Joe." She's crying now, hard, a scary loosening in her body.

He sweeps her toward the bed, the room reeling around her. He pins her against the quilt, holds down her wrists, his face transformed, blue veins pumping under his damp skin.

"You *will* talk to me, goddammit!" He screams at her, beads of spit raining down. She has no breath, no bearings, no sense that she might once have known him.

"I *slept* with someone, for God's sake!" He thumps her wrists against the bed. "And you have *nothing*"—thump!—"*nothing*"—thump!—"*to say!*"

Except for the scratches escaping breathless from her throat, and the hot tears running into the hair at her temples, Faith has no sense of her own body, no sense of being there, pinned under her raging husband. She doesn't struggle against his raging; she only stares into

53

his face, his pain like something she has come upon in the dark of a forest, frightening in its wildness, a ragged, bloody thing.

Suddenly he comes to, as if startled from a bad dream. He releases her wrists in horror, tries to stroke the red marks away. He opens his mouth and closes it again. No words. He lets her up, backs away from her as if she were armed. She doesn't feel armed; she feels bereft, resigned to what she is willing to lose.

"Forgive me," Joe says, staring at his hands. He covers his forehead and draws his hands back through his hair. Then he looks at her: "We're not going to make it."

Faith knows this. She has always known.

"Faith," Joe says. "This woman, she isn't—I don't want her, Faith. I want you. She—likes to talk. She talks. A lot. Until tonight that's all it was. We talked. That's all. Until tonight." He looks at her, pleading with her to say something. "Faith, it's you I want. Let me in."

Where is "in"? She wipes her face with the flat of her hand, her skin feverish and sweaty, hot with shame. Burning with the thought of this charming other woman, this woman who can't stop talking, Faith has to fight for breath, as if she's being crushed under the weight of all the women she knows—Phoebe, the sisters-in-law, Marion, the mothers at the boys' school—all of them armed with words, their pretty mouths moving.

"Why did you choose me?" she whispers, not looking at him, not expecting an answer, for she knows he can no longer remember. She watches her hands grab the wedding quilt and claw at it, but it resists her; the stitching holds. She rips the quilt from the white sheets and flings it to the floor. "Is this what you want me to do?" She picks up a book from the nightstand and heaves it across the room, scattering the porcelain birds off their shelf. "Is *this* what you want? *Is* it?" Her voice is rising on its own; there is no connection between herself and the things she is doing.

She clutches the quilt and tries to rip it again. Joe reaches for her and she shoves it against him. "Is *this* what you want?" She's shrieking now, her pulse thundering in her ears, throbbing all the way out through her fingertips. Joe backs away. She picks up one of the lamps and yanks it from the outlet, holding it over her head. How does she tell him what she has known all along? There hasn't been a day in their marriage that she didn't expect this, exactly this, her worst fear come true. She had made it come true, by simply being Faith. She catches herself in the mirror, looking horribly like her mother, then hurls the lamp into her own reflection.

In slow motion he blurs toward her and pulls her down. Daggers of lamp and mirror thud all around them on the carpet. After the echo of breaking glass fades from her head, she opens her eyes, and in perfect focus sees his giving up. He collapses on her, as he sometimes does after love; but this is not love, it is loss, and they are crying. "Who the hell are you?" He speaks into the hollow of her neck, his breath warm and rapid.

She gives him no answer, for she has none. She rolls him off her and he lies blankly on their carpet, staring at the ceiling. She gets up, fetches the wastebasket near the door, and begins to pick up their ruined room. She drops each shard into the metal wastebasket, piece by piece. After a time Joe gets up, slowly, and joins her, dropping in pieces of his own, each one loud as a gunshot, sharp enough to make her wince.

They spend the next hours in a helpless, remorseful silence, ensconced in different parts of what Faith still thinks of as Joe's house. Just before dawn, when Joe slips into bed beside her, she turns to him. They look at each other in the grainy dark for a long time.

"I don't want her, Faith," he whispers. "It isn't love, it's nothing like love."

"I know." She lies still, listening to her heart. "But you're right about us not making it."

"We'll talk. We'll get back to where we were."

"Oh, Joe. There's nowhere to get back to. Don't you see how little I ever gave you?"

"But you did."

"Joe," she whispers, "you made me up." She's crying softly now. "You imagined me."

"Faith—"

She puts her fingers gently against his mouth. "Please. I can't stand to hear my name."

She turns over, hugging herself, and he does not try to touch her.

55

She remembers how she watched her own wedding from a place outside herself, how helpless she looked, how inadequate to the work of being happy. Tonight, turning away from him, she believes she feels the dust of what was once herself return: a fluttering inside, a gathering. It is an unpleasant but strangely welcome feeling: her old, frozen self, finally delivered from the terrible trouble of love.

III

RITUALS

ONE

IT IS COLD COMFORT, these twice-monthly dinners at Faith's. For having this house to come to, Connie is grateful, but there are conditions: it is a place to come to only if you call first; it fills a need only if you don't need much.

Before going in, she stands for a moment in Faith's yard, looking at the house, its neat shutters, its tidy front porch. Bird feeders hang like ornaments among the trees. In the air, warm for April, Connie catches winter's final waning. Faith's preparations for spring are everywhere: flower boxes filled with soil; a rose trestle, newly painted, snugged against the end of the house; bits of string and yarn set out for the birds. Connie takes it all in with a sense of wonder; this annual act of hope is one of Faith's many mysteries.

Connie had moved back to Portland, into a one-bedroom condominium ringed by rhododendrons and unnaturally green grass, with a notion of setting down roots, and the proximity of Faith fed this notion. *I live a few blocks from my sister*, she pictured herself saying. *Oh yes, we see each other every day.* But it had not turned out this way. For one thing, Connie was never home. For another, their years apart had not made them any better suited to other people's rituals, and she discovered how inept they were at spontaneous visits. They were no more separate than they had ever been, and no closer, so they stumbled into a ritual that did suit them, another of their silent pacts: Connie began coming here two Saturdays a month, at exactly five o'clock.

She rings the bell. Joe and Chris appear at the door, on their way out, Ben and the dog behind them. Tucked under Joe's arm is a ruffled catalog of auto parts.

"Hey, Connie," he says, and kisses her cheek. The boys give her a brief hug, then the three of them seem to wait for her to say something. She looks from one to the other, vaguely uncomfortable.

"So, what do you think?" Chris says, finally.

"About what?" Connie looks him over, for a new haircut, the start of a beard, a tattoo.

"My *car*." He points to the driveway, to a blue car parked right in front of hers. The car is exceptionally ugly, yet somehow she'd missed it.

"Well," she says. "It's really something."

"Careful of your blood pressure, Connie," Joe says.

"No, really, it's nice." She frowns. "Isn't it something like that car you used to have, Joe?"

Chris places his hand on his father's shoulder, standing up straight. He's almost as tall as Joe, with Joe's big build, but he has Faith's fair hair—Connie's too, she likes to think—and the Spaulding green eyes. "Very good, Aunt Connie," he says. "What you see before you is a 1966 Corvair. A classic."

"Four on the floor," Ben says. "We're putting her back on the road."

"*I'm* putting her back on the road," Chris says. "You're not even old enough to get a license."

"So?" Ben says. He is short and stringy, with his father's black hair and deep blue eyes. "I didn't say it was my car."

Joe thumps cheerfully on the catalog. "It's nobody's car till we get it running."

To Connie, the Corvair looks hopeless. "Well," she says. "Congratulations."

Chris and Joe start down the steps, but Ben lingers, waiting while she pets the dog, a sweet-tempered shepherd-retriever mutt.

"What's new?" she asks Ben, running her hands over the dog's golden pelt. She doesn't want to go inside.

"I'm playing shortstop." He always offers her something. Chris is harder to talk to, his mind always somewhere else, his body in perpetual motion. Ben looks right into a person's eyes, focused, purposeful. To Connie it seems he has made a virtue of the pensiveness he inherited from his mother.

"Shortstop," she says. "Baseball, right?"

He laughs. He thinks she's kidding.

"How's school? Almost out, huh?" She has always felt a little foolish talking to children.

He smiles politely. "Yup."

"What grade will you be in?" She winces. As a child she hated this question: there were too many schools, too many grades.

"Eighth," he says patiently.

"Eighth. I keep forgetting."

Ben runs one spidery hand through his hair. "I'm gonna go help those guys with the car, okay?" He chucks the dog on the head. "Come on, Sammy."

Then he, too, is gone, and the dog is gone, leaving her alone with the house, and her sister. She tightens her grip on her purse, on the letter inside it. The letter contains just the sort of thing they're not good at.

She finds Faith in the kitchen, laying silverware around five plates.

"Sorry I'm early," Connie says.

Faith looks up. "Safe flight?"

"We got stuck in London for a while but we still touched down on time." She sits down. "How's work?"

"Fine. Marion's out with the flu, so it's pretty busy."

They have been having this conversation, more or less, ever since Connie first left this house to work for AtlanticAir. Connie considers how little her life has changed: she's had the same schedule — Portland to Boston to London to Paris; Paris to London to Boston to Portland — for years now. Her final return is always on a Saturday, when her routine is the same: she waters her one plant, puts on some coffee, calls her friend Stewart in Boston if she can get him home. From time to time she also has a boyfriend to call. She straightens her already tidy apartment, then lies down for a nap. When she gets up she takes a shower, puts on her makeup, and heads out to pick up her mail and drive the few blocks to Faith's.

"This is our first warm day," Faith says.

61

"It's freezing in Paris." Connie moves a fork next to one of the plates. "Is Joe eating with us?"

"Uh-huh," Faith says. "They'll be tinkering with that car half the night, by the looks." She rolls her eyes. "So far it needs nine hundred parts and a new tire."

Connie smiles. Faith's life hasn't changed much, either. She has worked at Dr. Howe's for nineteen years, ten as the office manager. And despite a divorce that's five years old, Joe is still a dependable presence. He lives with another woman but always seems to turn up here.

The aroma of chicken and ginger wafts out of the oven. Connie recognizes the recipe, one of Phoebe's. The table is set exactly the way Phoebe once showed them.

"Faith, can I talk to you?"

Faith looks up, startled, as if Connie has asked permission to remove her clothes. "Not if it has anything to do with Isadora James," she says. She opens the oven, then shuts it without looking inside.

"I got another letter." Connie fishes it out of her purse and presents it on the palm of her hand.

Faith looks at the letter as if it were a dead mouse. "What does it say?"

"The same. She thinks the first one got lost in the mail." She places it square on the table between the neatly arranged dishes. The handwriting is big and scrawly. "She thinks Billy's her father, Faith. She *believes* it."

Connie can almost count the shifting muscles in her sister's face.

"I don't want anything to do with her," Faith says. "She's probably nuts."

"Then what am I supposed to do with this?"

"I don't know. Send it to Armand. He can add it to his collection."

"His collection doesn't have anything like this, Faith."

"Yes it does. I bet she's writing a book on the theater. It's a mystery to me why any of these people want to include Billy and Delle anyway—they only had one legitimate hit."

"She's not writing a book on the theater, Faith."

"Maybe not. But you can bet she wants *something*. Besides, if Billy had another kid I don't want to know about it."

Connie watches Faith move back and forth across her kitchen, her meal materializing. It reminds her of when they were teenagers, trying to run a household around their mother.

Dear Connie, the letter begins. *My name is Isadora James and I believe I am your sister* . . .

She has carried the two letters back and forth to Paris three times now. The thought of another sister, another blood tie, is a cruel temptation, one that bares the pitiful ties she already has.

My mother was a dancer in a show called "Silver Moon."

Connie stares out the window, chin in hand. Faith's neighborhood looks solid, the houses and trees heavy and safe. Connie's condominium complex, though not far from here, has a temporary, antiseptic feel, its slim, well-formed trees no more than decoration. Faith's house is old and settling. What would it would be like to belong to a place like this? Connie's sense of belonging is more mobile: for years she has expected to find her true place in life at the other end of the next flight.

When the boys and Joe return, clattering through the door, the house begins to breathe. They gather at the sink to dip their hands in soap and sugar, their voices rising amiably over the running water. Arguing about what might be wrong with the car, they assemble at the table, Chris with an optimistic smear of grease across the front of his T-shirt.

"How long will it take to fix the car?" Connie asks him.

The three of them chuckle, a conspiracy of men. "Only all his life," Joe says.

Faith doesn't seem to hear anything. She stands with her back to them, tossing a salad at the counter.

"Everything okay here?" Joe asks, looking from one sister to the other.

"Just fine," Faith calls out.

Joe stacks plates and begins to serve from the stove. Connie gets up to help, grateful for the chance to move.

"I've been talking to Faith about meeting Isadora James," she says.

"Who's Isadora James?" Chris asks.

Faith shoots Connie a look: the surprise of betrayal, the look she gave every time Connie tried to make Billy and Delle behave kindly.

"Sorry," Connie says. "I assumed you'd mentioned it." She carries over the last plate and sits down, steeped in a miserable silence, her place at her sister's table ready, good food steaming into her face. She senses the boys' held breath, their fierce interest. Their mother's discomfort has not been lost on them.

"Is this any of my business?" Joe says. His voice breaks the spell and again everyone moves, taking up forks, reaching for bread and salad.

"Connie got a letter from somebody in Brooklyn, that's all," Faith says, as if that explained anything.

Joe stops chewing. "So?"

"She thinks she's our sister," Connie says.

"*Half* sister," Faith adds. "She thinks Billy was her father."

Joe lets out a long whistle, and the boys wait, their mouths parted.

"What does she want?" Joe asks.

"Nothing," Connie says.

Faith lays down her fork. "She probably thinks we have money."

"She says she wants to share our memories," Connie says. The thought is a cold hand on her shoulder.

"Another Spaulding sister," Joe says. "I'll be damned." His eyes darken with interest. "Why did she wait till now?"

"She didn't know. Her mother finally told her a few months ago, just before she died." Saying this, Connie already believes it. "She grew up thinking her mother's husband was her father. He's dead, too."

"How old is she?"

Joe's questions are a comfort; they anchor Connie to Isadora James's story in a way that makes it true.

"Let's see, they left *Silver Moon* in the spring of . . . she must be about twenty-six. I would've been ten when she was born. Faith, you were almost twelve."

Faith is taking tiny mouthfuls of food, one after another. The boys are vigilant, eating mechanically, suspended on the next word.

"I don't know why we're even talking about this," Faith says. She collects her plate, scrapes most of her dinner into the sink. "She probably works for a tabloid. 'Dead Crooners Speak from the Grave,' something like that."

"Crooners," Ben says, and he and Chris laugh. Their habit is to make gentle fun of their mother, but Faith never seems to mind. Connie watches her relax again, letting her sons coax her into a smile. She looks at them as she looks at no one else: she listens. It's the way she used to look at Joe.

"She might be for real, Faith," Joe says. "You never know. What about that stuff in the attic, all that stuff you moved from your mother's?"

"What about it?"

"Maybe there's a clue somewhere."

"Oh, for God's sake," Faith says. She turns to Connie. "Why are we falling all over ourselves just because some girl in Brooklyn says she's our sister?"

"I believe her," Connie says. Her words feel pronged, her voice hard; the recognition of something shuddering between them lends the smallest thrill to her discomfort. Their exchange has the texture of something living. Emboldened, she makes her claim: "I think we should meet her."

Faith closes her eyes.

"I've already talked to Armand about it, Faith. We could meet her in New York, in his office. Neutral territory. We'd never have to see her again."

"No."

"I just want to meet her once."

Faith shakes her head. "Connie."

"I hate to ask you, Faith, believe me." This truth presses on her like a soft wound.

"But I hate New York," Faith says. "I hate it there."

Connie keeps on: "I don't want to go alone."

"Then don't go." Faith looks away. "I'd have to inconvenience everyone at work," she says weakly. "I'd have to take the boys out of school—"

"Whoa, remember me?" Joe says, waving his hand. "They can stay with Brenda and me."

"We can take care of ourselves," Chris announces, indignant. Not quite seventeen, he's already bigger than most men.

"I'd rather go to New York with Mom and Aunt Connie," Ben says. "No offense, Dad."

Joe laughs. "None taken." He looks at Faith. "I think it's a good idea."

Faith leans back against the counter, her arms loosely crossed, staring into some thought known only to her. It's the mention of Brenda that has disarmed her, Connie knows; she can see it in the set of her lower lip.

"Meeting this woman will take what, an hour?" Joe says. "It might even be interesting. And look at the pluses: you get to do Connie a favor and the boys get to see New York City. Besides, you haven't seen Armand in years."

Faith flicks her eyes toward Connie, a green warning. "Armand will expose this thing in about five seconds," she says. "I hope you know that."

Is Faith saying yes? "I just want to know, one way or the other," Connie says. But it isn't true; she only wants to know one way.

Faith comes back to the table and sits down heavily. "Can you at least wait till school's out?"

Ben lets out a yip. "You mean we're going?"

"Thanks," Connie says softly. Faith has come through.

The boys talk through the rest of dinner about what they want to do in New York, but make no mention of meeting their possible aunt. By the time the plates are cleared, Faith is more herself, though she is quiet, even for her.

"Aunt Connie, watch," Chris says, standing at the refrigerator. He makes a clucking sound. The dog, who has been slumbering near the kitchen door, pricks up his ears. Chris opens the freezer and fishes out an ice cube.

Ben nudges her. "This is really good," he says as Chris tosses the cube into the air. The dog springs from all fours to catch it on its upward arc, then drops like a sack, intent on the meaty crunch of ice between his teeth.

Chris shuts the freezer and grins. "He thinks we buy them."

Connie laughs, slipping under the sound of the boys' voices, the crunching dog, the faraway neighborhood noises of the season's first warm night. These are only the motions of comfort, she knows, but for the moment it seems like enough.

All at once the boys are off: Chris to pick up his girlfriend, Ben to walk the dog. Joe stays.

"Another Spaulding," he says, shaking his head.

They're still at the kitchen table, the lights on. Eighteen years ago, Connie thinks, we'd be getting out a deck of cards.

"Faith, thank you," she says. "Really, I mean it. We can make it a quick trip. An overnight, if you want."

Faith looks into her lap. "I don't want another sister."

Connie can't tell how she means this. "Aren't you even a little curious, Faith? Imagine if she's really—I mean, if she's been out there all this time . . . "

Faith looks up. "I said I'd go. I'm sorry you had to beg."

Joe scrapes his chair back and looks at his watch. Connie has almost forgotten that he no longer belongs to this house.

"Thanks for dinner," he says to Faith, and presses her shoulders as he passes. "Don't worry."

"I thought you were going to work on the car."

"Tomorrow," he says. "Good night."

He tosses Connie a little salute, then he's gone, leaving her and Faith in their customary silence, a silence that has always come from not having enough to say to each other, until tonight, when it seems instead like too much.

TWO

FAITH SITS ALONE among a scattering of other parents on the bleachers at the edge of the ball field. The air smells of blossom and dirt and grass and boys. She spots Ben among the players on the Scouts' bench, his head bent toward another boy. Ben is a listener. He is liked by other kids, but lacks Chris's knack for attracting swarms of them. Ben has one or two best friends, and otherwise seems content in his own company and the company of the dog. She hopes he is happy.

He lifts a bat above his head — his hair squashed under a crimson Scouts cap, his skinniness masked by a bulky crimson Scouts shirt — and uses it to stretch, first far to the left, then far to the right. He does this exactly the same way before every game. A couple of the other boys join him, imitate him, bats hoisted, visors similarly curled, cleats dug into the sand.

"Hi, stranger," comes a voice near her. Joe Senior smiles out from under the brown visor of a FULLER MACHINE COMPANY cap.

"Well, hi." She smiles back. "Ben's playing shortstop again."

Joe Senior laughs, his face collapsing into deep lines. "I knew they'd see it his way. He was sleeping in the outfield. The kid needed action."

Across the field voices begin to ring out, the scratchy orders of the young coach, the higher, more urgent calls from the boys. They assemble into twosomes to pass balls, and words, back and forth, talking in their special code.

"Where's Phoebe?" Faith asks.

Joe Senior looks around. "Working the crowd, I imagine."

Eventually Phoebe appears, bony as a heron, in a cotton sundress flapping above a pair of red hightop sneakers. Her white hair, rolled into braids, glints against the sun.

"Hello there!" she shouts, working her way up the bleachers, hands in the air. "Let the games begin!"

She sits down and draws Faith against her fragile chest, her talc-scented skin pressed against Faith's hair.

"Where've you been lately? Your kids are always underfoot, but we never see you."

Joe Senior corrects her. "When do we ever see Chris? If he isn't working at the Shop 'n' Save then he's out chasing that girlfriend of his."

"Oh, I know," Phoebe sighs, shaking her head. "And Ben's right behind him. My last grandchild, all grown up."

Joe Senior squints into the sun-bleached field. "Seven great-grandchildren and she's moaning about Ben."

"But there's something about the last one of anything, don't you think?"

"There is," Faith says. She knows exactly what Phoebe means. As a child she never ate the whole of anything because she did not want it to be gone.

Phoebe leans close to Faith, one finger poised in the air. "Redpoll at the tube feeder."

"No. This late? I didn't get one all winter."

"Yessiree," Phoebe says, triumphant. "I almost called you, but I made myself wait till I could see your face."

Faith laughs. Phoebe had introduced her to birdwatching when she was home with the infant Chris, and they'd been engaged in a friendly rivalry ever since.

"Will you look at this," Phoebe says to Joe Senior. "Those no-good sons of yours are playing hooky."

Up through the bleachers bob two more FULLER MACHINE COMPANY caps. Joe and Brian. With them are Brian's wife, Maggie, and their oldest son, Jack, with Marilyn, his wife. They all greet Phoebe, Joe Senior, and Faith as if they haven't seen each other for months: the Fuller family axis has always turned on hellos and goodbyes.

"Greg and Will are covering the shop," Joe says to his father. He winks at Faith. "Slow day."

"The hell," Joe Senior says. "You just want to see how that kid of yours handles himself at shortstop."

Faith watches this scene as she has so many others. She still thinks of it as the family dance. The divorce halted the music not a whit, and when she sees them now they're as relentlessly cheerful as they were the first time she appeared at their door.

Faith is quiet at these games, especially amidst the noisy cadre of Fullers, who follow the nuances of every play with practiced fervor. For Faith the game is something that happens *around* Ben, whom she watches tenderly: his labored movements, his determination, his fierce will. He's not a natural athlete like his brother; he is gawky, a little hesitant, not entirely used to his body, but he tries hard and never gives up.

Whenever Ben leaves the field, Faith loses interest in the game, the score, who is next at bat. She prefers to watch the other parents, their feverish faces, the way their tightened fists and chewed lower lips seem to will the ball into the sky's farthest reaches. Faith wonders at them, for in Ben she looks instead for the smallest triumphs: a good swing, the *thwack* of connection. It doesn't matter to her where the ball ends up.

Today it's harder than usual to keep her head in the game. The trip to New York with Connie is looming, and there's a new horror in her constant worry over the boys: this morning she found a condom in Chris's laundry, casual as a gum wrapper in the pocket of his jeans. FOR HER PLEASURE, read the jaunty red packet.

The game ends and the Scouts lose. Faith picks her way down the bleachers to the balding grass and waits alone, watching the Fullers move in a pack to the Scouts' bench. In the thinning sunlight she hangs back, until they have made Ben smile in the face of defeat. As the crowd dwindles she lifts her hand to him, and he crosses the field: a trudging, crimson, backlit figure, her son. When his face comes into focus, his freckles standing out on his cheeks, she speaks to him.

"You were the best one," she says.

He squints at her, unbelieving. "Mom, I screwed up a zillion times. I muffed two grounders." So serious, so like her. Chris is like his father and will dance his way through the rest of his life. Ben will tiptoe, peering around every turn. One day soon he'll wake up a man. She missed the moment somehow with Chris; with Ben she'll be watching.

"No one else looks like you, Ben," she tells him. "You're a one-and-only out there."

He shakes his head, his father's black hair shivering out the back door of his cap. "You don't have to say that stuff, Mom. I sucked out loud."

"Isn't it all right if I think you're good?" She puts her hand on his shoulder and steers him toward the car. Joe is standing behind it, grinning, his forearms resting on the roof.

"Hey, lady, can I bum a ride?"

The sight of him — his limbs slung so casually from his torso — can both lift and sadden her still. She waves. No one can say they aren't friends. If she can't give him love, she can at least give him friendship. She has to, for Joe is her only friend.

"You came with a whole platoon — they couldn't fit you back in?"

"Nobody's going back to the shop. My truck's still there."

She turns to Ben. "What do you think?"

Ben rubs his nose, pretending to decide. "The man's desperate, Mom."

"Okay." Faith opens the door. "Get in."

"I owe you one, buddy," Joe tells Ben, and they climb in, Joe in front and Ben in back.

"Can you drop me off at the house first, Mom?" Ben asks. "I need a shower something wicked."

Joe glances into the back seat, but speaks to Faith: "Remember when we had to pay him to take a bath?"

"Just barely," Faith says, but she remembers it all. She remembers the instant of his birth, and Chris's. They came to her docile, ignorant, their crimped little faces expecting nothing, and she was the first one to love them. Her love couldn't be compared with anything else, for it was the only thing they knew. Loving Joe was different — so many people had already loved him first.

As she pulls up to the house, she spots Chris's bare stomach and

71

blue-jeaned legs sticking out from under the hapless Corvair. The huge, corrugated soles of his sneakers twist impatiently. His girl-friend, Tracy, sits on the edge of the lawn with Sammy. They both look bored. All around them, on the grass and street, lies an assort-ment of grimy tools. The Corvair's hood and engine cover are flapped open like the wings of some extinct bird.

"Not again," Faith says.

Ben is already out, on his stomach, peering at his brother, his own cleated shoes twisting in empathy.

"I thought that thing was all fixed," Faith says. "You said it was mint."

Joe looks amused. "This is a rite of passage, Faith," he says. "A boy's first car is supposed to break down."

She smiles. "Is that right."

"How else do you get to take off your shirt and show your girl-friend what you know about cars?" The light of sudden memory seems to lift up his face, peeling years away. She feels as if she's caught him at something.

"Huh," Joe says, and flicks it all away in a blink. "I loved that car."

He gets out and heads over to the boys. They slide from under the belly of the car to confer with their father, then all three of them as-semble at the Corvair's back end, the exposed engine their sole fo-cus. Watching them, Faith wonders about men and cars, one of the many relationships in life that she does not understand.

Her own car looks suddenly ridiculous: reliable, undistinctive, stodgy. Compared to Chris's Corvair it isn't zany or crooked or im-practical, there is nothing noteworthy about it in any way. A word comes to her, a word she types dozens of times a week at Dr. Howe's: *unremarkable*. At first she thought it a blunt, indelicate way to describe a person's hematocrit or glucose level or general physical state; she translated it to mean *Don't worry, you're fine.* But lately the word depresses her, as if in typing it she is somehow passing judgment on a stranger's chances for happiness.

Faith gets out of the car slowly, watching her sons and their father deliberate over an antique that is younger than she is. They are all talking at once, leaning over the engine. The tops of their heads—

Chris's blonde flanked by the dark of his father and brother—shine up at her like shells. She waits a moment, listening, basking in the sound of them, the shimmer of their hair as they move their heads, the way their shoulders bump together over the engine's dark hold.

Sammy trots over to escort Faith into the house. "Hello, Tracy," she says as she passes over the lawn.

"Hi, Mrs. Fuller." Tracy's brown hair is sporting some yellow strips, and she's had it cut short. She looks older, vaguely dangerous.

"Car trouble?" Faith says, just to make conversation.

"What else?" Tracy grimaces in a knowing way that gives Faith pause. The look is full of a smoldering knowledge: men, life, the future. Faith herself has never, as far as she can remember, looked like this. Tracy sits patiently, waiting for Chris to finish up, all the while exuding the unmistakable impression that it is she who is in complete control.

Joe and the boys stare at the car as if they expect it to move on its own. They stand in a semicircle, their hands stalled in their back pockets.

"What's wrong with it?" Faith asks.

Chris turns around, his gaze falling on Tracy. "Fuel pump. At least Dad thinks so," he says, then wipes his grease-blackened palms across his sweaty chest. The gesture is shockingly sexual, a rite of passage in itself.

"Me too," Ben says. "I think it's the fuel pump."

She hears a snort from Tracy. "It's the only major organ they haven't already replaced."

Faith looks at her watch. "How much longer?"

"Twenty minutes, tops," Joe says.

That means an hour, an hour and a half. Faith knows at least that much about men and cars.

"Are you staying for dinner?"

Joe nods. "Sure."

IT IS AFTER ELEVEN when Faith finally drops Joe off at the shop to retrieve his truck. Her bland gray wagon crackles over the gravel. She turns the ignition off.

"Got a minute?" she says.

"Two, even."

Outside the night is still. Though the shop is only a few miles outside the city, it is on a heavily treed, rural road. She fancies she hears an owl.

"What is it?" he asks. "Cold feet about going to New York?"

She reaches into her pocket for the red-wrapped condom. She hands it to him—its lurid message face up—as if it weighed a hundred pounds.

"I found this in Chris's jeans."

"Huh," he says.

"I suppose this means he's having sex."

Joe pushes his hair off his forehead. "Safe sex, at least. I suppose we should be glad the kid has a brain."

"A *kid*, Joe. Sixteen, God."

"Seventeen in a month. He'll be a senior next fall."

"So?"

Joe shifts in the seat, facing her squarely. "I just don't want to turn this into a crisis."

"What should we do?"

"Nothing, I guess." He doesn't sound convinced. She waits, expecting something more.

"Will you talk to him?" she says.

"Faith, I've talked to him." He looks surprisingly helpless.

"You have?"

"Of course. Ben, too."

She pushes some air through her lips and taps her fingers on the steering wheel, imagining the three of them together, the big talk.

She shakes her head. "I don't even like her," she says. "She's such a little know-it-all."

Joe is grinning slightly, the way he does when he wants her to say something, his eyes bright on her.

"You and your normal," she says, struggling to smile. "You and your rites of passage." She grips the steering wheel, pleading. "Joe, I'm losing him."

He slides over on the seat. "We're both losing him. Faith," he says, picking up her hand. "I think that's the way it's supposed to go."

She relaxes, leaning back. He smells like supper, her house, her yard. "Oh, Joe," she says. "That *car*. One of these days he's going to drive off into the sunset and we'll never see him again."

Joe squeezes her fingers, then lets her hand go. "He won't get far in that thing. Trust me."

Now she does smile. It astonishes her sometimes how much she still feels married. It's Joe who will leave someday, she realizes now; Joe who, in the absence of his sons from her house, will fade from her life.

In the glow of the shop's night lights, the dark looks purple. After a long silence she checks her watch, by now nothing but a gray shape on her wrist.

"I should go," Joe says. "It's late." He gets out of the car, then knocks on the window. Faith leans across the seat and rolls it down. He sticks his head in, his teeth showing through the dark. "Don't worry, Faith," he says. "We've got two good kids. We're doing fine."

She watches him get into his truck and rev it. As he pulls out of the parking lot, he sends her a friendly blast of the horn, and she listens, hard, until the sound of his engine disappears into the silence of the road.

THREE

CONNIE KEEPS the two letters from Isadora James in a dark pocket of her purse, hidden, as if they were parts of a treasure map. She carries them back and forth across the Atlantic as she goes on with her work, waiting for summer and the trip to New York, trying not to hope too hard. She reminds herself that Faith is probably right—Isadora James is writing a book, or crazy. Still, what would it hurt to meet a person like that?

Paris has been cold all spring, the flowers late, the sky low and solemn. Connie hardly notices. She's turned herself into a tourist, turned Paris into more than a place to sleep at the end of a long working flight. She visits the hushed cavern of Notre Dame cathedral, walks the Champs Elysées, roams through le Louvre committing names of paintings to memory. All this she does with an imaginary presence at her side; she's rehearsing for the day Isadora James asks to see this magnificent city. Connie has even thought of engaging a little apartment here, some high-ceilinged refuge with an ancient concierge guarding the door. She hopes Isadora will turn out to be the type to come to Paris by herself, to borrow Connie's keys and seek harbor in her big sister's rooms.

After one of these sightseeing excursions, Connie returns to her hotel—Le Perreault, the same one she's been staying in for years—with the frail hope of finding Stewart, who sometimes works the Paris run for Pan Am. Her eyes smart, and her feet hurt from too much walking. She peers into a mirror in the lobby; her hair needs another touch-up. She thinks of the crew she came over with, *her* crew—beautiful boys and girls with hair the color of copper, mahogany, dandelions, ink. Invariably cheerful, chatty, perfectly turned out, no matter how many sleepless nights. She calls them the New Guard. They are young. She is thirty-six and old.

She enters the lobby, looking around halfheartedly. It's been a month since she's seen Stewart, longer than usual—his work schedule is less routine than hers. She hears him before she sees him—a voice sputtering out of the lobby bar, emphatic cadences that make words sound like vows. She brightens, feeling lucky. Since Faith said yes, Connie's life has turned.

She finds him just inside the bar's arched doorway, talking to Frank and Debbie, two other Old Guards from Pan Am. His back is to her, but she can see he is trying to convince them of something. His shoulders move with his voice, his short hair quivers as he nods his head. Connie laughs out loud: Stewart has never been one to conserve energy, especially in the throes of an argument.

Frank sees her first. "Hey, Connie!"

Stewart whirls around. "Connie! Christ, I thought you were dead!" He picks her up and squeezes her, then lets her down with a thunk.

She pats his cheeks, frowning into his face. "Why didn't you tell me you were going to be on this run?"

"If you called once in a while, you'd know these things."

"You're never home," she says. "And I'm boycotting that ridiculous message on your machine."

Debbie groans appreciatively. "I *hate* singing machines."

Stewart looks perplexed. "It's pure kitsch. Old-fashioned glad tidings. You're supposed to love it."

"Sorry." Connie hooks her arm through his. "I won't hang up next time."

"You could take a lesson, Connie," he says. "Your machine sounds like a funeral home."

She laughs. Stewart is her best friend. They trained together and then flew together for years until he left AtlanticAir for Pan Am. Whenever she stays with him in his Boston apartment, they chat long into the night like girlfriends. He's the only man she knows who would never leave her.

"Where are you going?" she asks.

"It's under discussion," Stewart says. He grins. "I'm not getting my way."

Frank runs a brown hand over his tight curls. "He wants to eat at that place he likes on St. Germain."

"It wouldn't hurt either one of you to take a walk on the wild side," Stewart says. He turns to Connie. "Where's your crew?"

"Loose in the city. They asked me along, but the invite wasn't exactly fervent. I felt like their den mother."

Stewart caresses her arm, as if to soothe her feelings. "Kids today. Where are their manners?"

"Listen," Frank says. "We're going to Lucienne. You coming or not?"

Connie glances at Stewart. "Nah," she says, smiling. "I'll take the walk on the wild side."

She watches Frank and Debbie cross the lobby. Debbie's hair is dark at the roots. Connie lifts her hand to her own hair.

"You look fine," Stewart says. He always knows what she's thinking.

Connie twines a few strands around her fingers, then lets go. "What if we stay in, Stewart? A bottle of wine, room service, me. What could be better? Besides, I've got things to tell you."

"Two bottles and you've got a deal," he says, steering her toward the elevators. The doors open. "*Allons-y.*"

By the time they reach the bottom half of the second bottle of wine, the subject of Isadora James has been well worn and Connie is dressed for bed. Stewart lazes on the carpet, leaning on one elbow with his cheek pressed into his eye. He looks tipsy and bored.

"Look, you want to go out after all?" Connie asks.

Stewart shifts elbows, leaving a red scar on the other side of his face. "I'm not sure I can stand up."

Connie slips out of her chair and sits next to him. She pours the last of the wine and hands him a glass. He lifts it to her.

"Here's to finding it," he says.

"Finding what?"

"Damned if I know. Whatever it is we're looking for."

They drink. Connie sets down her glass and draws her knees up, wrapping her arms around them. She feels warm and safe, a little fuzzy.

"So," Stewart says. "Tell me some more about Isadora James."

"I told you everything. Two teensy letters, that's it."

"Think of something. This is the only interesting thing that's happened to me in weeks." His hair, normally blown back in soft waves, is sticking up in cowlicks.

Connie gets up and finds her purse, from which she plucks the two letters. She tosses them to Stewart. "That's the sum total."

"Why didn't you show me these two hours ago?"

Connie shrugs. She was guarding them. From what? Stewart reads the first letter meticulously, holding it close to his face. "She writes like Rebecca of Sunnybrook Farm." He reads the second one, frowning. "She doesn't sound anything like you."

"Why would she?" Connie says. "She doesn't even know me. I could have grown up on Mars for all we have in common."

"I'm just saying she doesn't *sound* like you. If she was really your sister I'd expect something to kick in, you know? Even in a letter. Haven't you ever read those studies about twins separated at birth? They both smoke Salems, own dogs named Fluffy, and work at meatpacking plants."

Stewart infuriates her sometimes, assuming her life is his business. At the same time his audacity links them—as does hers, for she has never been stingy with opinions about his life, either. She wonders if this is like being married.

"We're not twins, Stewart."

"Still." He tosses the letters on the carpet. They flap briefly, like moths. "I'd want something a little more convincing."

"Thank you, Stewart," she says. "Thank you for that bucket of water."

"Sorry." He takes a long draught of the wine. "I envy you, actually. I wish I had a sister to meet. I wouldn't mind trading my whole family." He stops, squinting into the air. "What if she doesn't look anything like you? What if she's black, or Chinese?"

Connie knows exactly what he's doing. Her friendship with Stewart is like a game of tetherball, one of them playing the pole, the other spinning wildly around, until it's time to switch places.

They pronounce judgments and make predictions about each other's love affairs, providing wine and solace at the end. After the initial diversion that a new man brings to her life, Connie sometimes looks forward to the breakup, knowing Stewart will be waiting on the other side, ready to talk all night about what went wrong.

But Isadora James is not a lover, and the possibility this time is something else altogether, having to do with flesh and blood, permanence, even healing.

"Can we talk about something else, please?"

Stewart sinks back on his elbows. "Fine. Let's talk about *my* thrilling life."

"All right. How's Craig?"

"Old news."

"That was short-lived."

He grimaces. "Story of my life."

He's trying to be his old playful self, but his spirits are low, gathered into his forehead, his held jaw. Connie understands, but she doesn't want to be part of it tonight. She wants to be happy.

She waits a while. "I met someone."

His head swivels toward her, a darting, chickenlike turn. "Is it serious?"

"I've seen him a few times. He lives right here in the city. Not far from here, in fact."

Stewart raises his eyebrows. "Oh ho, a Parisien. How's his English?"

"Good enough." She laughs. The last Parisien she dated, a commuter pilot named Luc, could barely say hello. Connie's command of French is all business: *What would you like to drink? May I see your boarding pass?* She can ask directions and order food, but can't discuss a movie or tell a man why she likes him. Stewart accused Connie, quite rightly, of having chosen Luc for his poor English. It is Stewart's theory that Connie prefers men with some kind of built-in obsolescence. Before Luc she dated a man who was two months from moving to New Zealand.

"So what's the guy's name?" Stewart asks.

"Marcel."

"Marcel. Hm."

"I like him."

"You're not in love, are you?"

"God, no."

"Don't let him get too smitten," Stewart says. He always says that.

The wine is beginning to give Connie a headache. She gets up, steadies herself against the TV, and retrieves Isadora's letters from where Stewart dropped them, succumbing to a compulsion to care for what she does not yet have. She smoothes the pages one at a time, staring at the innocent-looking handwriting.

"Doesn't she make you feel old?" Stewart says. "I mean, look at this. How young did you say she was?" He frowns. "This is the handwriting of a teenager."

"Don't be a pill, Stewart."

"I'll bet she's adorable," he says glumly. "A morning person, I'll bet. You won't be able to stand her." His face shows his full age and an indefinable sadness. "Cute and healthy," he says. "Worse than the New Guards."

"How many *bon mots* do I have to hear in one night?" Connie snaps, then a warning disrupts her irritation. "You're not sick, are you?" Stewart is a careful man, but they've lost too many colleagues not to be jumpy.

He shakes his head, his fire gone. "It's not that."

"What, then?"

"I don't recognize myself lately," he says. "I don't want the things I wanted." Connie creeps up close to him and holds his hand. Perhaps they are best together when one of them is unhappy. "I just want someone to *listen* to me."

Connie squeezes his fingers. "Don't I know it." There are other things she could say, about terror, exhaustion, loneliness. "Listen," she says, brightening. "How long are you here?"

"Another day."

"Perfect. Let's do something tomorrow. Have you ever seen Versailles?"

"Only ninety times."

"Will you come with me?"

He smiles. "Sure. We can rent a car, bring a picnic. It'll be fun."

81

They part with the promise to meet at noon, giving them ample time to sleep in. The next day dawns bright and clear, a good omen. Connie answers her door, expecting Stewart; instead she finds Marcel.

"Con-*stance!*" he calls. Her name sounds liquid and lovely in French. Though he speaks to her only in English he always calls her by her French name.

"How did you know I was here?"

He taps his temple. "I remember your schedule."

She had intended to pass him over on this trip, but decides she's glad to see him after all. She winds her arms around his neck. He is slightly built, barely her height. She loves his eyes, a rosy shade of brown. She's not in love, though Marcel is sweet, a graduate student living with his parents on Boulevard Malesherbes, not far from the hotel. He is young, unsettled, his life forever beginning; already she can see he will be in school for years. But she likes his uncomplicated company and the notion of beginnings. She looks forward to telling Isadora James about her Parisian boyfriend.

"I left my job," Marcel says. "Quit!" His accent is strong; his every phrase sounds quaint and dear.

"What are you talking about?"

He grins, his eyes crinkling at the corners, making him seem older, more attractive. "I said to myself, such a beautiful day, and the lovely Con-*stance* is here. My lady will come with me for a ride."

Marcel's mode of transport is an ancient motorbike that Connie finds charming, with the full knowledge that in a matter of weeks it will come to annoy her. It makes for a windy, noisy ride, and she's burned her ankle on the exhaust pipe already; but for the moment it's perfect, and she likes to ride with her body pressed close against Marcel's back, her hands fisted into his stomach.

"But you need your job, Marcel."

"There are other jobs, Con-*stance!* But how many days like this?" He stands back, admiring her. This part won't last long.

"Hello, hello," Stewart says, appearing at the door. A lumpy grocery bag, with two baguettes sticking out the top, crackles as he shifts it against his chest. He stops.

"Marcel, right?"

Marcel nods. "You are Stewart."

Stewart glances at Connie, pleased. Then his face darkens, figuring out the rest.

"This is a bit awkward," Connie says. "Marcel quit his job, Stewart. Just to spend the day with me." She lowers her voice. "How can I say no? Could you find somebody else—Frank or Debbie, maybe?"

"You mean I should let someone else have the pleasure of my company?"

Connie checks his face to tell how he means this, but his eyes don't move, and she doesn't have his talent for reading minds.

Stewart turns to Marcel. "May I have a word with your friend?" he asks, then steps into the hallway, where Connie follows him. "What, is he nuts?"

"For wanting to be with me today?"

"For quitting his job?" He shakes his head. "This guy's a case, Connie."

"You're mad at me."

"I'm not mad. Go break the guy's heart." He hands her the bag of food. "Have a ball."

"You've done this to me plenty of times, Stewart, in case you forgot." She watches him stride down the hall and bang the elevator button. "Fine," she calls after him.

The room is darker when she returns; the sky outside has cast over with low clouds. Another gray day after all. Her good omen is gone.

Marcel is sitting on the bed, smiling apologetically. "I have spoiled something?"

Connie shrugs. "Stewart likes to play the brother I never wanted." She checks the sky again. "Not much for riding weather."

He leans forward, his eyes fixed on her. "Then we stay here."

She peers into the bag—cheese, eclairs, a Bordeaux Stewart likes. "I guess we've just inherited a picnic."

They feast indoors. Marcel whips the bedspread off the bed and it floats down, white and bridelike. They drink, eat, make love, nap on the floor.

Connie stirs. She is naked, lying on her back, unwilling to fully wake. The spell of the Bordeaux is working its way out to her fingers and toes. Their picnic has taken a long time.

"Can I tell you a secret?" she murmurs.

Marcel turns beside her, propping himself up on one elbow, gazing at her.

"Of course. Anything."

She smiles. "This is my first picnic."

"True?"

"My very first."

"But a picnic takes place in the out of doors."

"Don't say that. We can pretend."

She rolls onto her stomach, trying to stay inside her half-sleep. Marcel places his narrow hands on her shoulder blades and presses down.

"Mm. Nice," she mumbles.

He kneads her back, her shoulders, her neck. He pets her hair. His hands, warm and insistent, cup her shape, moving down over the curve of her waist and hips, down over her thighs and calves and ankles. He holds one foot between his hands for a moment.

She rolls over. "Now do the front." She smiles at him, then closes her eyes.

For a long while she lies there, drifting under his moving hands. When she opens her eyes she finds him gazing at her as if she were a fragile, tender thing. She starts, fully awake, embarrassed to have him looking at her—not at her body, but directly at her face, into her eyes. She sits up and draws the blanket around her.

"Let's do something," she says. "How about going to Versailles?"

He gets up and begins to put on his clothes. "It is too late in the day." He winks at her. "I am not sorry."

She watches him dress, the way he moves, the way the soft cotton slides over his chest, whispery as a slip.

"My parents want to meet you," he says. He bends down and lifts her chin with one finger, kissing her chastely on the lips. "My mother would like to cook you a dinner."

"How nice," Connie says. "That's very nice."

"You will come?"

Connie looks around the room. "Uh, sure."

84

He puts his hands together like a prayer. "I knew you would."
"You mean now?"

He grins. "They will like you better if you put on your clothes."
His face is clean as an apple. She wishes she were him.

"Marcel, I can't. I'm sorry." Never in her life has she been to meet
a lover's parents. She can picture his parents' house: a sitting room
filled with modest heirlooms, a crucifix tacked to each wall. Thin,
happily worn carpets and a faint, musty smell, the smell of time. On
his mother's sewing table, planted among robustly colored spools,
a portrait of Marcel as a child. And his parents—he has spoken of
them so often she can see them plainly. His mother is short and
plump, a coil of auburn hair wound into a bun atop her head, a ro-
sary hidden in her apron pocket. His father is even shorter, his hair
combed back with water. They preside over their home, their son,
with the zeal of saints. How could she love a man who is already
this much loved?

"My parents are very pleasant," Marcel assures her.

"Of course," Connie says. "It's not that." She gets up quickly and
pulls on her clothes.

"You will love them," Marcel says. He is pleading. He is—all at
once—impossibly young. "You *must* come."

"No," Connie tells him gently. "No."

He leaves bewildered, and Connie watches him go without a
word. As soon as she hears the elevator's whine, she makes straight
for Stewart's room.

"She returns," Stewart says, looking at his watch.

Connie walks in past him, drags a chair from a corner and turns
on the TV. "I'm sorry about today, Stewart," she says. "I'm rotten
to the core."

Stewart folds his arms like a schoolmaster. "I take it Marcel is
history?"

Connie stares absently at somebody singing and dancing on the
screen. "Too young," she says. "Too goddamned happy."

"Hah! I hear you, sweetheart."

Connie kicks off her shoes and curls her legs under her. She
watches Stewart pull a new bottle of wine out of the dresser.

"Stewart, do you ever get the feeling you've lived the same year over and over for the last decade? The exact same year, time and again?"

"Yes," Stewart says. "But look on the bright side—that would make us about twenty-six."

They pass the bottle back and forth for a few minutes.

"We drink too much, Stewart."

"Speak for yourself."

Connie snaps off the TV. She looks at him. "I know you're not happy."

His voice is ragged. "Some night I'd just like to lie down with somebody, you know?" His eyes are such a mild blue, she thinks, like violets at the end of their season. "No sex, no nothing."

"True confession, Stewart."

"Shoot."

"I'm sick of sex. It's ready-set-go all night long with a guy you won't remember in a year."

"Bingo."

Connie grins, takes the bottle from him. "Don't you have any glasses?"

He gives her one. "You know what I wish?"

"What?"

"Nothing."

"Stewart," Connie says quietly. She puts her glass down and turns to him. "I'll lie down with you."

He waits a moment. Without a word he stands up and strips down to his shorts, while Connie turns down the bed and slips in, propping her head against the pillows. She opens her arms to him.

Stewart gets in beside her, wriggling down so that his head rests on the soft cotton of her blouse, in the warm hollow between her shoulder and the curve of her breast.

"This is so nice," he murmurs.

She closes her eyes. "I agree." His hair, downy as a child's, grazes her chin.

"Sing to me, Connie."

"I can't sing." As a child she listened to Billy and Delle many nights, always in some other room, their voices rippling over the scales, pelting the filmy quiet. She had wanted her parents so badly, without knowing what it was she meant. *I want, I want,* was as far as she ever got.

"Sing a lullaby. Anyone can sing a lullaby."

She waits, follows her memory as far back as it will go, until she finds a fragment, something half-remembered, in her grandmother's voice.

"All right," she says. "I'm warning you, Stewart, this won't be pretty."

It isn't pretty, and it doesn't put Stewart to sleep. Connie doesn't mind. Stewart's weight on her is substantial, even grave. But he is no burden, this man who expects her to do nothing but lie here and sing.

IV

ISADORA

ONE

FAITH CROSSES the white swatch of sidewalk in front of the Sheraton and enters the sumptuous lobby with a sense of relief. It's all so changed: the sidewalks fixed in her memory are gray and narrow, the lobbies strewn with mean, low chairs.

Within a few minutes she is walking down a long corridor with her sons and sister, their footsteps a dull drumming on the carpet. The boys install themselves noisily in the room next to hers, and Connie disappears behind the door across the hall. Faith can hear her sons on the other side of the wall as she unpacks: Chris's low, lively commentary punctuated by higher, tentative comebacks from Ben. She moves to the window. She is high up, looking deep into an alley. The last light of day clings to the brick in a sinister way, barely delineating some human or animal shapes—she can't tell which—from the wall they hunker against. She feels afraid, as if something down there were dead or dying.

In the books she read as a girl, beautiful heroines languished over their deaths, filled with exquisite regrets. She used to play at death herself, pressing the back of her hand to her forehead. She had seen Delle die this way on stage, swooning into Billy's arms. But when real death came, it was not the same. After Billy ran his car into the shallow depths of a pale Maine field, it was Faith whom Delle asked to identify the body. She waited till morning, lying awake, envisioning how he might look, and what she found was worse than everything she had seen in the fits of her sleep. She couldn't look long, but long enough. *Good*, she remembers thinking, then a rush of remorse and horror.

And when they found Delle on the couch one day, white, stinking of brandy, her mouth slung open to expose the steel-gray fillings in her back teeth, Faith was once again cowed by the ugliness of death. While Connie dragged a washcloth over Delle's unyielding face, Faith pulled the pant cuffs down to hide her unshaven calves. She picked up the bottles one by one and set them on the coffee table, labels facing front, as carefully as if they were her mother's stiffening fingers. No matter what she did, she couldn't make death look like anything else.

She and Connie had sat at the table of the kitchenette for a few minutes, staring at Delle's gaudy silence, her reproaches and admonitions and self-pity gone for good. *Are you glad?* she had wanted to ask Connie, but she didn't, for if Connie said yes there would be two of them in the world, two awful girls with no feelings.

A knock at the door startles her unreasonably, but it is only the boys and Connie, a trio of expectant faces. The boys seem younger in this monstrous city, a benefit Faith hadn't banked on. Connie is telling them about a baseball player she met on a flight. "William something," she says.

The boys look at each other.

"No, wait." She frowns. "William was his last name. It's *something* Williams."

Ben's mouth drops open. "Mitch Williams?"

"No . . . " Connie says. "I'm sure if you said the name I'd remember it. I think it might have been French." It touches Faith that Connie is trying so hard to please them.

"White or black?" Chris asks.

"Black," Connie says. "Really tall."

Ben begins to look suspicious. "Aunt Connie, are you sure he's in baseball?"

"Actually, no." The boys exchange a faint smile that Faith has seen a hundred times. It puts her instantly in cahoots with Connie: two ignorant adults.

"Wait," Connie says. "His first name is Donovan. Donovan Williams, is that anyone?"

Nothing registers on the boys' faces, but they're still trying. By now Faith is trying, too, though she knows very little about sports. "What did he look like?" she asks.

"Let's see, he was good-looking, with"—Connie puts her hands up around her head—"you know that squared-off haircut the black kids wear now?"

Ben slaps his forehead and groans. "Oh my God," he says—to no one, to God himself, to the world at large. "Aunt Connie met Dominique Wilkins and I bet she didn't even get his autograph."

"That's it!" Connie looks at Faith, then at the boys. "I'm sorry."

"Don't worry, Aunt Connie," Chris says. "He's only the best forward in the NBA."

"*Highly* debatable," Ben says, and Faith laughs. Her children are still children in some ways. She cheers up.

They all head for the elevator, Ben running ahead. "I just talked to Armand," Connie whispers. "He expects us at ten tomorrow."

Faith nods, holding her breath, trying to calm herself. Connie, too, is tense; Faith can see it on her face, though she looks beautiful, a fuchsia shirt blousing over her shoulders.

"You look so different," Faith says. "I guess I've never seen you dressed like that."

"Stewart calls them my go-get-'em clothes." She adjusts the comb that fastens her hair. "I get 'em, all right, but I can't seem to keep 'em."

"Who's Stewart?"

Connie looks puzzled. "My friend."

"Oh."

"He's my best friend, Faith. I've known him forever."

"Stewart . . . yes. I remember." But Connie has so many friends, Faith thinks. Dozens and dozens of colleagues, how is she supposed to know one from the other?

On their way down in the elevator, Faith steals a long look at her sister. She tries to picture Connie in an airline uniform, gliding among the passengers, chatting them up. As the elevator door opens, Faith says, "You look pretty, is what I meant to say."

"Well, thanks."

They take a cab to Little Italy. The boys choose a restaurant:

93

busy, authentic, filled with families. While they wait for the food, Ben tells Connie his favorite joke.

"These two monks live in a cave," he says, shouting a little to be heard over the bustle and chatter.

"*Three* monks," Chris says. "You've told this joke a million times."

"Aunt Connie's never heard it, have you, Aunt Connie."

Connie smiles. "I'm sure I haven't."

"See?" Ben looks at his brother, then starts over: "These *three* monks live in a cave. One day a horse walks by. Five years later the first monk says, 'That was a nice-looking horse.' Ten years later the second monk says, 'That wasn't a horse, that was a zebra.' Fifteen years later the third monk says, 'If you two don't stop this endless argument, I'm moving out.' "

Faith, who has also heard this joke a million times, chuckles politely. Chris groans and tips back on his chair.

Connie puts down her wine glass, snickering softly. She clamps her hand over her mouth, shoulders shaking, until her hand drops away and she begins to laugh out loud, her cheeks going pink, the day's tension draining from her features, her laughter musical, warm, filled with relief. Suddenly she's howling, clutching her stomach. "Monks!" she shouts gleefully. "Monks!"

Faith is struck still: has she ever seen Connie laugh like this? Is this how she is with her friends?

"Get a hold of yourself, Aunt Connie," Chris says, looking around self-consciously.

But she doesn't, or can't, stop. Faith watches her, puzzled, until, infected by Connie's melodious giggles, she herself gives up to a fit of laughter. She covers her face and lets it go, bubbles of sound released like a fistful of balloons. They laugh together, helpless, their voices crossing in the air like a two-part song.

Chris is still monitoring the crowd, as if he expects somebody he knows to catch them, but Ben looks as pleased as a game show host. "It's all in the delivery," he tells his brother. He pats his chest a couple of times.

This triggers another howl from Connie. She puts her palms on the table as if she's afraid of falling. "Hoo!" she sighs, wiping her eyes. "That was a good one, Ben." She giggles again. "Faith, those monks remind me of us." She fishes a tissue out of her purse and blows her nose.

Faith isn't sure how Connie means this. "I suppose," she says. Her laughter drains away, she already misses it. "That felt good." She remembers sitting across the kitchen table from Connie and Joe in her new married home, the three of them laughing over a poker game.

"Can we please act like normal people now?" Chris asks. After all the years of helping his father get Faith to move, loosen up, let go, he's looking at her as if she might spontaneously combust. Dressed in a shirt and tie—a deliberate try at sophistication—he's the soul of decorum. She's the unpredictable one, foisting her laughter on strangers. This fleeting reversal amazes her. She wishes Joe were here to see it.

When dinner comes they eat heartily, mounds of spaghetti, lasagna for Faith, baskets of bread. For the moment, Faith forgets why they've come to New York in the first place. For the moment, they might be a family from Indiana on their first vacation.

After dinner the boys want to stroll down Broadway. Though it is nearly July, a chill has blown in from the river, out of season. The cab drops them off a few blocks shy of Times Square so they can walk the rest of the way to the hotel.

Ben sings "New York, New York" over and over as they stroll among the lighted theaters. The city has lit something in him; Faith can't recall his ever singing out loud.

"Start spreadin' the newwws," he begins again.

"Shut up, Ben," Chris says. "Mom, which one of these theaters did my grandparents act in?"

"They're my grandparents too," Ben says. He looks at Faith for confirmation.

For a bizarre instant Faith thinks they mean Joe Senior and Phoebe.

"Mom?"

"I don't know," Faith says. "Lots of them."

"But which ones, specifically?"

"I don't *know*, Chris."

"We were young," Connie says. "They all looked the same, really."

The simple pleasure Faith felt at dinner is gone. Again she feels a certain dread dragging itself through her, vague as those shapes in the alley. The boys hurry ahead, gawking at posters and marquees and the pulsing throng of passers-by. With Ben and Chris out of earshot, Faith and Connie don't talk much; the city swells up in a noisy battle around their silence. Their laughter already seems years away. Faith watches doorways for muggers, or worse. Connie is looking up and down the buildings, peering down cross streets. It takes a while for Faith to realize what Connie is doing; it comes to her when something—perhaps the smell of must and urine floating up from the subway, or the long-forgotten shape of a door or window—stings her unconscious. They stop at the same time.

"It's gone," Connie says, staring up at a new-looking building with a glass storefront. Faith catches their reflection among mannequins dressed as characters from the stage: Mame, Gypsy, King Arthur, Lady Macbeth. Faith and Connie could be characters themselves, remarkably alike, their tallish, angular silhouettes poised in the same surprise.

"Site of the old Prince Theater," Connie reads underneath the neon proclaiming PRINCE COSTUME COMPANY. She turns to Faith, her eyes wide, amazed. "We stood right here. Exactly here, on this very spot."

Faith looks down at the dirty sidewalk and imagines her white shoes, her pretty white dress, her braids, her parents' cold hands on her shoulder, the heat of several cameras flashing at once.

Connie is watching her, her lips poised for a word, as if she means to explain where they are, as if she thinks Faith might not remember.

TWO

Armand is not much changed. He still has attentive blue eyes and a shiny, accommodating face. Round, slow-moving, bald as an oyster; a reassuring, unlawyerly presence. It surprises Faith how happy she feels to be near him. Although they have never been out of touch, she has seen him face to face only once since her wedding, when Ben was just a toddler. Armand had taken it into his head one fall to do a foliage tour and turned up on her doorstep. She showed him to the Fullers as if he were the generous, forthcoming, hidden part of herself. *See?* she wanted to say to them. *See?*

Here they are again, more than ten years later. Connie is standing near him, her hands clasped inside-out, the stance she used as a child.

Armand shakes the boys' hands. "You won't remember me," he says to Ben, "but I remember you." He beams at Faith. "He spent most of my visit varooming around the yard in some kind of home-made contraption."

Chris laughs. "My father's go-cart. It's still in the basement. Dad can't stand to get rid of anything with wheels."

Armand's office — deep chairs and oiled wooden surfaces — brings back a comfort Faith had nearly forgotten. It comes back in the piney scent of these high and heavy walls. She remembers a time in this very office, when she was six or seven years old. Standing near the window, she clutched the soft, brown drape as she watched the people darting across Columbus Circle, no bigger than cats from so grand a height. Behind her, in their musical voices, Billy and Delle listed a string of cities and dates for a tour. Their mood was giddy,

97

their gay laughter spilling into Armand's office like something tipped from a bottle. They were happiest at the start of a tour, before the endless bus rides and ungrateful audiences began to take their toll. This time they were leaving Faith and Connie behind, with a series of dour babysitters in the Connecticut house whom Armand would oversee. As with everything else in her life, about this turn of events she was both glad and not. Her parents' voices—staccato, tinged with hysteria—already seemed a distance away. While they wouldn't allow Armand to take Faith and Connie himself—a single man, how would it look?—he would come out to Connecticut every Sunday, bearing gifts, smelling of this cozy office.

A middle-aged woman comes in with a tray of coffee and soda. "This is Louise," Armand says. Louise smiles cheerily as she herds them all into a grouping of stuffed chairs arranged around a low table. The chairs are not the same ones Faith once sat so far, far into, but they feel the same. She tips her head back and hides between the wings.

Louise nevertheless catches Faith's eye.

"Handsome boys."

Armand nods, gracing one hand toward Chris. "This one is the picture of his grandfather." Faith looks at her son. *No*, she thinks. *He looks like me.*

When Louise goes out, the door whispers closed behind her, and the air in Armand's office changes from welcome to uncertainty. "I take it she's not here yet," Faith says.

Armand has to lean a little to see around the wings of the chair, and his eyes glitter over her. "An hour," he says. "I thought it would give us time to talk things over. To get ready, if we need to."

But Faith doesn't talk; she hides in her chair while Connie and Armand talk. She said she would come, and here she is. Connie can't expect any more than this.

Faith settles against the quilted back of the chair, shreds of memory filtering in and out. These memories have no context or story, they are just little puzzle pieces turned over at random: the deliberate penciled line of Delle's eyebrows; the tiger's-eye ring Billy wore on his little finger; the dimpled chrome trim of the refrigerator in the Connecticut house. From time to time she returns to Armand's office, almost surprised to see her grown sister here, wearing grown-ups' clothes.

Armand is sifting through the contents of a manila folder which bears the name *Isadora James*. Faith is only half listening, but from the words that glint through her faraway thoughts she comes to understand that Armand has done some kind of check and Isadora James came up just fine.

Faith sits up, her reverie draining away.

"In any case," Armand is saying, "I'd advise you all to view this with an open mind." In his slow way, he strolls to his desk and tucks the folder into one of its many holds. Faith steals a glance at Connie, whose face is a soft glaze of appeasement, wonder. The boys stare at their sneakers to conceal a somewhat guilty look of expectation.

"Armand, what was Mom like?" Chris says suddenly.

All eyes turn to Faith. She freezes, watching a stripe of sunlight shiver across Connie's lap as she turns.

"Oh my goodness," Armand says. "Your mother and aunt were funny little girls. Very sweet and serious, even businesslike. Especially you, Faith." Chris is hunched forward, listening. Ben flashes Faith a reassuring grin. "I remember bringing them dresses one time, during the tour of *Smythe and Smythe*, I believe. I had some business in San Francisco, which was where the show was playing. Two green dresses with little bows, exactly the same. Quite brave of me, I thought—what did I know about dressing up little girls?"

The boys are enthralled, their chins raised, hungry for more.

Armand fusses his hands in the air. "I managed to get the sizes right, more or less. The two of them disappeared into the bathroom with the boxes and came back in, Lord, a minute it seems to me now." He shakes his head, chuckling. "Your aunt Connie came flouncing out like a princess bride, but your mother stepped right up and looked at me, I'll never forget how suspicious you looked, Faith, you said, just as practical as you please, 'Are these for us?' "

Ben and Chris look at each other and laugh, but before Armand can say anything else a shadow crosses his polished round face, as if he understands too late that he has told a sad story.

"They were blue," Connie says. Her mouth is turned up, but she is not exactly smiling. "It was my favorite dress, wasn't it, Faith?"

99

"Yes," Faith says, and for the first time since they arrived in this office, their eyes meet. Connie's irises have gone a hard, hard green. She is a woman with either nothing or everything to lose.

Armand ticks his fingers together. "You were good little girls."

"Didn't they ever do anything wrong?" Ben asks. He's hunting— he wants the kind of story his father might tell on him, about broken windows, pilfered change.

Armand thinks a minute. "No," he says. "They were good little girls."

A brisk knock sounds on the door and Louise pokes her head in. "She's here."

Before Faith can get her bearings, before she can plan what she might do or say depending on what Isadora James might do or say, Billy Spaulding's third daughter steps into the room. The recognition comes quick as a fall, and Faith is knocked nearly windless, her hands fly to her mouth. The boys stand up—their father's old-fashioned manners. No one speaks.

She is short, fragile, birdlike, with a cloud of yellow hair. Her eyes are green. She is wearing a simple, sleeveless black shift that exposes her body type: sharp and angled, a smaller version of Faith and Connie. Her arms are long, bony as rakes. She takes a few steps into the room, an enormous satchel hooked over one arm, a stack of tiny bracelets tinkling down the other. "Oh," she says. "You really came."

No one seems able to move. Armand resorts to the rituals of polite company. "Miss James," he says, "may I present Faith Fuller and Connie Spaulding. And these handsome fellows are Faith's boys, Chris and Ben." Faith can feel her sons' wary eyes on her.

Isadora is welded to her spot on the rug, her eyes frozen open. "Oh my God," she says. She turns her back, her narrow shoulders shaking.

Connie gets up. "It's all right," she says. She grips the back of her chair, her knuckles whitening. Faith can see that she's a little dazed.

"Miss James," Armand says kindly. "Let's all sit down. This is a sensitive situation, we all realize that."

Isadora turns, wipes her face with the flat of her hand. "I'm sorry," she says again. "I didn't think seeing you would—oh, here we go." She drives the heels of her hands across her cheeks.

Armand leads her into a large leather chair directly across from Faith. Her walk is noiseless on little flat shoes. She sits for a minute, wiping her eyes. Up close Faith sees less of a resemblance. Isadora's full-lipped mouth is most unlike Billy's, and the heart of her face—a gently pointed chin and rather broad brow—is not familiar. But these differences are little comfort: there *is* something, in her carriage, her silent walk. Her green irises are heavily flecked. And though the shape is wrong, her face in repose reminds Faith of Connie as a child.

"Well," Isadora James says. "Here we all are."

Her voice is husky and matches neither her slightness nor her blondeness. She sits with her toes pointed down, twisting them into the carpet. Her face is unsuspecting, earnest as a tourist's, framed by a short tangle of curls. She digs into the satchel and hauls out her wallet. On the table she places her driver's license, an ASCAP membership card, and a charge card for Bloomingdale's.

"Just so you know I'm me," she says.

Armand makes a pretense of examining the cards.

"I know you didn't want to see me," she says to Faith, talking very fast, "but really, I'm so glad to see *you*. I'm not kidding, this is the happiest day of my life."

Faith stares at Isadora, looking for all their differences and cataloging them over and again, but there is no escaping the coloring, the precise angles of her elbows, the long, narrow hands, the green, flecked eyes.

"Paternity can be difficult to prove, Miss James," Armand is saying. "And in this case I'm afraid it's quite impossible."

Isadora shakes her head vehemently. "Billy Spaulding was my father. My mother would never lie to me. I'll do anything. You can even have my blood, O-positive, does that prove anything?"

"I'm afraid not," Armand says.

She is quiet for a moment, then turns to Faith. "I've imagined what you must think of me," she says. "That I was looking for money or something."

Faith speaks then, her mouth barely moving: "Or something."

Connie moves in quickly. "We wanted to give you a chance to speak your piece."

Isadora looks at Faith a moment longer before responding. "But I don't have a piece to speak."

"You think Billy was your father," Faith says. "That sounds like a mouthful to me." She sounds meaner than she intends to.

Isadora waits, a long, solemn pause. Then: "My mother had cancer. She knew I had two sisters out there and didn't want me to be alone. She even knew where you were. I found a whole scrapbook of clippings—not just about Billy, either. I have a clipping of your wedding announcement, Faith."

Faith flinches: here is an invasion she did not expect. Had she been watched from afar somewhere, without knowing? Was Isadora's mother some kind of guardian angel? All of a sudden a host of strangers seems connected to her life. What if she had met Isadora in the grocery store, or the bank, or Dr. Howe's office? Would she have noticed the shallow earlobes, the pointy elbows? It's too late now to ever not recognize her, too late for this fidgety young woman to be just a face on the street.

Isadora's color is high, her hands flail; the chair groans around her as she speaks. "Please," she says. "My mother was a sweet woman." She smiles at the boys. "A dancer."

"Yes, they know," Faith says, not unkindly. "I didn't mean to insult your mother."

"We weren't shocked about, you know, the situation," Chris assures her.

Isadora releases a short, crackling laugh, and Faith realizes that they've all been holding their breath. For a moment they simply sit, breathing, while Isadora reaches into her satchel and pulls out a bumpy manila envelope.

"Here's her picture," she says, drawing a large photograph from the envelope. "This was before she had me."

Connie takes up the photograph eagerly, then places it on the table for everyone to see. A young woman about Isadora's age, dressed in a sequined dancer's costume, stares out from an eight-by-ten-inch glossy. She is tiny like Isadora, but dark-haired, dark-eyed. Her form is perfect, if a bit staged. She reminds Faith of Delle, except for the expression on her face, which is decidedly unprofessional. She is like a woman madly in love trying to look serene: ready to burst into laughter, or song, or tears. Faith can't fathom this woman keeping track of her and Connie's whereabouts, and yet she has a single-minded look, much the same as her daughter.

"She's very pretty," Connie says. She smiles easily at Isadora. Faith can see she's convinced, not that it would have taken much.

Isadora holds up another photograph. "Here's one from *Silver Moon*."

Another publicity shot. Billy and Delle—Billy in overalls and Delle in low-cut gingham—are posed cheek to cheek, surrounded by six chorus dancers in similar garb. Isadora's mother is easy to pick out, smiling directly into the camera.

Isadora lays the photograph reverently on the table next to the first one. Faith stares at it, shaking her head.

"Is that—" Ben begins.

"Yes," Faith says. "It's them."

Ben picks up the photograph, then hands it without a word to his brother.

"I have something else," Isadora says.

She takes out a creased letter and hands it to Armand. He reads aloud: " 'My dearest Marie.' "

"That's my mother," Isadora says. "Marie Lazarro. She married my father—the man I thought of as my father— when I was a baby."

Armand looks at Connie. "I can have the handwriting verified," he says.

Faith takes the letter, then hands it back. "It's his." Connie is looking straight at her. *Please*, she seems to be saying, *pleeease*.

Armand scans the letter, then gives it to Faith. It reads:

My dearest Marie—
How you float when you dance. You take my breath away.
Here is a small token of appreciation for your graceful presence
in "Silver Moon."
—All my love, Billy

103

Isadora folds her hands. "Listen, I've got a couple of aunts who adore me, and a few cousins. Bucketloads of friends. I'm not alone, not at all. But the thought of having *sisters* . . . "

Armand breaks in. "Miss James," he says. Faith can hear the strain as he speaks a functionary's words. He feels sorry for Isadora, perhaps for them all. "These things—this so-called evidence, your mother's testimony—I'm afraid if you tried to go forward with some kind of claim—"

"Claim?" Isadora says. "I'm not talking about claims or evidence or testimony." She gestures with one of her fluttering hands. "I'm not *claiming* anything. I have everything I need. My mother married a beautiful man who took good care of us." Her eyes rove briefly over the photographs. "I don't know what I thought would happen here. I thought maybe when you *saw* me . . . I thought . . . this might sound stupid, but I thought somehow we'd all *know*." She pauses. "I believe in signs. Do you know how my mother met the man I called my father?"

Connie shakes her head no, answering for them all. Ben and Chris are still.

"The day she took me home from the hospital, this man moved into the apartment across the hall. An older man, a widower, no kids. There he was, alone in the world, and his name turns out to be Rudy, the name my mother had picked out for me if I was a boy, after Rudolph Nureyev." She looks at them as if she expects applause. "That was her *sign*, see? That everything would be all right. And it was. They got married on my first birthday."

She tucks her fists under her chin. "I don't want your father," she says. "I had a wonderful father. I just want to know *you*, is that so much to ask?"

For some reason Faith is thinking about the second step of the Long Point trailer. Thin and rotting, it never broke through only because she and Connie always skipped it. They stepped from the first to the third step every time, at first deliberately, then without thinking about it at all. Eight, nine, ten times a day they skipped that rotting board until it became part of the way they moved. All that time Isadora James was a clean and thriving child, the apple of somebody's eye in Brooklyn, New York.

104

"What was the token?" she hears Chris say. He is hunched forward, his forearms resting on his long thighs, his hands loosely clasped.

"Token?" Isadora says.

"The token of my grandfather's appreciation."

"Oh." Isadora points to the photograph from *Silver Moon*. "A gold heart on a chain." They all peer down, and there it is, sparkling on Marie Lazarro's chest.

"He gave it to her just before he left the show," Isadora says quietly. "She was already pregnant."

"Did he know?" Connie asks, staring at the picture.

"Yes." She adjusts the photograph, squaring it with the edge of the table. "He gave her some money, then left her on her own."

"But he was well known then," Faith says. "At least in the theater crowd. Why didn't she—"

Isadora gives her a long look. "She wasn't that type."

Faith catches herself breathing with her mouth open; there is simply not enough air in this heavy, heavy room. It is filled with Billy and Delle, their mean and petty life.

"I know I'm your sister," Isadora says.

For a few moments no one speaks. Finally Armand clears his throat. "You've done your part here, Miss James." His voice is careful; Faith realizes that again he is being kind. "If Faith and Connie wish to pursue a relationship with you, then it's up to them."

Isadora stands up and gathers her things. She glances around. "To be honest, this isn't what I expected," she says. "I thought we'd just—well, fall into each other's arms."

"I'm sorry," Connie says. Her cheeks are red. "We're not very— we're not like that."

Isadora writes her phone number on a card, shaking her head, her hair shimmying in the slanted light. "I thought it would be so clear." She offers the card to Connie. "Will you take this?"

"Of course," Connie says, casting an eye in Faith's direction. A flutter of panic flits through Faith's chest, as if her future were somehow dangling from a cliff; this is the way she felt when she said yes to Joe, that she was about to be engulfed by ordinary life and its terrifying requirements.

"If nothing else, it was nice meeting you," Isadora says. She offers her hand all around and comes last to Faith. "I mean it."

Faith can't think of anything to say. *Goodbye* doesn't seem quite right. She shakes the cool, small hand and watches Isadora James walk out the door, her satchel bumping against her hip like a sack of holiday mail.

SHE WANTS TO be home. She wants to see Joe, tell him it was nothing, it was just as she had thought, some silly girl with a notion. But now she has witnesses. She can refuse to believe her own eyes, she has done it before, but hers are not the only eyes.

"Do you believe her, Armand?" Connie says. She sounds like a little girl.

"Yes."

"Faith?"

"I don't like this," Faith says, finding her voice.

"But she's here," Connie murmurs. "She exists."

"Mom," Chris says, "she looks exactly like you two."

Faith closes her eyes. There's nothing she can do to stop this now; the snowball is already rolling down the hill.

"I don't think she looks like you, Mom," Ben says then. He looks around guiltily, at his brother, his aunt, Armand. He is lying. Faith puts an arm around him and for the first time recognizes that he is going to be tall.

"I thought she was kind of sweet, Mom," Chris says. She knows he's trying to be gentle, trying to make her see, as he has at other times, that there is nothing in the world to be afraid of.

"She has no reason to lie," Connie says.

"I'm not calling her a liar," Faith says. She is suddenly exhausted.

"Then you believe her?"

"I can't think of any reason not to."

Armand takes her hand. "It's a strange turn."

He sees them to the elevator. His lips are cool on Faith's cheek, and she holds him an extra moment. When the doors close in front of him, Connie says, "Why did you let her walk out?"

"Why did I—"

"If you believe her, why did you let her go?"

The boys are watching. "Maybe I just didn't like her," Faith says. "Do we have to waltz into her arms just because she says so? Just because she's related to us?"

"We could give her a chance," Connie says. "She's not asking for much."

"How do we know how much she's asking? We've only known her for five minutes."

"Faith—"

"I have all the relatives I want," Faith says. She looks at her sons, their solemn faces. "There's no room for her." If she sounds harsh she can't help it. The truth is, Isadora James reminds her of the Fullers, all the vociferous sisters-in-law bubbling in one slight body.

"There's room," Connie murmurs. "You *make* room."

The doors open on the lobby, where Isadora James stands waiting. She darts over to them, her satchel swinging in her wake.

"Please, can't we go somewhere for coffee?" Her face still has a rosy cast. "Just for a few minutes? Please—all of that upstairs was so formal."

She is looking mercilessly at Faith. They are all looking at her. Connie mouths a word: *Please.*

And again, Isadora: "Please say yes."

Please, the word Faith refused to speak as a child. Why are they even asking her? She can already see how it's going to go: this pixie woman has come thundering into their lives and means to stay.

Faith grimaces. "All right."

She lags a step or two behind as the others follow Isadora across Columbus Circle to a cafe on Eighth Avenue, where Isadora is greeted by a waitress who apparently knows her. They hug and kiss, falling instantly into a frenzied conversation that Faith can't begin to comprehend: a flurry of names and places and arbitrary exclamations. Faith glances at Connie and the boys; they don't seem to mind waiting. Faith does mind—she's getting tenser by the second. Still, it interests her to see these young women, their animated faces, the way they want to catch up on each other's lives. "I worked here for a couple of months last winter," Isadora explains after she finally extricates herself. "We got really close."

The tables—placed among a formidable snarl of potted plants—

are round and spindly, with copper tops. They drag two together and still there is not quite enough room. They have to huddle in close, shoulders touching. A redheaded waiter, who also seems to know Isadora, comes over to take their order.

"Don't get the guacamole, it's canned," Isadora cautions the boys, as if in their wildest nightmares they'd order such a thing. Ben exchanges a wry look with his brother, who then passes it to Faith. This small intimacy cheers her.

"I'll have a Coke," Chris says. They all order Cokes (something quick, to Faith's relief), then there seems to be no place to begin. Isadora laughs nervously.

"I practiced a hundred speeches," she says. "My roommates were ready to kill me."

It is Connie who finally gives shape to the conversation. "Where do you live?" she asks, and Faith notices how the boys, both of them, square themselves to listen.

Faith listens too. Isadora lives in a big apartment in Brooklyn with several roommates and a bobtailed housecat. She calls herself a blues singer.

"Not that it's a living yet," she quickly adds.

"Blues?" Chris says.

Faith feels an unexpected flash of tenderness for Isadora James, who looks about as much like a blues singer as Ben. She must spend half her time in the wrong skin. Faith knows exactly how that feels.

"I've got a guitar," Ben announces, then glances at Faith as if checking the rules.

"Well, good for you," Isadora says. "Maybe we can jam sometime."

Ben flushes scarlet to the tips of his ears. "I only know a couple of chords." He checks again with Faith. "G and C."

"First position?" Isadora asks.

"I guess so." He looks mortified.

"Three fingers or four?"

Ben thinks a minute, still blushing. "Three."

"Four's better, I'll show you sometime," Isadora says. "But listen, you have to start somewhere."

Chris asks Isadora what she does with her time.

"Right now I work at a copy place," she says. "It's a bitch of a job but I like my friends there. Every once in a while I get a decent gig. I did a show at the Back Door last week." She pauses, as if expecting everyone to know the place. "I used to send demo tapes through the mail, but I get better results taking them around myself. It's kind of embarrassing—I mean, there you are, your whole *life* on the line, and you just stand there trying not to swear out loud while some tone-deaf bar manager sticks the tape in a machine and listens to it, not even looking at you."

Faith can't imagine such a thing; she can't imagine being related to someone who could.

Isadora asks Connie about being a flight attendant and listens, chin in hand, as Connie tells stories that Faith has never heard, peopled with names to which she connects no faces.

"What do you do, Faith?" Isadora says suddenly.

"I—well, I run a doctor's office."

Isadora raises her pale eyebrows. "How do you run a doctor's office?"

"Well," Faith says. She pauses. "You'd probably find it boring."

"They're switching the office over to computers," Ben says. "Mom's running the whole show. Tell her, Mom."

Faith tells a little, for Ben. She understands that he wants to be proud of her. Isadora looks interested in a way that seems like an effort, but the boys are paying attention, their generosity an unexpected gift.

"Mom's a computer nerd," Chris says, grinning. He taps her arm, as if to say *You're doing fine.*

Eventually the boys and Isadora take over the conversation: music they like, movies they've seen, teams they follow. Isadora reveals herself to be an avid baseball fan; she and the boys pass names back and forth, waiting for each other's reactions. *They're playing catch,* Faith thinks. She feels her life giving way beneath her like loose rock. She sits there, helpless, watching the future change.

Isadora has a friend—she seems to have friends everywhere—who works the Yankee Stadium box office, and after a minute's discussion Connie agrees to let Isadora take her to a game that night with the boys.

"Is that all right, Faith?" Connie asks. Her face is flushed; happiness looks peculiar on her, like a costume.

"I suppose so," Faith says. She's outnumbered, choiceless.

"Come with us, Mom," Ben says. "You'll have fun."

"I only have fun when you play." She forces a smile, but her head is pounding. When she gets up from the table her bones shiver ominously, ready to fly apart and take up residence in a more accommodating body.

FAITH HAS Joe on her mind—a vague and troubling sense of him, of their worst times, the times at the end of their marriage when he would rail at her, frustrated beyond his considerable limits, telling her to *face things*. "Why are you letting this happen?" he would shout, his face transformed by anger. "I can't do it all myself!" Then, as now, she would find herself immobile, unable to act, not even in her own interest.

There was so much she hadn't told him for so long, back when telling might have made a difference. How her baby boys had terrified her! She was stricken by love, and feared its unbuckled force, as if it might kill her; she feared it in the most literal way, her heart making dangerous fluttery pats just under her skin.

"Tell me something," Joe used to ask her. They'd be sitting somewhere, at the beach, say, watching the boys clamor in the surf. He'd look at her, desperate: "Tell me something."

She told him nothing, for everything she knew embarrassed her. Everything she didn't know embarrassed her more. She had taken him once to a snowy field—for an owl she wanted to see—and found herself walking behind him, setting her feet one after another in his deep prints. She was grateful for them, and at the same time troubled by the sense that this was the way her life worked.

She lies in the dark on top of her tightly made bed in the hotel, her sister and her sons wedged somewhere into the thin-air section of Yankee Stadium with Isadora James, all yelling their heads off at a couple of baseball teams. She closes her eyes and tells herself, in Joe's voice, to *face things*: Connie wants a different sister.

She gets up and goes to the window. From the eerie gradations of dark below comes the suggestion of movement. She saw the hope in Connie's face. The need. What ever happened to Rule Number One? *Dump them before they dump you.* Faith sighs. Connie was never good at following even her own rules. A sudden, tender flash stalls her thoughts: Connie, cross-legged on the floor of Chris's bedroom before Chris was born, when the room belonged to Connie. She had six or seven airline brochures laid out like a hand of solitaire in front of her. They were exactly the same size and almost all of them had a red border. "These are my plans," she said, picking up the brochures one by one until they came together as a small deck in her hands: neat and finite, with a precise weight and order, with red edges. Faith wonders now if Connie sees Isadora James as a plan she can pick up and hold in her hands.

She hears them in the hallway outside her door, scuffling and whispering. Chris and Ben are in high spirits, and Connie sounds surprised by her own laughter. They rap softly on the door. Faith remains at the window, hugging herself, until they go away.

THREE

THE PHONE is ringing when Connie comes through the door.

"Don't say a word," Stewart says. "I'm on my way up and I want every last detail."

"Stewart—"

"I called every hotel in New York."

"We were at the Sheraton Centre."

"Except that one. Damn!" He pauses for breath. "Just tell me one thing—is she or isn't she?"

"Well—"

"No, no, don't say it! I'm on my way. Should I bring cannoli?"

"Stewart, I'm exhausted. It's been a long four days." She checks her watch. "There's no way you can get here before ten."

"But I've been *dying* here."

"I'm practically unconscious, Stewart. How about tomorrow instead?"

"Connie, don't do this to me."

She gives up. "All right."

"Two hours, sweetheart."

She hangs up, then rises heavily, wandering around her apartment, struck by what she thinks of as its hardiness. She hasn't been gone long enough for the apartment to need her. There is food in the freezer and milk in the fridge. The furniture is exactly as she left it and there is no dust. Her coleus plant, long accustomed to sporadic watering, hasn't even begun to droop. This is how her apartment looks in her absence. She lifts one of the plant's leaves: it would take a long time for something to die here without her.

By the time Stewart arrives she is desperate for company and flings open the door. "Jesus, you look awful," she says.

"Why, thank you." He hands her a box of cannoli and two bottles of wine.

"I'm serious, Stewart. Are you sick?"

"Listen to the Mistress of Doom." He smiles faintly. "I'm not sick, just depressed."

She follows him into the kitchen, where he immediately finds a couple of plates and a corkscrew. It pleases her unreasonably that he knows his way around. He has not come for the story of Isadora James; he has come for solace to this apartment, these self-sufficient rooms.

"What's going on in Boston?" she asks.

He divides the cannolis and puts three on each plate. "Everybody's out of town." Stewart has a lot of friends, gives a lot of parties.

"Lonesome?" she asks.

He shrugs. "James and Michael moved out to Brookline, can you believe it?"

"A regular Ozzie and Harriet." She sits down next to him at the table. "You want some dinner? I thawed some chicken."

"Nah."

"Come on, Stewart, what is it?"

"Forget it. Is Isadora James your sister or what?"

"I think so."

Stewart's eyes fly open. "Oh my God."

Connie laughs. "I know, I can't believe it either. She's only about five feet high, but other than that she looks just like us."

"Then she must be gorgeous." He's trying.

"She sings blues, can you imagine?" Connie can't stop smiling. "I'm supposed to call her tonight, late, after her gig. She wants to make sure I made it back safe, isn't that sweet?"

"Sweet," Stewart says. "This is amazing. I was sure she'd turn out to be some kind of wing nut with a theater fixation." He pours some wine, staring into the glasses. He looks up, frowning. "Listen, are you working Thanksgiving?"

"I guess so," she says, puzzled. She always works holidays. "Stewart, Thanksgiving's almost five months away."

He hands her a glass. "With all this business about long-lost sisters in the air I've been thinking about my own family."

"And?"

"Things haven't been the greatest since I came *bursting* out of the closet last year. I mean, I think Mom still loves me"—he offers a sheepish smile—"but I'm not so sure about Dad and David. David the house builder, David the procreator, David the real man."

"They don't think that." But they probably do. People think all kinds of things.

"I offered to come home for Thanksgiving—it's been years—and I got the brush-off from my own mother."

"Ouch."

"David's going to be there, of course, with his precious wife and precious son. And Aunt Hallie, who still thinks I'm looking for the right woman. I guess Mom figures I'd rain on everyone's parade."

"She knows this five months ahead of time?"

"It might as well be five years. Some things don't change."

Connie looks at Stewart's eyes, his frail blonde lashes. "We could have Thanksgiving together, Stewart. I haven't spent a holiday on the ground in years."

He brightens. "You think?"

"Sure. We can invite Isadora, too." It's an exhilarating thought.

"Jesus, a real holiday. Would Faith come? And her kids?"

"I doubt it." She picks up the plates of cannoli and sets them on top of the refrigerator.

"Hey," Stewart says.

"First you have to eat some real food." She takes some chicken out of the fridge and places it on the counter.

"Do you have any idea how compulsive you are?"

"Yes," she says, chopping the chicken into neat cubes.

"I think it's neurotic. This place is so clean it's creepy."

"You're a fine one to be talking neurotic, Stewart."

"Too true." He gets up, opens a cupboard, and slides the wok from its shelf. "So, what about Thanksgiving? You, me, and Isadora? That's it?"

"Faith always goes to the Fullers'."

"Even though she's divorced?"

"Old habits, I guess." She pours some oil in the wok. "Besides, Faith isn't exactly sold on Isadora."

"Why not?"

"I don't know. You should have seen her, Stewart. You'd think Isadora had fangs."

"Maybe she's jealous." He pauses. "I am, a little."

"Oh, come on."

"Maybe she thinks Isadora will take you away from her."

Connie gives Stewart a kiss on the cheek. "Stewart, you always make me feel wanted." He smiles. "Anyway," she says, "Faith's not jealous."

"How do you know?"

"Because we're not like that." She throws the chicken into the wok and steps away as it hisses against the oil. Phoebe taught her to do this long before woks were popular. She remembers learning fondue, how elegant she thought she was, dipping pieces of bread in hot cheese.

"But it's been just the two of you, Connie, and now you're three."

"Just the two of us doesn't mean what you think, Stewart. It's two chairs in the same room—sometimes I think it's no more personal than that." She's amazed at how this sounds. "That's just the way it is." She thinks of the day she left Faith and Joe's for good, her inexplicable sadness.

"All right, it'll be just you, me, and Isadora. Oh, this is going to be great! We'll get a big turkey, some pumpkins—give me a piece of paper."

While Stewart writes out a detailed menu for a five-months-away dinner, Connie sets out two place mats, some silverware, and cloth napkins. She scoops out some food from the wok and arranges it just so. She sets the steaming plate in front of him. "Here, eat this." She gets a plate for herself and lights a candle.

Stewart stops writing and raises his glass. "Here's to finding it."

She clicks her glass with mighty purpose.

LONG AFTER THEY have eaten, Connie closes herself in her bedroom and places a call to Brooklyn, her hand tight around the receiver, afraid to find Isadora changed overnight.

"Isn't this just the most amazing thing," Isadora says. "Here we are talking on the phone like any sisters anyplace in the world, and a week ago we hardly knew the first thing about each other."

"It *is* amazing," Connie says, relieved. She loves Isadora's voice; it's so dark and musical. "I was just telling my friend Stewart that."

"I've thought of a thousand questions since you left, Connie," Isadora says. "I've been looking at the pictures of Billy, and somehow after meeting Chris I can *see* him better, I can see just what he must have been like in person, so tall and dashing, and his voice, I can imagine that, too, smooth and syrupy, a music-hall voice, not a bar voice like mine, but just as strong, as sweet and golden as a voice can get."

"I suppose so."

"Did he sound like that?"

"It's been such a long time, Isadora."

"Was he a tenor or a baritone?"

"Tenor."

"Democrat or Republican?"

"I think—actually, they weren't much on politics."

"Did he bring you gifts when he came back from a tour?"

"No." She hears Isadora waiting. "They brought us with them."

"No kidding? Wow, that must have been something, going to all those cities, meeting all those people . . . "

"Well—"

"Did you ever meet anybody famous?"

Connie is getting the feeling that Isadora has her thousand questions written on a piece of paper. "Well—"

"How did he dress? Did he dress up? I bet he dressed up—I love that."

"Everybody did in those days. It was all a lot more formal."

To Connie these questions have nothing to do with Billy. What does dressing up have to do with a man whose presence could be remote and stultifying at the same time? What do gifts have to do with the things she ached for?

"What famous people did you meet?"

"Let's see . . . Helen Hayes once. And Jessica Tandy. Hume Cronyn was in—"

"Aren't those people all dead? Did you meet anybody who's still alive?"

"Actually, they're not all—"

"Did he sing you to sleep? I can just imagine being sung to sleep by a *singer*. My father's voice was about as musical as traffic."

"Speaking of music, how did your gig go?"

"The manager stiffed me for half the pay."

"Isadora, that's awful." Connie draws herself up like a mother cat, ready to protect and defend. She's glad Stewart isn't here to see how foolish she looks.

Isadora laughs. "I'll make him sorry someday when he's dying to book me. So, did Faith like me or what?"

"Well—"

"I know she didn't. I've been racking my brain ever since but I can't imagine why not."

"It's not that she doesn't like you, Isadora. Faith does everything slow."

"Well, you'd know better than me." She stops for breath. "Was Billy religious?"

And round they go, until Connie is exhausted from evading answers. Finally they run out of talk.

"What if I call you tomorrow night?" Isadora says. "We can take turns."

"I'm working tomorrow, but I'll call you the minute I get back."

"Just a sec," Isadora says. Connie hears the rustle of paper. "Tell me your schedule."

Connie tells her, flattered at being pinned down to paper. This is even more than she expected. She likes the idea of being tracked. When Isadora hangs up, Connie stays on the line, listening to that odd pocket of silence before the dial tone fully disconnects them.

She finds Stewart propped up on her sleep sofa, reading the paper and drinking wine, the shadow of his eyelashes skewed across his face from the light of a single lamp. She climbs onto the blankets, accepts a glass, and sits with him.

"A little sister," she says. "I can hardly believe it."

He puts the paper down. "You get to start all over again."

They are silent for a while. She listens to the hum of the refrigera-

MONICA WOOD

tor, the tick of the living room clock; she suddenly feels her apartment might give over to the most domestic impulses.

"Stewart," Connie says. "Sometimes I wish you weren't gay."

"Hah! You and me both, sweetheart."

"Do you think we'd still be friends?"

"Of course."

"I mean do you think we'd be lovers instead?"

"Can't you be both?"

"I never have." She pours some more wine. "Isadora's got tons of friends. She lives with four or five roommates and a cat. She just seems so, I don't know, normal."

"Because she has lots of friends?"

"Yes."

"You have lots of friends," Stewart says. "So do I. A lot of good it does us."

She looks at him.

"Where are they when you really need them?" he says.

If he's talking about her she doesn't want to know.

"Stewart, I'm not sure I know how to do this."

"Do what?"

"Be Isadora's sister."

"But you're already—oh, right, chairs in a room."

"I want to, though. It feels good."

"True confession, Connie."

"Shoot."

He sits up. "I've been having this little fantasy."

"Go."

"About having a kid." His face is still.

"You're not serious."

"Why not? You've thought about it, too."

"I think about a lot of things."

He smiles shyly. "What I mean is, I'd want you to be the mother." Connie sits back on her haunches, staring at him. "Of course we'd have to figure out a way to do it without actually having sex," he says.

"Thanks a lot."

He laughs. "Don't take it personally."

118

"I don't. It's the sweetest thing I've ever heard. Ridiculous, but sweet."

He drops back against the cushions. "That's only one of my fantasies, anyway." He grins. "The other one involves that new guy at Air France."

Connie laughs. "I saw him first." She cups her glass fervently, as if the wine contained information. "You know what, Stewart? I'm glad Isadora's so young. I swear I feel almost motherly. Big sisterly, anyway."

Stewart nods. "I'd spend more time with my nephew if they'd let me near him."

After the bottle is gone, she tucks him in and kisses his forehead. "Here's to finding it, old friend," she whispers, and goes to bed.

Near morning, the deep sound of Stewart's breathing lazing in through her bedroom door, Connie opens her eyes in the dark. She has been dreaming of stage curtains rising and falling, too quickly to see what they hid or revealed. In the gray light appear the familiar shapes of her room: the nightstand, its brass knob, the lacy hem of Grammy Spaulding's doily, the slim profile of the table lamp. In her half-sleep she reaches for the telephone, and by the time she has dialed the first digit of Faith's number she recognizes where she is, that it is too late to call and too early, and that she hasn't the smallest idea what she might have wanted to say.

FOUR

THE CLUB IS SMALL and dusky; it smells of spirits, dark wood, the hot street. Armand loiters over a whiskey and water while Connie and Stewart share a bottle of wine. Connie lolls in their company, in the sight of her little sister, who is curled over a well-worn guitar, her blonde hair cloudy under the weak stage light. Her voice, its low timbre drowsing over old blues, quiets the scattered crowd. Behind her a thin black man thumps on a bass guitar.

This is the last set. Connie watches Isadora's slender fingers, the fragile arms, the soft lines that appear between her eyebrows as she sings. She is small, but mighty somehow, transformed under the light. Billy and Delle had been able to change like that, and Connie is aware of wanting Isadora in the huge and foggy way she had once wanted them.

Armand leans over, touching Connie's shoulder. "She reminds me of Billy, so help me," he whispers. She nods dumbly. She claps until her palms sting, the room a gentle, wine-tipped whirl.

Isadora lays her guitar in a case and steps down from the stage. She aims a bright smile at Connie's table, then steps past them to greet a gathering of friends, late arrivals who have commandeered several tables in the back. Connie listens to them laugh and talk, a society all to themselves, their voices pumped with the amplitude of a shared and careless past.

"She's great, isn't she great?" Connie says to Stewart and Armand. "She's the best damned singer I ever heard, I swear, she's great."

120

Stewart regards her patiently. "Gee, Connie, have another drink."

"You don't think she's great?" Her question is a challenge, one she finds exhilarating; she's defending her little sister. It's an unnecessary bravado, a throwback to her adolescence. She is speaking loudly and knows it, hoping Isadora can hear.

"She *is* good," Stewart says. "I'm impressed."

Armand smiles, lifts his drink. "I'm still here, an old man out past his bedtime." He cranes his neck. "Is she coming over?"

"Give her five minutes," Connie says. "You have to keep the fans happy." She speaks as if from a store of intimate knowledge — about performance politics, psychology, and Isadora.

But Isadora has happily installed herself amidst a stable of friends, a boisterous, adoring throng. They rock their heads back, wave their hands around, transforming themselves into a kinetic cloak of movement that seems almost calculated to isolate Isadora, who sits somewhere in its center.

"I'm done," Stewart says, rising. "I've got to be at the airport by nine." Armand gets up, too, rubbing his eyes, the skin over his fists loose, the knuckles swollen. He is indeed an old man.

Connie wants to stay, in the hope that she and Isadora might enjoy last call together, just the two of them, but she can see this is not going to happen. She has imagined over and over just such a scene: a late-night unburdening over a glass of wine in a restaurant, or a bar like this one, or Connie's hotel room, or a private corner of Isadora's apartment in Brooklyn. In this scene, Isadora's face opens into a smile, her features obscured by smoke (the bar) or low light (the restaurant, hotel room, apartment), except for her eyes, which are trained on Connie with the clarity of an emerald while she expresses her deepest needs and dreams.

Their phone conversations have become more sporadic, even a little stilted. Connie's made-up answers are beginning to contradict themselves. One night she told Isadora about a family outing to the zoo, and a few nights later manufactured an anecdote about Billy's fear of large animals. Isadora even sounds bored sometimes, though it could be her late hours.

A burst of laughter detonates at the back table. "New Guard,"

121

MONICA WOOD

Stewart mutters cheerfully. "They're everywhere." Connie turns around. They are one merry bunch, Isadora dead center.

Connie is beginning to suspect that her existence in the world has turned, for Isadora, into a mild, possibly unimportant disappointment. Still, she visits whenever she can, staying in a hotel uptown a couple of blocks from Armand's apartment, commuting to and from Brooklyn by taxi to see Isadora. Isadora, who is weary of the subway, doesn't come into Manhattan any more than she has to. On the one night she persuaded Isadora to meet for dinner in the Village, Connie waited nearly an hour at Washington Square while a heavily dressed man, with the precision of a robot, smashed an endless supply of light bulbs one by one on the sidewalk half a block away. Isadora eventually arrived, out of breath and aflutter with explanations having to do with roommates, phone calls, a neighbor's lost keys. They went to a cafe on MacDougall Street that Isadora liked: noisy and crowded, bereft of intimate corners.

Connie follows Armand and Stewart to the door, knowing that if she stays there's a possibility she won't be wanted. They stop by the noisy group of tables on their way out. Isadora jumps up.

"Where are you going?" she says.

Armand chuckles. "Home. This old boy needs some sleep." He looks at Isadora and her friends kindly, but from the other side of a chasm of age and sensibility. Connie knows just how he feels. He takes Isadora's hand. "You were marvelous, dear."

"You were," Stewart adds. "Loved your stuff."

"Did you really?" She is flushed and shameless. "You're not just saying that?"

They repeat their compliments, while Connie waits, watching the table of friends. Finally she says, "I'm Connie."

"Oh!" Isadora says. "Everybody, this is Stewart and Armand, and my sister, Connie. Connie, this is—" She scans the dozen or so faces. "Well, this is everybody." More raucous laughter erupts from the friends.

"Hi," Connie says. Most of them have already turned to each other. She remains, thinking of the next thing to say. She somehow expects something momentous to happen, having been introduced as Isadora's sister.

"Well, I guess we're off," she says to Isadora after no one else speaks. "You were the best."

Isadora, a hugger, hugs Connie. Connie breathes the fluffy hair, presses her hands against the delicate wings of Isadora's shoulder blades. "I'm so proud," she says, hoping Isadora will catch some import there, layers of meaning.

Instead, she makes a face. "It's a dumpy club. But life gets better." She smiles. She believes it.

THE NEXT DAY Connie, unannounced, drops by Isadora's apartment, a sunny, two-story shambles in Park Slope where a bewildering number of roommates parade in and out. The rooms are large and cluttered, presided over by Isadora's enormous tail-less cat, Bob. He sits in Isadora's lap, his claws dug into her skinny thighs, staring at Connie with a cat's hard judgment.

"Nice cat," Connie says. She is perched at the edge of a plaid couch, wearing a red sun dress and heels, feeling overdressed. Isadora is the picture of comfort in a long T-shirt cinched at the hips with a scarf. She barely looks eighteen.

Isadora kisses the top of Bob's head. "He's my little baby. You should get one, Connie."

"I'm always away."

"Oh, right." Bob shifts his weight and anchors himself to one of Isadora's knees. The claws look painful but Isadora doesn't seem to mind. "Do you ever get sick of traveling?"

It sounds like small talk. It is. Connie makes a noncommittal gesture.

"When I get my big break I'll have to travel a lot," Isadora says. "Poor Bob won't like it one bit." She kisses the cat's head again, nuzzling the fur with her mouth. "What did you think of my bass player?"

"Oh. He's good." She can hardly remember what he looks like.

"We used to go out," Isadora says. "We're still friends."

Connie laughs. As far as she can tell, Isadora has gone out with a lot of men, including at least one of her roommates. It's a familiar business, except for the part about staying friends. She thinks of

123

Marcel, young and callow. "I know a guy in Paris who would adore you."

Isadora waves her hands. "I'm off men for a while."

"I don't blame you," Connie says. She sounds more cynical than she wants to.

Two of the roommates emerge from upstairs, shouldering bicycles. They wave on their way out the door but do not stop to be introduced. Connie has an unexpected urge to run after them, asking *What does she say about me? Does she say anything about me?*

"Don't you think it was sweet of Armand to come last night?" Isadora says. "He reminds me a little of my father."

Connie looks up.

"Not Billy." She rearranges Bob once again. "Anyway, I think Armand's an old sweetie."

Watching Isadora, Connie wonders if, had she lived Isadora's life, she herself could have turned out this way: lounging in a deep chair with a big cat, friends calling at all hours, a belief that life gets better. She can't imagine how she would function in an apartment like this one, even for one night.

One of the roommates pokes her head in. "If Timmy calls, I'm on my way."

Isadora laughs. "Don't blow it, Rosie."

The roommate makes a face and disappears. It occurs to Connie that Isadora must have things to do, that sitting here is a courtesy. She gets up. "I've got a plane to catch."

Bob spills out of Isadora's lap as she stands up. She calls a car service while Connie waits, studying her quick movements, the way she drums her fingers in the air, rehearsing without the guitar. "Come on, I'll walk you down," Isadora says, and Connie follows her into the hall and down the stairs, still watching her, the way her bracelets slide along her arm, the way her feet tap each step, barely making contact.

Isadora reaches the street long before Connie, bouncing slightly on her toes. She's been out half the night but her skin is bright, her eyes alert.

"I was going to ask you something, Connie," she says. "I've been thinking about my brilliant career." She grins—a charming, self-deprecating twist of her lip—then turns abruptly serious. "I need a manager. Someone who knows people in this town, someone who can get me off this *plateau* I've been sitting on."

Connie considers her: the tiny smile, the self-conscious way she draws her hand through her hair. Is she asking for something? A succession of cars moves through the light at the corner but Isadora takes no notice. Connie watches, not wanting to miss her ride but also not wanting to catch it. Next door to Isadora's building, the polished vegetables of a Korean market are piled into bins above the grimy sidewalk. Connie moves closer, lured by their simple beauty.

"I thought you might know somebody here," Isadora says. "Maybe somebody who worked with Billy—with your parents." She sounds casual, but her eyes don't move from Connie's face. "You know, a show biz type."

Connie wheels back through time as a myriad of faces appears before her, dim and nameless. She tries to remember, desperate to come up with something. "I don't know anyone but Armand."

Isadora makes a face. "He was no help. He doesn't run in those circles anymore."

"Oh."

"I thought maybe Billy had an agent or something."

"He did." Connie frowns. "Garrett Reese. But he was a theatrical agent. I don't see how he could help you."

"Connections, Connie," Isadora says. "Believe me, these guys all know each other."

"He must be at least sixty by now," Connie says. "Probably retired. Besides, Billy and Delle weren't exactly his favorite clients. He despised them at the end, and the feeling was more than mutual. He dropped them after they left *Silver Moon*."

Isadora plunges one hand into her purse and comes up with an envelope and a pencil. "Anything's worth a shot," she mutters, writing down Garrett's name. "Maybe I can get *something* out of being Billy Spaulding's daughter."

Connie steps back, blinking hard, as Isadora blathers on. "Being a performer is a bitch," she says. "Maybe he wasn't the nicest guy in the world, but I have a lot of respect for Billy, just for surviving. Your mother, too. They didn't pick an easy path."

But they *didn't* survive, Connie wants to say. They're dead. She catches an incongruous whiff of fields and earth from the market's colorful harvest.

"It must have been exciting," Isadora says, "growing up with all that *commotion*." She sounds envious, as if she thinks with Connie's life she'd be already famous.

"They were quite the days," Connie says. "I sat in Marlon Brando's lap when I was five."

Isadora smiles politely. "Really?" Apparently Marlon Brando has lost some stature since the last time Connie told this story.

A car slows. Isadora's hand goes up instantly; she's been watching after all. Connie moves toward the curb, staring hard at the street, ashamed of her long-ago lie.

FIVE

SETTLED ON the porch steps, the dog's soft head in her lap, Faith looks out over her yard: the bountiful feeders, the red impatiens crowding their pots, the hydrangeas' snowball flowers already tinged with their dying pink. Mums and marigolds line the walk, solid and mute.

It sometimes occurs to her that, unlike most people she knows, she has no inner life, no poetic core of certainty, no burning dot of conviction from which springs a lifetime of heedless, unaccountable choices. But her flowers and trees contradict her: surely her inner life is here, in this tended yard, in these colors that are doomed to disappear after the cold of autumn. Come spring she will begin again, digging in the dirt. Planting is her private tradition, her secret belief that life, in all its passages, contains the possibility of beauty, even hope.

Before Faith hears the car, Sammy propels himself off the porch to wait at the end of the walk, ears pitched forward. More than once Faith has wished for an animal's finely tuned senses, that talent for knowing what's just ahead. Connie pulls over, waving out the window, her radio on. Since Isadora's arrival in their lives, she has taken to dropping by Faith's house unexpectedly, sometimes just for minutes, just long enough to say hello. Their conversations together are spare, as always, but Connie's tone has become nonchalant, almost breezy, as if there were nothing between them but good fortune, as if the thing they had in common were happiness of an inherited kind.

"I was in the neighborhood," she says, coming up the walk.

Faith smiles. "You live in the neighborhood." She reaches for the dog. "Down, Sammy."

"He's all right." Connie pushes the dog away gently, petting his head to calm him. "Where is everybody?"

"At the Fullers'. The end-of-summer barbecue."

"You didn't go?"

"I had things to do."

Connie sits down next to Faith. "I'm going to New York tonight and wondered if you wanted anything."

"What would I want?"

"I don't know," Connie says. "Some decent wine? Some good chocolate, maybe." She looks out at the yard. Faith wonders what she sees there. She wonders if sometime far from now her children might see a chrysanthemum in full bloom and think of her.

"I don't need anything. But thanks."

Connie makes an odd gesture with her wrist—an exacting little flick—that Faith remembers from long ago. It means she is disappointed.

"Some chocolate would be nice," Faith says. "Now that you mention it."

"Great." Connie rummages into her purse for a pad and pencil. *Chocolate for Faith*, she writes, then keeps the pencil poised. "Any messages for Isadora?"

Faith shakes her head. "She called here last night. Chris was the only one up."

A goldfinch lights on one of the feeders, then another.

"Musicians' hours," Connie says.

"We keep regular people's hours." Faith pets the dog, glad of his smooth fur, his silent company. The phone rings inside the house, but she makes no move.

"Do you want me to get it?" Connie asks.

"Let it ring." She knows it's Phoebe, or maybe one of the boys, wanting her at the barbecue. She listens until it stops.

"Faith?" Connie taps the pad with her pencil. "Can you think of anything I could tell Isadora about Billy?"

"You mean something good?"

128

"Yes," she says softly. She's watching the finches, a band of them now, squabbling at the feeders. "Something good. A family story."

A blue-black grackle descends, scattering the flock. "I can't think of anything, Connie," Faith says. She wishes she could, but it's like looking into a store window at the perfect gift that's thousands of dollars out of reach. "Really. I'm sorry."

Connie keeps silent awhile, fidgeting on the step. "Didn't they take us to a zoo or something once?" she asks finally. "I think I remember that." Her tone contains that new nonchalance. An old image pierces Faith's vision, an image of Connie trailing Billy, her blonde hair snarled behind one ear.

"I can't think of anything," Faith says again.

"I should go," Connie says. But she doesn't, yet. "Does she ever say anything about me?"

"Who? Isadora?"

"I just wondered." She tucks her purse under her arm. "Sure you don't want anything besides chocolate?"

"She said she thought you were sweet." This is a lie, and Faith is amazed at herself for telling it. When Isadora calls she talks mostly about herself.

"Really?" Connie says.

"And brave, too, going all over the world the way you do." Faith thinks a minute. "She says you're lucky to have so many friends. She thinks it's a good reflection on you, that a lot of people like you."

"No kidding," Connie says. She looks five.

"And she likes your hair. It's beautiful."

Connie takes a long swipe through her hair. "Well."

Faith follows Connie to her car and then waves her down the street. It is late now, fall just days away, a chill sweeping in from the bay which she can feel this far into town. Fall used to be her best time of year, the boys coming home from school with their stories. She had taken every step of childhood with them, and as they grew up, so did she; she thought of herself as a slow bloomer, still a bud. Now it is different: their adolescence has turned more private, the remaining steps a mystery.

The finches are back, small and fierce and directed. She is suddenly cold. "Come on, Sammy," she says. "Let's go in."

She thinks about the barbecue, the voices shouting back and forth across the volleyball net. As if it would be gone by nightfall, Faith again takes in the sight of her burgeoning yard. She snaps a pink-tinged hydrangea from one of the bushes, then hurries up the steps, the flat, painted wood yielding nothing under her weight. She considers how immobile a house is, how everything you put into it stays there, how immune it is to change, how much more solid than a person.

SIX

WINTER COMES swift and early. Fall is long buried, its auburn leaves lost under a few hard inches of snow. In the stinging cold of her back yard, Faith braces herself against the icy air, shivering, one glove on, the other hand bare and held out, a scatter of sunflower seeds shining like onyx on her palm. Still as death, clucking softly, she watches the chickadees flutter around their preferred feeder—three tubes with a cover and bowl—a few inches from her outstretched fingers.

This simple ritual, which she has been repeating twice a day, will, according to the book, bring the chickadees and perhaps the siskins to light on her hand. Bundled in an old, royal blue parka (*something in a bright, recognizable color so the birds will come to know you,* the book says), she stands the cold, the birds' indifference, and the inherent foolishness of this act with the patience of one who has no time but a well—a whole canyon—of faith.

The chickadees dart back and forth, in their habit of taking one seed away at a time. Their lispy, quarrelsome voices connect her somehow to the world, and she loves them for their noisy presence, their beauty, their unflinching predictability. They give her an occasional glimpse of the world's design.

"Mom, we're leaving," Ben calls from the house. "Dad's here."

It is Thanksgiving Day. She has told the boys she is going to Connie's so they won't feel bad leaving her alone. She returns to the house and shepherds them out the door with a couple of pies—her traditional contribution to the Fuller Thanksgiving—hoping to have them gone quickly, to spare them from witnessing whatever

131

she is bound to feel. This will be her first Thanksgiving without them. Joe lingers on the porch, full of silent questions.

"You know you're welcome," he says.

She shakes her head, looking beyond the front door to where Brenda sits waiting in a green car. Joe's truck has been banished for the day, unable to accommodate them all. Last year at this time there was no Brenda, no one Joe wanted to take into the family. He'd been dating, but the women were just names. Marianne. Gail. Then Brenda. The boys must be talking to Brenda from the back seat, for she smiles and nods without looking at them. Her hair, black like Joe's, sprays out from her face, aimless in the dry, staticky cold. A finger of resentment lays itself on Faith's heart as she imagines this woman at Joe's table, in his bed, talking and talking, arms permanently outstretched, making it all look easy.

Chris likes Brenda, Faith knows, but Ben will never say, thinking he's being kind. She looks like a nice woman, and of course she must be.

"Don't you have to go?" Faith tells Joe, lifting her chin toward the car.

"Right."

"Say hi to everyone."

Joe hesitates. "Are you okay?"

"I'm great. The day's all planned."

"I'm sorry I brought Brenda," he says. "I didn't know how else to do this."

"For God's sake, Joe, you've been living with the woman for months. Why are you apologizing?"

"I don't know." He looks perplexed. "Stupid, I guess."

It still surprises her that he found Brenda, that it's possible for a human being to surrender to love more than once. To again wander through the slow motion of turning toward and turning away, shaping out of words let go and words taken back a language you could both understand. Hadn't that always been the difference between them? Joe would surrender again—and again, a believer.

He starts to leave, then turns back. "Don't you ever miss me?"

She knows he expects no answer. *Yes*, she could say, but the specter of the road that had been their marriage—steep and dangerous, full of switchbacks—freezes the word in her throat. After the divorce, their house seemed empty and forbidding, and she recognized all at once how little of it had ever been hers, how heavily she had borrowed from Joe's life. He had taken little away—his clothes, his gadgets in the basement, a couple of pieces of furniture—but even with the boys still in it, the house had an echoey quality, the sound of moving day. She resorted to an old comfort, a superstition she'd devised as a child: in every new room of every new place on the road she would walk the whole of the floor in a crabbed, deliberate way, imprinting every square inch with the soles of her feet. It would take a long time, and a lot of concentration not to lose her place. Then she would hide something—a button, a penny, a marble—in a secret place, to be left there forever or until some lonely person found it. Even now it pleases her to think of the trail of treasures in places she has long forgotten. She repeated her childhood ritual in this house after Joe left, walking every inch—the space behind the stereo speaker, the narrow corridor between the bed and the dresser, each stair from side to side. But she hid no treasures here; her children were her treasures, and if she hid no others perhaps they would belong to this house forever.

"If you change your mind," Joe says, "you know where we are." He turns again and finishes his leaving.

She watches them drive away, the snow so dry it kicks up like flour behind the tires. Her sons' dark and light heads bob against the back windshield.

The day endures. She reads, naps, walks the house. Finally she returns to her birds and stays there a long time. Her fingertips turn numb and bloodless, but she persists, in the waning sunlight, her second attempt in the day, holding out her gift to the ignorant birds. By now the turkeys at the Fullers' have long since been cut, the white and dark meat doled out. She can almost see it, the aftermath, the decimated pies, wishbones drying on the stove, the sound of voices sparking out from various parts of the house.

This is Joe's year to say the Thanksgiving grace. She pictures him standing at the table, his simple words of thanks, his good-natured voice. She sees the assemblage that she once tried to believe was hers, bowing their heads in some tacit and immutable notion of

133

themselves as a linked body. In years past she would open her eyes, raise her head, and peer over the fragrant abundance at the ring of good faces, as if to separate herself from their version of love.

An easy loneliness settles in: gossamer, weblike, so familiar it is almost a comfort. And nostalgia, too, a peculiar longing for the holidays of her childhood, stripped of ceremony or decoration, just she and her sister left behind again, a desk clerk or babysitter for company, and always a small diversion: a hot turkey sandwich from the room-service girl, or a long-distance phone call, just for them, from Armand. A far cry from the Fullers' picturesque holidays, but at least she had always known, more or less, what to expect. At the Fullers' she never knew what extravagance was coming next.

"Faith?"

Birds explode from the feeders as Faith jumps, the seeds spilling from her hand and disappearing into the white ground. At the edge of the house stands a man, a stranger.

"Sorry," he says. "I'm Stewart. Connie's friend?"

Connie and Isadora come up behind him. Dressed for cold weather, Isadora looks a little bigger. Stray hairs trail out from under her hat in a filmy veil.

"What are you doing home?" Connie asks.

"I live here." *I was just thinking about you*, she wants to say.

Isadora takes four long strides and plants a kiss on Faith's cold cheek. "I was dying to see where you lived, Faith. I asked Connie to bring me over here."

They stand in a loose cluster, looking at her, something breathless and happy about them, as if they've been drinking, or running fast. Isadora notices Faith's one bare hand. "What are you doing?"

"Feeding the birds." She thrusts her hands into her pockets. "Looking at them."

"Faith's a birdwatcher," Connie says, her voice big and hearty.

"Me too," Isadora says. She is beaming; they are all beaming.

"Really?" Faith says.

"I've watched birds for years." Isadora regards the creatures in question, who are already returning to the feeders. "You have quite a bunch."

"What are they?" Stewart asks. The birds flit back and forth

again, not bothered by the presence of a crowd. Faith waits, out of
habit and politeness, for Isadora to answer first. The wait is long
and then awkward, until it becomes clear to Faith that Isadora
doesn't know a thing about birds.

"The little striped ones are pine siskins," Faith tells Stewart. "And
the ones with the black caps are chickadees." She points out a
nuthatch near the fence and a cluster of house finches on the far feeder. "If you wait long enough you might see a couple of woodpeckers
at the suet bell."

They're all smiling as if under direction, especially Connie, who
seems ready to burst out of her clothes.

"They're pretty," Isadora says. "I saw a big blue heron once, right
in Central Park."

"You're kidding," Connie says. She sounds amazed, as if Isadora
were reporting on a recent trip to the moon.

Faith pushes her frozen hand deeper into her pocket. "You probably mean a great blue." She meets Connie's eye briefly.

"I thought you were at Phoebe's," Connie says.

"I came back early." She feels her face go red and with some relief
understands herself to be a bad liar. "Actually, I didn't get over
there."

"You didn't?" Connie says. They're all shivering, standing in the
snow of Faith's back yard as daylight fails them by seconds. "You
mean not at all?"

"I didn't feel like it."

"You didn't get any turkey?" Stewart says.

"I didn't want any."

Stewart's long arms float out from his sides. "And here we were,
eating like the three little pigs!" He holds his hand out to Connie.
"Give me your keys. I'm going right back there for some food."

Faith takes a step. "Oh, no, please—"

"Don't even say it," Stewart says. "We had a veritable food orgy
over there, and there's plenty left."

Isadora laughs. "We cooked enough for ten."

"Really, I don't want anything," Faith says, but Stewart runs off,
with Isadora and Connie yelling after him not to forget the pies, the
wine, the cranberry sauce.

"We had a ball," Isadora says. "I wish we'd known you were here."

Faith makes a noncommittal sound.

"My mother used to feed the birds," Isadora says, gazing at the feeders.

"Isadora lived near Prospect Park in Brooklyn," Connie says. "Remember that park, Faith? Armand took us there once. Remember the beatniks?"

"No."

"Playing the bongos? You don't remember? You were scared of their beards."

Isadora is nodding. Apparently she has heard this story already today. "No, really. I don't remember that," Faith says.

"Anyway," Isadora says, "Prospect Park is loaded with birds. Spring and fall, my mother would go crazy. She had feeders everywhere." She sweeps the scope of Faith's yard with one hand. "Just like this. Of course our yard was smaller."

Connie and Isadora are fading into the dusk, their smiles luminous, similarly shaped. Billy and Delle used to fade that way at the end of each act, and for a long time Faith suspected they possessed the ability to literally disappear. It was one of the many things she never confided to Connie out of the fear it might be true.

"Is anyone else cold?" Connie says.

"Oh. Sorry. Come in," Faith tells them, and they follow her into the house. She doesn't quite know what to do with them. In the warm hall she flexes her frozen fingers, stamps her feet, stalling.

"Oh, I *love* dogs," Isadora says, scooching down and peppering Sammy's face with kisses. "Aren't you a sweet old boy."

Faith hangs up their coats while they stand in the hall, not talking. Isadora wanders over to a calendar, which features for November a color photograph of a willow ptarmigan.

"My mother had one of those in the yard one day," Isadora says.

Faith smiles awkwardly. "That would be an amazing sight."

"Oh, it was. Fat and pretty." Isadora measures its breadth with her hands; she's off by half a foot or so, but the bird materializes anyway, its white feathers fluffed out, protecting itself. Faith half believes Isadora could have seen such a thing.

She invites them into the living room, but when she retreats into the kitchen to put some water on, Isadora follows her, and Connie follows Isadora. Isadora pulls out one of the kitchen chairs and straddles it, her arms folded over its back. Connie stands, her hands in her pockets. Faith feels their eyes on her as she fills the kettle and turns on the gas.

"I've been trying to get the chickadees to eat out of my hand," she says. She turns to look at them, to see if she has really confessed this.

"I didn't know birds did that," Connie says.

"Oh, yes," Isadora says, the soul of authority. "They're much tamer than people think."

Faith stares at the kettle, the watched pot. Suddenly Stewart is clamoring at the front door and Isadora skips out to let him in.

Connie appears at Faith's side now, one hand tentatively perched on her shoulder. "You don't mind that we came?"

"No," Faith says. "I don't mind." She doesn't, somehow; she's glad of the company, and recognizes that it has been a long, dark day.

Stewart comes in, the cold evening wafting off his clothes as he sets a stack of foil-covered plates on the kitchen table.

" 'Over the river and through the woods,' " he sings, and Connie and Isadora join in: " 'To Grandmother's house we go . . . ' " Faith can barely hear Connie, but her mouth is moving. " ' . . . The horse knows the way to carry the sleigh, da dum da dum dee doe . . . ' "

Connie unfurls the turkey wrappings. "Remember that song, Faith?"

"We could only come up with the first three lines," Stewart says. "And a loose approximation of the melody, as you probably noticed."

"I know it ends with 'Hooray for the pumpkin pie,' " Connie says, her forehead furrowed with remembering. "Grammy Spaulding used to sing it. Faith, how did it go after 'carry the sleigh'?"

"You don't remember Grammy," Faith says. Isadora's small fibs have made her ill-disposed to large ones.

"Yes I do."

This is an old argument, their only one. It began ludicrously long ago, in some grade school in California where Connie was asked to write an essay about an unforgettable person.

"Connie, you were two years old."

"I remember that far," Connie says. "I can't help it." She turns to Stewart. "It's 'Hooray for the something/something something/ and hooray for the pumpkin pie.' Isn't that it?"

"Connie, you were *two*." Faith sounds more agitated than she means to, and the three of them regard her uneasily.

Connie begins to open the other wrappings, revealing pies, cranberry sauce, stuffing. "She used to go to bed with her hair in a braid," she says. "This thin white braid down over one shoulder."

It is quiet, gravelike. Somehow they have all gotten into chairs and are seated around the table, listening to Connie. The festive remnants on the table remind Faith of pictures of airplane crashes, bright bits of clothing flung over the evil ground.

"Don't you remember the braid?"

"No," Faith says.

"You're the one who used to talk about her when we were little," Connie insists. "You're the one who told me she was in heaven."

Faith strains to remember, tries until her head hurts, but it's no use. She remembers a million things, but not that. "I don't see how you can remember her, that's all," she murmurs.

Connie lowers her eyes. "I don't see how you can't."

Faith has changed the temper of the room and she's sorry, but she can't help herself. Quite unexpectedly, she feels protective of her grandmother's ghost, unwilling to let her be resurrected into Connie's new, painted-over family.

"I don't remember any further back than my first day of school," Stewart says. "I got to be the crayon boy, my first job." He divides the remaining cranberry sauce into four portions with an earnestness that Faith finds touching. The kitchen lights are on, and she wonders what this gathering might look like to someone passing silent in the snow.

"I fell off a table when I was one," Isadora says. "I remember that."

Faith accepts some food from Stewart with a polite smile. "It doesn't matter. We did have a nice grandmother, by all accounts. Armand adored her."

"He used to call her our guardian angel," Connie says.

"He did?"

"Armand told me that," Connie says quickly. "I don't remember it myself."

"Did Billy adore her too?" Isadora asks. She's cutting into one of the pies, but her body is stiff with listening.

"Oh my God, he *worshiped* her," Connie says. "He dedicated all his shows to her." Faith stops eating, stunned, as Connie studiously avoids her eyes.

"I love that," Isadora says. "I bet he carried something around with him, you know how people do, a brooch or a hair ribbon or something." She stretches out her thin hand to show a gold ring. "This was my mother's."

Faith watches as Connie examines the ring, taking Isadora's hand in hers. "Did you notice the lace doily on my bedside table?" Connie asks.

"I didn't happen to," Isadora says.

"It's Grammy Spaulding's. I got it from Billy."

This is not exactly a lie, Faith thinks, but it is certainly not the truth.

Isadora sighs deeply. "Oh, I *love* that. I bet she made it for him when he was just a baby."

Connie pauses. "Think how long he carried it around. Think how old it is."

Faith is staring full at Connie now, but Connie won't budge. Instead it is Stewart who catches her eye, an ironic smile quivering on his lips. Faith acknowledges his message gratefully, relieved that she is not the only one here who understands how badly Connie is bending the truth.

"Memory is a magnificent thing," he says, one eyebrow arched.

Isadora nods vigorously. "We're nothing without it." She reaches down to pet Sammy, who has taken up residence at her feet. "I pity animals, really. They don't seem to remember past their last breath."

"Oh, I don't know," Faith says. "The birds come back every year.

They nest in the same trees, feed in the same yards, leave again when it's time. They remember better than we do."

"So," Isadora says. "What about you, Faith?" She places a hunk of pie on her plate with the rest of her food and begins to eat it all at more or less the same time, which gives Faith's stomach a turn. "What do you remember about Billy?"

"I'm sorry, Isadora," Faith says gently. "I have no stories for you."

She hears the slamming door of Joe's truck outside, a sound she would recognize anywhere.

"That's okay," Isadora says. "He's not important anymore." She waves her fork. "We're the important ones."

"He was a wonderful actor," Connie says.

"It's true," Faith says, mostly to herself. "They both were." She turns to Isadora. "They could make you cry."

Footsteps thunder on the street, the walk, the front steps. Joe and the boys appear, a burst of clean cold. They're a magnificent sight, the unadorned truth marching through the door, as real as the weather they bring in with them.

"Hey, it's Isadora," Chris says.

Isadora trots over and gives everyone a hug, including Joe. "I take it you're the third sister," he says, grinning.

"You guessed it," she says, and suddenly everyone is talking at once. To Faith it sounds like a language she has long studied but never spoken.

"Did you have fun?" Faith asks the boys.

Ben holds his stomach and groans.

"He ate a whole pie," Chris says. "He was disgusting."

"Did not," Ben protests. "Mom, I didn't."

"Do you guys know the words to 'Over the River and Through the Woods'?" Stewart asks.

Chris frowns. "Say what?"

"It's a Thanksgiving song," Isadora says.

"We're not very musical," Chris tells her. "You should hear us at Christmas."

Joe laughs. "My mother has Von Trapp delusions. We indulge her the best we can."

"I have a guitar," Ben says, as if that might redeem them.

"Well, bring it on out," Stewart says.

Isadora produces a well-worn bottleneck and a guitar pick. "We'll just make it up as we go along."

As Ben goes after the guitar, everyone else assembles in the living room. Joe moves to join them as if he has all night. Faith doesn't ask about Brenda.

"Why did you tell her those things?" Faith whispers to Connie as they sit down.

"What things?"

"Connie." In the background she can hear Isadora telling Joe and the boys about the dinner at Connie's, the visit to Faith's back yard, even the story about the willow ptarmigan.

"He left her mother high and dry," Connie says. "Why not let her think he could be decent once in a while?"

"But it doesn't seem fair to make up a bunch of—"

"Faith." Connie looks away, toward the sofa, where Isadora is still chattering as she tunes Ben's guitar. "Not wanting her won't turn her into somebody else's sister."

Faith falls silent, for this is the first thing Connie has said since arriving that has the ring of truth. Isadora clears her throat and beams at everyone, then begins to coax some languid blues out of Ben's cheap guitar. Her voice is dark and husky, yet plaintive, astonishingly clear. Faith listens.

Isadora's singing brings the surprise of memory, for there is something in her voice that is reminiscent of Billy's, and Faith remembers how she felt as a very young child, watching Billy and Delle on stage, listening to their entwined voices, filling herself with the sweetness of the characters they played. For the longest time she thought these charming people who sang and danced and said funny and romantic things to each other were her real mother and father, however fleetingly they appeared. Billy and Delle were some sort of stand-ins, altered somehow by the darkness of life offstage.

When Isadora finishes her song the room erupts. "Yeah!" Ben calls out. Stewart and Chris whistle through their fingers.

"Wow," Joe says.

Without a word Isadora begins again, another song about love.
Faith moves her eyes slowly around the room, at the ring of faces
transfixed by Isadora's music. She has to admit to being transfixed
herself, not so much by the music as by this brief glimpse of what
they all might have been, given a different life.

V

SECRET LANGUAGE

ONE

GARRETT HAS NOT done well. His waiting room is small and stale, its one window looking down on the wintry rubble of Times Square. Behind a flimsy desk sits a secretary, a girl barely out of high school, with heavily made-up eyes. She has the aspiring look of an out-of-work actor and is reading an unbound script. Her head moves oddly, as if she is walking the stage in her head.

Photographs jam each wall. Many of them are old, including one—the largest, almost poster-sized—of the cast of *Silver Moon*. Isadora gets up to inspect it. She is quiet, obviously disappointed by Garrett's poor quarters. Connie wanders to a different wall, sorry to have brought Isadora here, to have presumed she had anything to give her.

She scans the photographs, dozens of obscure faces—musicians, actors, comedians, dance troupes, rock bands: a parade of hope and frustration in which she recognizes no one but her parents. In one photograph Billy and Delle stand side by side, dressed as a count and countess. Connie recalls the costumes but not the show, though she thinks she might remember a choking heat, a vapid audience, a bitter, ongoing argument. In another photograph they are posed in evening clothes, flanked by Garrett and some cast members in front of the Barrymore. The marquee reads *Smythe and Smythe*. Their smiles are huge and gluttonous, for this is their first Broadway show.

She blinks at this photograph and, as if they have just appeared, finds two tiny girls hovering like dust motes at the fringes of the small crowd. They stand close to each other, but nothing touches except the frilly hems of their white dresses.

A shadow appears behind the milky glass window of Garrett's office door. As it swings open, the letters on the window, GARRETT REESE, MANAGEMENT/PROMOTION/PUBLIC RELATIONS, appear backwards behind him. The secretary doesn't flinch from her reading; in the twenty minutes Connie has waited, the phone hasn't rung once.

"I'll be goddamned," he says, putting his hand out. "Connie Spaulding."

His smile strikes Connie as unnervingly forgiving, as if she has come here for restitution. His face, mostly unchanged, triggers a clutter of eavesdropped memories: screaming phone calls, accusations back and forth, threats and counterthreats and ultimatums. She'd had some foolish notion of cashing in on his nostalgia, but realizes too late that there is nothing to collect.

"This is Isadora," she says.

Isadora offers her hand, a little stiffly, Connie thinks. She looks like a person aware of wasting time.

Garrett looks from one to the other. "Amazing." He shakes his head, chuckling softly. "Amazing. Come on in." To the girl at the desk he says, "Hold my calls."

He ushers them into his office, a roomier, more cheerful space with two windows and a smaller explosion of photographs on each wall. He sits down and teeters back on his chair. His hair is almost gone, but otherwise he is not much changed. His clothes are casual, but expensive and pressed, and he moves like a man who knows what he's doing. He is still slim, slight, and his eyes contain the narrow gleam that Connie had once taken for whimsy and recognizes now as hunger.

"So this is the love child," he says, looking at Isadora. If he is being indelicate, Isadora doesn't seem to mind. She opens her hands as if to say *That's me.*

"You do blues?" he says.

"I do blues." She regards him evenly. "A lot of people think I'm good."

"A lot of people don't mean shit."

146

Isadora shrugs. "Depends on who they are."

"Maybe." Garrett seems to be playing a game to which Isadora already knows the rules. He looks pleased.

Isadora points to the wall behind Garrett, at a photograph of the curtain call of *Silver Moon*. "My mother's the one on the end," she says. "The pretty one."

Garrett doesn't look. "Don't remember her." He glances at Connie as if they share a secret. "I had my hands full with the leads." He leans back a little farther, lacing his fingers behind his head, his eyes glittering out at them—a man with a plan. "It was different then," he says. "You got *involved*. Nowadays you book your gig and take your ten. It's a lonely business." He unlaces his hands, taps the picture frame behind him without looking. "I produced the whole shebang, raised the money, hired the director, babysat the whole tour. I did half the rewrites on this thing; did you know that?"

"No," Connie says. She doesn't understand what it is she is witnessing, but the room feels sepia-toned all of a sudden, quiet in the way of house lights going down.

"We had a ball on that tour." He looks beyond her. "Tours lasted forever back then. It was one big party when you knew you had a real show. Even Billy and Delle behaved themselves; they could smell a hit." His teeth are showing but he does not quite smile. "Everybody wanted in on that tour, even the backers. One of them might pop in for the Houston run, then another one in San Francisco. That's how it was, a family deal."

Connie tries to remember the tour, but it fades into other tours, other shows, dim hotels and pink backdrops and curtain calls and fold-out couches and Faith tossing all night next to her.

"We *worked* with it," Garrett continues. "Rewrites every couple of weeks, fine tuning, you understand? It wasn't like that other crap we patched together. No sir, this one was *the* one; it fit them like white on rice." He stops for a moment. Connie has clearly underestimated Garrett's capacity for nostalgia. "That was the thing about that show," he says. "The *fit*. They'd been parading around the country for years playing ball-busting aristocrats, and it worked fine, we'd get to Broadway, last a respectable six or seven months, then off we'd go with another drawing-room comedy or musical about dukes and duchesses." He rubs his chin, looking off again. "See, no one ever thought to plant them in a cornfield to sing about the moon. Billy and Delle? Please. But it worked. Star-crossed, dewy-eyed lovers, Jesus. They looked sixteen."

He finds Connie again. "You remember this stuff? Seems to me you and your twin were always underfoot. How is she, by the way?"

Connie hesitates. "You mean Faith?"

"Faith, right." He grins. "Faith and Constance. How is she?"

"She's not my twin."

"No? I thought you were twins."

"No."

"So how is she?"

"She's fine. Two kids. Boys."

His eyes for a moment lose that angling look, and he seems to take her in for the first time. "Glad to hear self-destruction doesn't run in the family."

A needle of bitterness sticks in Connie's throat at Garrett's presumptions, his cynical recollections. She remembers him now: always in a rush, predicting disasters, starting fires. She is helpless here, at the mercy of her parents' ghosts.

"That show was a little gold mine," he says. "By the time we got back to New York we really had something."

"A hit," Isadora says.

He sits forward on his chair with a clunk. "You know it, dear. A hit like you wouldn't believe."

Isadora looks around Garrett's office. "So how come you're not rich?"

Garrett tips back in his chair again and raps on the glass over the photograph, on Billy's face. "Two years, ladies," he says. "Two years on the Great White Way. We could've gone four, five, even more. A movie, maybe, who knows." Without turning around, he lifts the photograph off its nail and sweeps it down gently onto his desk. Billy and Delle, Marie Lazarro, and a host of strangers smile desperately out at them. "This, ladies, is the big fish. The one that got away."

He gives Connie a sudden, searing look that seems to blame her for something. "I own this show now," he says. "Every once in a while some community theater or high school acting club produces it." He purses his lips, his mood darkening. "I sold a couple of the songs. Patti Page did 'Making Up,' ever hear it?"

Connie shakes her head.

"Course you didn't, it was a B side," he says. "The thing is, *Silver Moon* was a mediocre show, just like all the others. Forgettable music, stupid script." He presses his hand into his desk and his voice drops. "It was the *fit*," he says. "When they started missing performances, the jig was up. People wanted to see *Billy and Delle* playing virgins, not a couple of understudies covering for a hangover." He stops, as if he expects Connie to say something.

"They were difficult," she says. What else can she say? What else does she know?

He looks away, out the window at the magnificent, tacky billboards of Times Square. "They were set to be the Lunts of the sixties, the new first couple of Broadway." She hears a stream of air escape his lips. "And they took us all down with them." The photograph seems to be moving, as if the cast is ready to burst into song. Christmas music drifts into the office from somewhere else in the building.

Isadora taps one red nail on the desk. "So what can you do for me, Garrett?"

"Wrong question," he says. Connie feels the weight of all the photographs and their sense of failure. She understands Garrett to be a bitter man. He crosses his hands on the desk like a schoolteacher, looking at Isadora. "What've you done lately? Let me guess. A more or less steady gig in Jersey? Some East Village coffeehouse crap?"

"Close enough," Isadora says. "I played the Speakeasy twice last summer. And the Bottom Line once."

Garrett raises his eyebrows. "You get those gigs yourself?" Isadora nods, and settles further into the chair. She is either getting comfortable or getting ready.

"She really is good," Connie says, but her words sound irrelevant. Garrett and Isadora apparently expect something of each other; Connie is the go-between, with no real business here.

Out of nowhere Isadora produces a tape and places it in front of Garrett. As he picks it up, she rips a piece of paper from a pad on

149

his desk and writes down an address. "I start at nine-thirty, tonight and tomorrow." She makes a face. "East Village coffeehouse crap, but who's complaining?"

He looks at the address but doesn't touch it. "Ever do show music?" Isadora laughs dismissively. He opens a lower drawer and produces an old hi-fi record. "I brought you a present." He hands her the record, on its jacket a hand-colored moon over a cornfield. In the foreground Billy and Delle sit smooching on a porch glider. Connie remembers the record, an entire box of them in fact, left for the Salvation Army when she and Faith packed up the trailer.

Isadora turns it over in her hands. "Listen to it," Garrett says as he escorts them to the door. The phone is ringing and the girl at the desk picks it up. "We'll talk," he says, then takes the phone.

Out on the street the noise and motion appear random and faintly menacing. Connie follows Isadora to the end of the block.

"He's a classic," Isadora says. She holds the record across her chest like a shield, its colors cartoonish, lurid somehow, against her dark clothes.

Connie looks out at the traffic, the thin, dirty patches of snow. "I'm sorry. He was the only person I could think of."

"Don't be sorry yet." Isadora's eyes slide over.

Connie is struck by her self-possession. What on earth ever made her think Isadora needed her? When they first met Isadora had seemed almost frail—she might have been constructed from the hollow bones of a bird. It seems to Connie now that those bones must be stuffed with gunpowder.

When the light changes, Isadora charges ahead, her garish shield at her chest, her walk purposeful and titanic. Connie hurries after her, barely keeping pace, the grimy street soughing under her shoes.

TWO

IN HIS HOTEL ROOM at Le Perreault, Stewart opens another
bottle and offers Connie the first glass.

"Chestnuts roasting on an open fire," he says. "New snow,
Mom's plum pudding . . ."

"What about precious David and his precious wife and his precious son?" Connie reminds him.

"Cinnamon buns, eggnog, Bing Crosby . . ."

"I take it you weren't invited."

Stewart lifts his eyelids, a sly gleam in his eyes. "Connie. Sweetheart. Haven't you ever crashed a party?" He drains his glass. "My
mother, bless her soul, said I could come for New Year's. The
homophobes will be cleared out by then."

"So wait till New Year's."

"Nope. Christmas morning. Can I borrow a dress?"

She laughs, pours more wine. "I saved the best news."

Something shines fleetingly through the dull cast over Stewart's
eyes. "Tell me."

"Remember *Silver Moon*?"

"The toast of Broadway."

"Garrett's resurrecting it."

"You're kidding."

"I'm not."

"How's he pulling that off?"

Connie pauses, milking the suspense. "By casting Isadora James
as the female lead."

It takes him a minute. "Who's going to want to see this master-piece?" he says. "Besides you, of course."

"A lot of people remember Billy and Delle, Stewart. Isadora is Billy's daughter; her mother was in the chorus. People will be curi-ous at the very least." She folds her legs underneath her, the carpet's soft pile a familiar cushion against her skin. "Think of it, Stewart. Here she comes, an unknown with a huge talent, reviving the show that broke her father. People love this stuff. Plus she's rewriting the music."

"A blues musical?" Stewart says. "I thought it was about a farm couple in Nebraska."

"Don't laugh, Stewart. They've raised half the money already. They even have the posters designed." She sets down her glass and squares her hands to show him. "Here's a faded replica of the origi-nal poster with Billy and Delle and a handful of the chorus, includ-ing Isadora's mother. Juxtaposed over that is a picture of Isadora with a guitar slung over her back and a small caption: 'The *Moon* Is Blue.' What do you think?"

"I think it's got a snowball's chance in hell."

"You're wrong," Connie says. "They're angling for a big, fat nostalgia trip." His cynicism can't touch her. She's already thinking ahead to hearing about the casting, the rehearsals, the tour. She's already beginning to see how close it will bring them.

"Doesn't this bother you even a little?" Stewart asks.

"Why should it?"

"It smacks of opportunism to me."

"What's wrong with that?" Connie says. "How else do you make it in this world?"

"Can we talk about something besides Isadora for a change?"

She raises her eyebrows.

"Isadora this, Isadora that. You sound like a first-grader with a new friend."

Stung, she shrinks from him. "Go to hell."

He hangs his head like a bad dog. "I'm sorry. I'm just jealous." He thumps on his chest. "Hit me, go on. I deserve it."

"Stewart."

"No, really. Hit me, go ahead."

"Forget it, Stewart. I forgive you, okay?"

He lifts his glass to her, empties it into the carpet, and with the magnificence of a cymbal player smashes it between his hands.

"Jesus!" Connie leaps up, tears his hands apart, blood spattering. "Jesus Christ! Stewart, goddammit!"

He is bent in two, whimpering. Her pulse thundering against her temples, the liquor lurching through her body, she helps him into the bathroom and runs cold water over his palms to see better what he's done. She picks slivers of glass from his skin as the water runs. "Jesus," she says, shaking all the way out to her fingertips. "Oh, Stewart." His blood runs in a pink swirl down the drain.

"I'm sorry," he keeps saying. "I'm drunk." The water begins to reveal his white palms. One hand is miraculously unscathed. The cuts on the other are lightning-shaped, shallow but cruel.

"You're a lucky goddamned bastard, Stewart." Even her teeth are quivering. "What *is* this, anyway? Your family? Make up a new one, for Christ's sake. Come home with me." She places his cut hand on the counter, palm up, and presses a washcloth into his skin.

"Connie?" His head hangs down and blood seeps up through the cloth. "Do you love me?"

"Hold still so we can see what we've got. I might have to take you to the hospital." She peers under the cloth. "You're going to have to explain all this in French."

"Say 'I love you, Stewart.' "

"Shut up."

"Say it."

She heaves a long-suffering sigh, pressing his palm. "I love you, Stewart." She used to say such things in high school to any boy who might say it back, and then she discovered Rule Number One.

"Say 'I love you enough to have your baby.' "

"Will you shut up? Why didn't you tell me you were this drunk?"

His eyes rove over her, glazed in their sockets. "We'd be a real family, Connie, close as close. You and me and the baby, Aunt Isadora coming in from New York—"

"Not now, Stewart."

He's quiet for a moment, watching her hand on his hand. "Close as close," he repeats. "Close as . . . close as those brothers and sisters you hear about who have their own secret language. That's how close we'll be."

"You're raving."

"No, no, I read this. They make up their own language so nobody can bother them." The cloth is blood-soaked now and she lifts it. To her relief the cut has stopped spurting. She grabs a clean towel and presses. "I'm not kidding," he says. "You ever hear of that?"

"No."

"Can you imagine being that close to someone?"

"No."

"What about you and Faith?"

"We weren't close."

"No secret language?"

"Not unless you count silence."

He's laughing now, leaning heavy against her, drunk and blood-drained. She watches the towel for signs, but it's still white on the surface. She keeps pressing, thinking about silence, and words.

"What about you and precious Isadora?" he says.

"Stewart, just keep your hand still, would you?" She thinks of all the words that have careened back and forth between her and Isadora, over the phone, over a restaurant table, over the bulky form of the cat, Bob. All those words, and her little sister is still a dream, something she has made up, a new friend she has a crush on, a stranger who shares some of her blood and none of her memory, and Stewart is a bastard for knowing it.

THE ATLANTICAIR BOEING 747 hits a wall of sleet over the English Channel. The seat belt signs flash on, but there is no word from the cockpit except a cryptic instruction for the attendants to buckle up. The crew is all New Guard, including one skinny novice in her first month of flying. After a stomach-gouging drop in altitude she begins to cry softly. "Just strap yourself in and *sit* there," Connie snaps, nervous herself over the wild rocking and bumping. She has a reputation for being rigid, and this is a good time to invoke it. The girl sits, humiliated and petrified, smoothing her plum-colored skirt over her knees.

After a few more minutes of bucking and heaving, during which several collective gasps escape from the cabin, Connie leaves her seat, raps on the cockpit door, and marches in.

"You're supposed to be sitting," the captain says, not turning around. His face glows eerily over the control panel.

"I think the passengers could use some reassurance, Evan," she says. The copilot, a novice himself, looks up.

"What do I look like, a fucking tour guide?" Evan mumbles. She has heard him say this before. He hasn't much use for the crew; he refers to all of them, even the men, as "the waitresses." Connie dated him for a while a long time ago, and then his brother, and he's held it against her ever since. She sometimes entertains herself with thoughts of having to land the plane herself someday, the way beautiful stewardesses once did in the movies, after Evan suffers a type-A, stress-related, particularly painful heart attack at the controls.

"*I'll* speak to them, then," she says.

"That's what they pay you for, honey."

She whirls around and snaps the door shut behind her on her way back into the cabin. The jet retches again, nearly knocking her to her feet. She straps herself in and reaches for the PA. Her voice, even through the crackle, is calm. Her own anxiety settles as she hears herself; she has always been good at this, and she can see the relief—perhaps even gratitude—in the faces of her charges. Her blood still pulses against her ears, but she senses the change, the slowing, the collective relief.

After a bumpy landing at Heathrow, the connecting passengers file past, pallid and subdued, nodding at her with small smiles. Word comes then to unload everyone, there will be a delay before leaving for Boston.

The skinny novice approaches after all the passengers have deplaned. "I'm sorry," she whispers.

"It happens," is what Connie discovers herself saying. It once happened to her, when she was twenty-two, her first emergency landing. "You'll do better next time," she tells the girl, and believes it.

In the flight lounge she sits around with the crew, their young voices shimmying mawkishly, as if they had just saved the inmates of a burning orphanage. She pretends to listen, but her thoughts are

155

elsewhere, with Stewart in Paris, his bandaged hand and six stitches and a promise to call when he reaches Boston. Only now does she begin to shake, the terrifying flight and the scene with Stewart behind her.

She looks out at the slushy runway. She murmurs a prayer for a short delay, for she wants to be home. She thinks of her hollow apartment, Isadora arriving to fill it with her rickety laughter. She imagines a Christmas visit to Faith's house, a blue snow cloaking its eaves. Perhaps Faith will say something surprising, something about all of them being there together; perhaps she will have bought a present—not a bottle of perfume or more towels, but a prettily wrapped bauble, some small surprise that Connie does not yet know she wants. She hopes Joe will be there, she hopes the boys will run the dog through its tricks.

She imagines herself walking through the door of the house she once lived in, joining the gathering in the kitchen, and in this vision they can't stop talking. Their words rain into the room, a downpour of voices, a lifetime's worth of catching up. And if this part is merely a dream, Connie thinks, the people in it are not; they exist, an ocean away, and she knows exactly where they are, waiting for her to come home.

THREE

"THIS IS THE ONE he wants," Chris says. He holds up an electric guitar in an eye-destroying shade of blue.

"This one?" Faith asks, hoping he's wrong. "Are you sure?"

"Positive." He shrugs, not looking particularly regretful. "Sorry."

The guitar is shaped like a crescent moon, and the tuning pegs are black, with eyes—or what look to Faith like eyes—painted on each one. Joe looks it up and down as if he's planning to run it through a lathe.

Faith examines it helplessly. "Chris, it's hideous."

"Hey, I'm only the messenger," Chris says. "And I hate to clue you, but you can't get the guitar without an amp. We're talking major bucks here, folks."

The store is full of last-minute Christmas shoppers, mostly teenaged boys in denim jackets, black T-shirts. The few adults, like her and Joe, look as though they've just gotten off a tour bus. She wonders what kind of Christmas they are readying for in their homes, what their homes look like. Near the window a man is trying "Chopsticks" on an electric piano with his daughter; they have the same red hair. She hopes they could likewise spot Chris as her son.

"Well," Chris says. "I'm outa here." He hands off the guitar to Joe, who holds it by the neck like a chicken. "Meet you at the truck."

"Wait a minute, I thought you were going to help us with this," Joe says.

Chris backs away, lifting his arms the way Joe likes to. "Hey, I did my part. All you guys have to do is pay for it." Faith watches him saunter out the door. She hopes he will always look this at home with himself, so like his father.

Joe turns to her. "I vote we get it."

"Did you see the price?" She taps the tag. "That's not even counting the amplifier."

"Just give me what you can," he says. "I'll pay for the rest."

"If we'd done this earlier we could've shopped around a little."

"Faith, I've been busy, okay?"

"Fine." She doesn't look at him. "I just hope he uses it." She runs her fingers over the strings, the knobs on the body. "Isadora taught him a few chords and now he thinks he has some kind of destiny."

"Maybe he has." She hears him trying to make up. "He's got music in his genes, after all."

They buy the guitar, and the amplifier, and a beginner's book on blues. As they walk out to the truck, struggling with the boxes, Faith turns her lineage into notes across a staff: tuneless, indecipherable, their identifying stems snapped off.

"Any plans for Christmas Eve?" she asks.

"Nope. Not a one."

It is snowing, light and grainy, gathering on Joe's black hair, turning it white as his mother's. Faith watches this soft aging and wonders if she had ever, even in the first blush of love, believed they would grow old together.

"I thought you and Brenda might be doing something," she says.

He slides the boxes into the back of the truck and closes the door of the cap, yanking once on the handle. "Brenda's gone, Faith." He sounds bitter. "As if you didn't know."

She watches him, her blood moving. "What do you mean, gone? For good?"

"Don't your sons tell you anything?"

She sets her lip. "Not about Brenda, no. Apparently they've gotten the idea that I'll die."

"They didn't get it from me." The snow is falling harder now, fine and heavy, ricelike beads ticking at the pavement. He's looking at her but she can't quite make out his eyes. "We're fighting," he says. He sounds pleased.

"*You're* fighting. This has nothing to do with me."

"No?" he says. "Brenda left me because she thinks I never left you."

More hushed, pebbly snow seething on the ground. Faith remains in it, the hard, dry flakes pelting her face. Something she can't see is being revealed to her, something she ought to know, or already knows but can't listen to.

"I'm sorry," she says softly. "I can't help what she thinks. You have two kids who need you, what did she expect?"

"You're right," he mutters. "It has nothing to do with you. She left me fair and square."

The accusation in his voice disarms her further. The snipe about the boys not telling her anything stings belatedly. He makes to turn from her.

"Fair and square?" she says, holding him there. "There's nobody else?" She really wants to know. She's curious about how people leave each other. Too late, she realizes she also meant something else.

"Are we back to that?"

She doesn't answer.

"*Are* we?"

"I didn't mean us."

"Let me set the record for you, Faith. I *paid* the price for hurting you." He is nothing but a misty shape in the weird parking lot light, half obscured by falling snow, a shape she knows. "I *paid*."

"Joe, I'm not—"

"And let me tell you another thing." His outline sharpens somewhat as his voice picks up. "I know you, Faith. I know that somewhere in that mind, that *mind* of yours, we were doomed no matter what I did. I *know* you. You didn't plan on us making it."

"Joe—"

"I'm not defending myself. I realize what I did. I'm talking about what *you* did."

"What did I do?" she asks, defensively, then realizes she is really waiting for an answer. "What did I do?"

He thinks a minute, the snow calling *shhhh*. Then he answers, matter of fact, all accusation gone from his voice: "You didn't love me."

He disappears around the front of the truck. She hears him wipe the snow from the windshield with his sleeve and knows exactly how this looks, the way he pulls the cuff of his jacket over his bare hand.

Faith waits awhile in the hard, insistent snow, under the tinsel-trimmed lights of the parking lot. A carol stammers out from some-body's car radio and she listens, numbed by Joe's words, numbed to the depths of the empty bucket that is her heart.

She wanders over to the cab of the truck, stopping for a moment to watch Chris, a few yards away behind the lit-up storefront of a sporting goods store. He moves through the equipment, hefting basketballs, fingering warm-up gear. He retracts his elbow, bends slightly at the knees, and pushes his arm forward into a graceful, im-aginary free throw that swishes through an imaginary basket. He bends his knees, eases forward, releases again. He performs this ritual year-round, with or without a ball, in the kitchen, in the yard, standing next to his car. Muscle memory, he calls it: you do it enough, it kicks in when you can't afford to stop and think. She be-lieves him: that elegant arc looks exactly the same, every time.

When she opens the door to the truck and slides into the seat, Joe is staring at his son through the snow-dusted windshield.

"Sorry," he says. "It's the damn holiday. 'Jingle Bells' and all that crap."

"No, I'm the one. I'm sorry." She wants the word to cover almost twenty years, but it doesn't. It's just a word.

They lapse into silence as the snow covers all the windows, encas-ing them. It seems they have been this way—together and apart—all their lives.

His voice comes cutting out of the dark. "Can't you at least deny it?"

She draws her coat around her. "I didn't have the faintest idea how to love somebody—not even you." She sounds darker than she means to, but her failures are rearing up again, all the everyday in-timacies that had made her ashamed, for she didn't know the words, the steps, she could never quite keep time.

She's back at her first bicycle ride, Joe's sneakers slapping the street behind her as he holds on, then lets go. "I don't know how!

I don't know how!" she had screamed, even as she maneuvered the bike down their green street, even as she made the corner and came to a safe stop. He came upon her in a few minutes, yipping joyously, she thinks she remembers him skipping, *that* pleased with her small triumph.

"I did love you," she says suddenly. This much, at bottom, she knows. "I did."

He doesn't answer. His soft breathing sifts through the snow-lit dark.

"I'm sorry you had to go through it again," she says. "With Brenda. I'm sorry."

His face is a shadow. "It wasn't the same. It wasn't even close."

Faith sinks lower in the seat, pressed against the door. "At least you tried again, Joe. And you're not done trying, I know it. I admire you for that."

"I can't blame her," Joe says. "She's right, I wasn't home much." He laughs, a painful bark in the hush of the cab. "I didn't want to smother her. I was so determined not to make the same mistake twice that I made a new mistake once."

They sit in silence for a time. Faith finally stirs. "Do you mind if I turn the heater on?"

He starts the truck and the wipers come on, too, revealing Chris coming out of the store.

"He broke up with Tracy again, did you know that?" she says.

" 'Tis the season."

She leans over and taps on the horn so Chris can find them. He flings open the door and jumps in, squeezing her between them. "Yow," he says, snow falling off the fringes of his hair. "Looks like this is never going to stop."

A CALM SQUARE of light defines her kitchen window as they pull up, and from the living room flash the white lights of a hopeless, spindly tree the boys found according to her expressed wishes. "Five bucks," Ben had said, dragging it over the porch steps. "We got robbed. *Free* wouldn't have been a bargain."

That same tree is a picture of welcome, one of her own making.

161

She's learned something over the years, she thinks, more than Joe realizes.

"Mom?" Faith suddenly finds herself squashed next to Joe, Chris's empty place stretched out on her right. She slides out of the cab.

Joe puts the truck in gear. "I'll go get Ben."

"Thanks. Say hi to your parents for me." She touches his arm and leaves her hand there. "And be careful driving in this stuff."

"Hey, someone's here," Chris says as Joe drives off. Faith looks toward the porch. A small figure huddles there, arms folded tightly across her chest. Behind her, Sammy's face appears at the window of the front door.

"Tracy?" Chris calls. He sounds suspiciously hopeful. They'll be back together in two days, three at the most. He has several presents for her under the tree.

"It's Isadora," Faith says. Though she has a hat pulled down over her forehead and is buried inside a big coat, Faith recognizes the tilt of her head, the way she sits with her feet perched on their toes.

When they come upon her she doesn't move. "I kept thinking you'd be back in a minute," she tells them. "The lights were on and the dog was in."

Isadora appears paralyzed with cold, leaning against the dark shape of her suitcases. Faith pulls her gently to her feet, surprised at the strength of Isadora's gloved hands.

Once inside the house, Isadora begins to shake visibly. The dog whines and walks circles around her.

"My God," Faith says, "I think she's hypothermic. Let's get her out of these things. Chris, get a blanket." She works automatically now, as she does sometimes in the office. She has attended to fainting spells, insulin shock, panic attacks—all the little dramas of a doctor's waiting room. She ushers Isadora into a chair and yanks off her hat, jacket, gloves, boots. Chris appears with a blanket and a pair of Faith's slippers, his face taut.

"She's all right," Faith says.

Isadora peers at them from inside the cave of blanket. Her lips are blue. "I feel like a jerk."

Isadora looks unexpectedly helpless and young. Faith turns to

Chris. "Put on some water, honey. She needs something hot." Chris goes out like a man possessed.

"Were we expecting you here tonight?" Faith asks politely.

Isadora grimaces and shakes her head. "Connie was supposed to meet me at the airport. When I got in I waited awhile, then called her and got the machine. Then I called you and didn't get anybody, so I took a cab to Connie's." Her nose begins to run. Faith hands her a tissue. She honks on it a couple of times, sounding like a man. "Anyway, when I got to Connie's, I don't know why I was surprised to find all the lights out. I had the cab bring me here, figuring you'd show up sooner or later."

She looks like a small animal in a burrow, and when Chris arrives with tea her hands reach out slowly, like paws.

"She probably got delayed," Faith says. "She doesn't always call."

Isadora lifts her eyes over the rim of the cup. "Thank God you were here."

"I wasn't."

"I mean eventually. Thank God you were here eventually." Faith glances at Chris, who appears to be containing a laugh. He has his father's fondness for the absurd.

"I feel like such a jackass," Isadora says, "plunked on your doorstep on Christmas weekend."

"It's all right," Faith says. "You can stay here tonight."

"I don't want to put you out."

"We have room," Faith says. She tucks the blanket under Isadora's feet.

Isadora smiles. "I love your tree," she says. "I love ugly trees."

FAITH SETTLES Isadora into the guest room, her favorite room in the house. Because it is rarely used, for she rarely has guests, she keeps it exactly the way she likes it. Everything is pink and white, a room she thinks a daughter might have liked. It's a room she herself would have loved.

She watches Isadora unpack, her movements sinewy, catlike. Isadora talks the whole time, barely pausing for breath. In this sense she's easy to be with; Faith doesn't have to worry about holding up half a conversation. She begins to see what has captured Connie so

163

completely: an enthusiasm for living that Billy and Delle might have once possessed before they twisted it into something else. Faith begins to believe there might be something pure in her heritage, something worth passing on.

"We got Ben a guitar," Faith says.

Finished unpacking, Isadora pulls the pillows from under the pink spread and props herself against the headboard, as if she plans to stay for years. "What kind?"

"Blue," Faith says.

Isadora's laughter cracks into the room. "I meant what brand. Strat? Gibson?"

"Oh," Faith says. "I don't know. He's been practicing from that book you sent him. I think he might be good."

"He's a Spaulding, isn't he?" She pauses. "The show's going great, by the way. We've got most of the money and Garrett's got a casting director ready for next week. I was born for this part, Faith." She laughs. "In more ways than one."

She looks childlike, her hair hazy and angelic under the pinup lamp, and yet the mention of the show puts Faith back on guard. She can't shake the feeling that Isadora has been sent to show her how unseemly it is to borrow from other people's lives, the way she once borrowed from Joe.

"This has worked out quite well for you, then," Faith says. She knows how stingy this sounds, but the revival, and all it will revive, is caught in her throat like a pill she has swallowed by accident.

"Why shouldn't it?" Isadora says: a simple statement, not a challenge. If this is Isadora's philosophy of life, Faith is hard-pressed to refute it, although Faith herself has never thought along these lines.

"You'll feel better when you see the show," Isadora says. "You *are* planning to come?"

Faith says nothing.

"You don't like me much, do you?"

"I like you fine, Isadora."

"You never answer my questions."

"I don't have answers you want to hear."

"You think I don't know what a creep Billy was? I can tell when Connie's making it up, Faith. I'm not as naive as you think."

"I didn't say you were naive," Faith says. "Believe me, I never even thought it."

Isadora looks surprised. "Anyway, Connie makes up Billy stories for my sake, which makes me feel good, and then she begins to believe them a little, which makes *her* feel good."

"Well then," Faith says, trying to sound as neutral as possible. "I guess it works all the way around."

"See?" Isadora says, sitting up with a lurch. Faith moves back. "That's just what I mean. You don't like me one bit. I've tried to figure it out, Faith, but I'm damned if I know why."

Faith sighs. "I don't feel related to you, Isadora. It's not the same thing as not liking you." Isadora looks disappointed. She might be nothing more than a lonely girl who misses her mother.

Snow-muted footfalls rumble on the porch. "Joe and Ben," Faith says, relieved to have an excuse to go downstairs. Isadora follows her, talking.

"I don't mean to put you on the spot or anything, Faith. It's just that as long as we *are* sisters, whether it *feels* like it or not, we might as well make a stab at a relationship."

Before she gets to the landing, Faith senses something wrong. Joe's expression reaches her from the door. Ben comes in behind him, his boots dripping, his face white. When he pulls off his hat his hair stands up in needles of static.

"How's everything here?" Joe says. The words hobble out, carved clean of meaning.

She nears him now, breathing the cold off his jacket, trying to see in his face what his words are hiding.

"Everything's great," she hears Isadora saying behind her. "Connie's late, which nearly killed me, literally, but Faith and I managed to make the best of it, didn't we, Faith? We were just getting to know each other a little better." She pauses, her words slowing. "Weren't we, Faith?"

Faith knows this man; she knows his voice, his many voices. She places her palms on the front of his parka, a cold wall of blue, then digs in, crunching great hunks of goose down under the thin, silky fabric. She does not let go.

She stares into his face. "Is it Connie?"

165

"Sit down, sweetie," Joe says, but she knows already. She knows. He walks her to a chair and sits her down, her fingers caught like a cat's claws on a sweater, and like a cat she watches him, unblinking. In her periphery she catches moving bits of shirt, a hand, the fleeting halo of Isadora's hair. She hears the eerie hush of held breath.

"The plane crashed in Boston a few hours ago," Joe tells her, and she anchors herself to his voice, the way he forms his words, trying to hear everything. "That's all we've got so far." She is aware of his hands on her face, their cool calluses, their width and pressure, their dogged tenderness.

"We heard it on the news at Grammy's," she hears Ben say. His voice is high and heartbreaking. And Chris, sounding like a man: "There could be survivors, Mom. There could be, it happens all the time."

Joe's hands press her skin gently. She can feel the shape of her own face by the shape of his hands on it. He is speaking slowly, tenderly. "Mom's been on the phone trying to get some information."

Faith can hear Isadora's quiet whimpering, but she does not turn her head. Her hands relax, drag themselves down Joe's chest and drop into her lap. "Oh." She looks at her hands. "Oh, Connie."

Joe shucks his jacket and reaches for her. Faith presses her face into the soft cotton of his shirt. She feels his hands again, one on her back, the other snugged against her neck. It is here she waits for news.

FOUR

THE STRANGERS in this hospital remind Faith of all the Christ-mases she has spent in the company of strangers. She remembers one Christmas—after Delle's death and before she met Joe—when she and Connie sat mutely in a corner of Armand's brother's house in New Jersey, listening to one of Armand's grand-nephews recite "The Night Before Christmas." She thinks of herself at all the Fuller Christmases—with their vaguely military rituals—trying to fit somehow into their warmth and vigor, knowing herself to be at heart a stranger there.

It is past Christmas now, two days or three, and Connie has not woken up. Faith has lost track of time, place, herself. She yearns to do something—anything—familiar: buy some potatoes, type a let-ter, fill a feeder. Without her own rituals she is bereft, alone with the quiet of her sister's dying.

Even here, however—with nurses and doctors roving in and out with news or no news, random trips to the cafeteria, reliance on the kindness of strangers—she has managed, more or less, to keep a schedule. She measures time by the breaths Connie takes, her trans-lucent form lying deathlike under horrifying white sheets; she mea-sures time by the lunch carts squeaking down the hall, the shift change at the nurses' station; she measures time by the peculiar gra-dations of Boston light: from the russet morning to the cindery dusk, she measures time.

Connie sleeps.

At noon Faith calls home, talks to Ben or Chris, still on Christmas break but staying near the phone. One of them is always there,

167

which may or may not be orders from their father, who arrives at the house after work and stays all night. Either way, it touches her. She wants Connie to know all this, that people are waiting for her to wake up.

Each night, late, from Stewart's apartment, she calls Joe, and they talk for a long time. He gives her the details she craves: what the boys ate for supper, how many birds at the feeder, how far up the porch the snow has banked. He relays good wishes from Dr. Howe and Marion, love from Phoebe and Joe Senior and the family, hellos from some of Dr. Howe's patients. He asks her, always, how she is.

"Joe, if there's anything I could have done differently—" she begins.

"Shh," he says. "You're a good sister. Hey, remember those card games the three of us used to play?" But she hadn't meant Connie. She meant Joe. She hangs up with the grimmest sense of disconnection.

She and Stewart and Isadora keep watch over Connie's lusterless presence. Her skin is pulpy and blue across the eyes and up into the forehead where a swatch of hair has been ripped out, the exposed scalp stitched. Faith has been waiting for her to open her eyes, but isn't sure how she will know when they open. The rest of Connie's face, what Faith can see of it around the tape and feeding tube, is eerily white and unscathed, making the unbruised part of her the part that doesn't fit.

The sheets are tucked under her arms, and her arms fall straight at her sides, in casts from just below the elbow. From the end of the right-hand cast, the chipped red nails of her middle three fingers stick out like broken suckers; from the left, a little more of the hand shows: four fingers, swollen and purple-green. At the end of the bed where the sheet wells up, Connie's foot, swathed in another cast, lies unseen.

Talk to her, the doctors tell Faith. She thinks of the other things they tell her, about the swollen brain, the collection of blood, and the things they will not know unless, until, she wakes up. *Just talk to her.*

Stewart and Isadora have no trouble talking: they talk and talk and talk. Words march out in platoons, timely, apt, voluminous. Stewart, bleary-eyed, gaunt with grief, tells Connie about their friends, entertaining little stories he unravels like ribbons. He tells about Christmas at his parents', about the precious nephew who turned into a devil-boy and behaved only for Uncle Stewart. His own hand sports a thin bandage, which he waves in front of her face. He tells her that his cut hand was a big hit with his family, that he made up a story about defending Connie's honor on Boule Miche. His mother kept referring to "Stewart's injury." He tells Connie these things with great glee, innuendo, irony, revealing to Faith an old and intimate friendship. He speaks passionately, his face close to hers, as if the tube were the only thing preventing him from kissing her.

He does not say anything about the eight crew members who died. He does not mention the 182 passengers.

Isadora goes on, and on, about *Silver Moon*: the new music, the big-time director, the tour Garrett's planning, the promotion. She'll be appearing on "Good Morning America," she tells Connie, but the husk of her voice cannot penetrate the husk of Connie's sleep.

Isadora, like Stewart, seems to know about Connie's friends, seems even to have met them, and offers more: Debbie's husband came back; Grace quit in a huff; a passenger proposed to Frank and meant it. Perhaps she has these stories second-hand, from Stewart; in any case she has thought to arm herself with them, these stories that expose Faith's meager knowledge of her sister's life.

But Isadora always manages to come back to the show, and Faith understands that it is her way of telling them she must leave.

"You don't have to stay here," Faith says. Says it for her.

Isadora turns from the bed as if Connie is already dead. "I feel guilty leaving."

"Of course you do."

"I have to be there for the casting."

"Of course you do."

Stewart looks up sharply.

"I know this might seem a little weird to you, considering everything," Isadora says, madly yanking her sleeves up and down. "But really I've got to be there. The show must go on." On this last she

169

drops her voice, as if to imply that the show's going on will wake Connie up.

Faith begins to laugh. She can't help herself. "Why are you laughing?" Isadora says.

Faith stops. "That expression. It's the dumbest expression in human history. Even Billy and Delle never said that." Then she giggles again, an undignified crack in the climate-controlled air. "The Show Must Go On. I'm surprised they never said that, it's so — it's so apt."

Isadora is shrinking into her sweater. "Don't feel guilty," Faith says. "Go do the show, Isadora. The Play's the Thing." Another ripple of laughter clangs against the antiseptic walls.

"Faith," Stewart says. He's standing next to Isadora, horrified.

"I'm sorry," Faith says, her lips close together. "Is this mean?" It gets out in spite of her, another cruel snap of laughter that springs tears to Isadora's eyes. Faith is not surprised at her capacity for meanness: it has been coiled in her, all her life. She listens to Isadora's soft crying and turns from it, toward Connie's unearthly repose.

Her meanness then doubles back on her: instead of cutting Isadora away, she instead recognizes her own desire to flee. Her terrible mirth drains from her in an instant. She sinks to her chair, next to Connie's bed, her eyes trained on Connie's ravaged fingers. "It's just that I don't want you to go."

"If I didn't have to . . ." Isadora begins. "Garrett needs me right now."

"I'm sorry I made fun of you."

"I wish I *had* to be here, Faith," Isadora whispers. "Some burdens are good."

Isadora's voice seems to come from far away — far from this little prison Faith has fashioned for herself, as if her ankle were tethered to Connie's bed. She wants it and doesn't, this prison of blood ties, duty, history. Isadora remains outside, her hands barely fitting through the bars.

"I'm going," Isadora says.

Faith says nothing.

"She's going, Faith," Stewart says.

Faith stands up, accepts Isadora's arms. She holds her — such a

170

tiny person, Faith thinks, who would not have been one of the survivors—and waits until Isadora stops crying. Faith herself does not cry, has not cried, her crying is waiting in line behind everyone else's.

"Goodbye," she says. She does not want Isadora to go away. She looks at her hard, in case she never sees her again.

"I'll be thinking of you," Isadora says.

Stewart offers to walk Isadora to the lobby, leaving Faith alone with Connie and the doctor's instructions to talk.

Faith puts her hands on Connie's sheets, over her chest. Connie's metronomic breathing spirits Faith's hands up and down, up and down. *It's Faith*, she says. Up and down, again, again. *I'm here*. She is not sure she is saying these things out loud. *I'm right here*, she says again. Up and down, up and down. *I'm here, I'm here*. This is all she has said in two days or three: *I'm here*.

ALTHOUGH THEY ARE seldom in his apartment at the same time, Faith gets to know Stewart by virtue of shared quarters. His friends call and stop by at all hours. He likes nice things, including nice wine. He's tidy and organized, but not like her and Connie. After each shift of their vigil and a noisy bus ride from the hospital, a gift waits from one to the other: cold chicken with a garnish, clean laundry, a small Bible with a chapter marked. For Faith, who doesn't know if there is a God and is inclined at the moment to believe there is not, Stewart has underlined Ecclesiastes, Chapter 3: *To everything there is a season, and a time for every purpose under heaven* . . . Her dry, burning eyes can read only the first two lines, but she recognizes the passage, almost remembers it whole.

By the time Faith gets to the hospital, on the fifth day or sixth, Stewart is on his way out with a grocery bag full of food: brownies, homemade bread, mufins, pinwheels. He smells like Phoebe's kitchen, which is how Faith knows that Phoebe is there and that Joe has brought her.

"Where are they?" she asks.

He shifts the bag on his hip. "In the room. No change." His eyes flicker over to the nurses' station. "I had to clear the visitors with the hospital Gestapo."

She smiles. Faith has forged a peculiar intimacy with Stewart, as if they were strangers stuck for days in an elevator between floors. One of the signs of their forced complicity is the code they've devised. They have words for everything, nicknames for the nurses. Stewart dubbed Faith the Keeper of the Gate: as next of kin it fell to her to define immediate family. She had gladly let Stewart in.

She stares down the scoured hall to where it turns abruptly, a clean hook in the architecture braced by a grid of windows, the wintry sun steeled against the panes. The light is intense, but bearable; she can look straight into it. She wonders if this is the sort of light people mention, back from death.

"Have you seen the doctor?" she asks Stewart.

"Once."

"Did he say anything?"

Stewart rolls his eyes, exposing smeared red veins. "Too soon to know anything. Wait and see. Blah blah fucking blah."

Faith starts to go.

"What'd you leave for me?" he says.

"A surprise. Thank you for the candy."

"You liked it?"

"The arrangement was interesting."

"It was a self-portrait."

"It was? Then I guess I ate your ears."

"Faith." His voice drops, and he peers at her over the rim of the bag. "I thought I saw her fingers move."

The candy curdles in her stomach. "Did you tell them?"

"The nurse was there. She couldn't see it."

Faith wonders if he's hallucinating. He's been here on the night watch, and considering how often his phone rings, he can't be sleeping much during the day.

"It looked like she was shaking," he whispers, checking the nurses' station as if he were doing something subversive. The grocery bag rumbles under his arm. "I thought maybe she was thinking of something, maybe remembering the crash, something like that."

"Okay," Faith says, patting his arm over the bag. She's afraid he might cry, or fall down. "Okay. Go home, Stewart. Get some sleep."

He grips her hand hard. For a moment they simply stand there in the cold gleam of the hospital, and Faith considers that holding Stewart's hand is the closest she can get to Connie. Except for that brief and painful hug when Connie left Portland to start her life, they have never held each other.

By the time she crosses the distance of the corridor, she has forgotten about Joe and Phoebe, her thoughts blighted by the idea, the prayer, of Connie's moving fingers, and so when she enters the churchlike quiet of Connie's room she believes she sees her father there, his yellow hair a spectral shimmer in a gloss of light.

She makes some sound.

When the ghost turns around it is not her father but Chris.

"Hey, Mom," he says. His voice is strained. His eyes have the glassy look he gets watching those rented horror movies with his friends: mummies gone wild, their tattered wrappings unraveling as they chase a band of teenaged archaeologists. Connie, with her purple face and mummified arms, is, Faith realizes, a horror.

She reaches out to hold her son, but his arms are bigger, he holds her. He is no apparition, and against his clothes she catches the scent of other clothes squashed against them in the closets of her own house; that, and laundry soap, cedar, the dog, the musk of boys' bedsheets.

"Were you shocked?" she asks him.

He moves. "A little. Mom, I feel so *bad*."

He sits now, in a chair far from the bed, staring at the hummock of sheets. He is sad, she realizes, and surprised by his sadness. He wants his aunt back, not because he loves her, not because he's made memories with her or confided in her or traveled with her; he wants his aunt back because she is his aunt. His mouth seems slackened by the loss of expectation, a surrender to the earth's vagaries.

"I missed you," she tells him. She squeezes the back of his neck, the way she used to when he snuggled next to her, pajama-clad and out of the bath, to hear a few pages of *Mr. Popper's Penguins* until he fell asleep. Unlike Joe, who read in expressive grumbles and squeaks, she used an earnest monotone, and the boys preferred her voice to his.

"Dad and Gram went to call you," Chris says.

She hardly hears him; she is watching the battered, trembling tips of Connie's fingers. At first she believes she must be sharing Stewart's hallucination; she has seen one ghost already, after all. But it's there, a subtle tremor, as if a spider were spinning a web between her fingers. She has seen this before, exactly this, in her mother's spiny hands, whenever she was desperate for a drink.

She drags a chair to her spot at Connie's side, and begins to talk the ghosts away.

"It's Faith," she tells her sleeping sister. "I'm here." She tries to chuckle, manages a dry riff in her throat. "Connie, remember that doll you had with no hair?"

She hears Joe and Phoebe come in behind her, but she doesn't move, doesn't stop, afraid that if she stops talking Connie will die. Joe's hand lands on her shoulder, and she takes it, still talking, her lips close to Connie's face. "Remember that card game we used to play on the tour bus?" she says. "Remember when Armand took us to Coney Island, that man who let us on the roller coaster for free because he thought we were twins?" Another clicky rasp from her throat that sounds like a crow laughing. "Remember the bees on that big bush in the Connecticut yard?" She holds the four chipped fingers of Connie's left hand between her own fingers and thumb, and it is not clear to her whose pulse she feels. She goes on and on, stumbling in and out of the years, show to show, school to school, back and forth and back again. When she stubs against *Silver Moon* she stops short, and though she cannot sing she sings the only thing she remembers from the show, the chorus of the title song. It comes out in a talk-singing whisper, but in her head she hears her scrub-faced, gingham-shrouded parents as they two-step cheek to cheek:

The day is dying, my darling.
Evening will be here soon.
On this star-filled night
How we'll welcome the sight
Of the sil-verrr moo-oo-oon.

Her shoulder is warm where Joe holds it. She's ashamed of her awful voice and wishes she could be talking to Connie of her friends, her job, her present life, but she doesn't know anything of Connie's present life, nor Connie of hers, and she must talk to keep her alive, and so she offers the only part of her life that somehow belongs to them both.

FAITH GETS TO Stewart's apartment very late. Joe and Phoebe and Chris have gone back home, after persuading her to leave the hospital long enough to go out to a restaurant, and though she wanted them to stay they had to go back to Ben, who had somehow figured out he wasn't ready for this kind of sadness and stayed home with his grandfather. She steals in, suspecting that Stewart has decided to sleep this night, but finds the light on, the place vacant, another gift on the table.

A tape, unmarked. She puts it in Stewart's tape player, turns off the lights, lies on the couch, and waits. She hears the heads turning, but no sound, and is about to get up when the first strains of Isadora's guitar drift into the dark like a salve.

Like most of Isadora's songs, this one is about losing love and then coming back for it, over and over again. Faith closes her eyes, awash in the warm timbre of Isadora's voice, a resonance that lends the briefest shape to the most wild and shapeless wants.

FIVE

ARMAND HAS SENT Connie a present, which means today—or yesterday, or tomorrow—must be her birthday. Without ripping anything, she undoes the brown postal wrap, the purple ribbon, the orange dotted paper, and reads the card, a huge card with a cartoon lion on it. HOPE YOUR BIRTHDAY IS A ROARING SUCCESS, says the lion. She isn't sure if she is seven, or six.

She shows the card to Faith. For some reason Faith likes lions. "What's the present?" Faith asks. Armand always sends something they have to share.

In the box are two big plastic things that look like hair dryers. ASTRO-PHONES, the box reads. One astro-phone is red, the other yellow. Connie sits down; she takes a bite of the chocolate bar the desk boy brought up with the package, and lets it melt on her tongue as Faith reads the astro-phone directions. When he doesn't send books, Armand sends things with directions you have to read.

"Stand over there," Faith tells Connie, "and put your astro-phone so that round thing faces me." Connie runs to the window, holding her astro-phone in front of her. The lights of the city are just coming on, all at once a lot of blinking, making the city look like the scrim in Billy and Delle's new play. In the play the city is New York, but they're really in Los Angeles.

"Hold it up like this," Faith says. Connie does.

Across the room Faith adjusts her astro-phone, the yellow one, so that the round thing on hers lines up exactly with the round thing on Connie's.

"Press down on the button and say something," Faith says.

176

Connie does. "Can you hear me?" she asks.

"Not through this."

Connie takes a couple of steps.

"Don't jiggle it," Faith says. "It has to line up exactly. It's an invisible light beam."

"I'm not jiggling it," Connie says. "Can you hear me now?"

"Are you pressing the button?"

"Yes. Can you hear me?"

"Step closer. Try it now."

"Now can you?"

"No. Come closer."

Connie steps, one, two, three. Another, just in case. "*Now* can you?"

"Not through this. Line it up again."

And on, and on, until they are a few inches apart. Connie presses again, speaks again, and when she's close enough to touch, Faith hears her.

They play with the astro-phones all evening. Connie asks the questions, her mouth close to the red plastic, which smells like a new doll. She asks, "Can you hear me?" and "How do I sound?" but also other things—"What color is your hair?" and "How many letters in the alphabet?"—just to get some garbled voice noise through the round thing on the astro-phone. Connie hopes her questions aren't too babyish, hopes Faith isn't getting bored, but the astro-phone is irresistible, even to Faith; the voices through them are otherworldly. Connie pretends they're martians meeting on the moon but doesn't tell this to Faith.

When Billy and Delle return, it is long past midnight, but Connie is still awake on the fold-out couch, Faith asleep next to her, the astro-phones on the end table in their box, the orange dotted paper folded underneath it, Armand's card placed on top like a cover. She closes her eyes, listening to them fumble and whisper. She hears the astro-phones being lifted out of the box, hears the card being sifted open, the orange paper being picked up and put down.

"Damn," she hears Billy say. They whisper some more and go back out.

Connie gets up and puts the astro-phones back in the box, folds the orange paper, tucks Armand's card into the envelope.

Connie is sleeping. Suddenly the lights come on with a burst of noise. She sits up, cowering. She can only get one eye open at first but she recognizes the noise as Billy and Delle singing "Happy Birthday" in harmony. Their teeth gleam, bigger than the light. Connie sits up, her nightgown twisted around her legs so badly she can hardly move. Faith is up, too, just behind her, a startled cool breath on her neck. Billy is holding a cake, a perfectly square cake with coconut frosting that looks like it was put on by a machine. Connie counts the candles and finds out that she is seven. Delle hands her three books, unwrapped, books she read when she was five.

Billy and Delle settle onto the bed, balancing the cake, laughing, the smell of brandy floating over the blankets. Connie moves over, squashed against Faith, to make room for them all. Billy lights the candles one at a time and they look beautiful.

"Make a wish," Billy says to her, but she can't think of anything that has the barest hope of coming true. She wishes anyway: for a pony, for glass slippers, and for her grandmother to come back.

"What *are* these things?" Delle says, waving the yellow astro-phone in the air.

Faith plucks it from her hand so fast it seems to disappear. "We'll show you." She sits on her knees. "Get yours," she says to Connie.

Connie fumbles for the red astro-phone, hers, and sits back on her haunches, twirled into her nightgown and assaulted by the stink of liquor and bought cake, waiting for Faith to tell her what to do.

"Can you hear me?" Faith says, and her voice comes groggily through the round thing.

"Yes, can you hear *me*?"

"Yes."

"What color is your hair?" Faith asks.

"Yellow. What color is *your* hair?"

"Yellow."

Billy and Delle are laughing, hearty as sailors. But Faith's voice remains straight and stony, her little questions monster-big. They are inches apart, alone together by the grace of Faith's gargly voice through the astro-phone, in a slender capsule of space that does not include anybody else in the world.

HER NIGHTGOWN becomes more and more tangled and the hazy static of the astro-phone falls away from Faith's voice. Connie can't move her feet and somehow the sleeves of her nightgown have trapped her arms in the way its hem has trapped her feet. The astrophone is gone, but Faith's voice is still there, ringing, clear as anything she has ever heard: "Can you hear me? Can you hear me?"

She lifts her leaden eyelids, a slow and painful fluttering. The voice continues. At first she can see nothing but a whitish blur, reminiscent of a face. She has lost all sense of place and time, she cannot feel her own body, she cannot remember her own name. Panicked, she fights her way through this disconnection, willing the image before her to resolve itself into something she might understand. Finally, she sees it: the oval of pale skin, blessedly familiar. And the green eyes, inches from hers, watchful, wary, unbelieving. Her name returns to her, and then the other name: Faith.

VI

MUSCLE MEMORY

ONE

FAITH DOESN'T LIKE Nancy, the home-health nurse who mixes up the dishes, puts back the newspaper in the wrong order, leaves wet tea bags to dye the bottom of the kitchen sink. Even as she retreats to the comfort of work — the stellar gleam of her computer screen, the austere hunk of telephone at her elbow, the plain wants of the faces in the waiting room — Faith imagines her house being plowed up like a cornfield by the scarecrow form of Nancy, her short stalk of a body and strawlike limbs zigzagging through the rooms like a chicken in a barnyard. Faith's one comfort is the certain knowledge that Connie, imprisoned in the guest room, is somehow making Nancy pay.

After the transfer from Massachusetts General Hospital to Maine Medical, where the doctors ran more tests and finally pronounced Connie cured, they'd handed her to Faith with a sheaf of instructions, a fistful of appointment cards, and peculiar, self-satisfied smiles, as if the New England medical community had brought her back to life, saved her blood-swollen brain. Faith knew better. Connie had saved herself: Faith saw the way her skin moved upon waking, pulsing weirdly as if her spirit had been working itself up through a dream.

There had been some small discussion about where Connie would convalesce. With her lower arms, both hands, and one foot rendered useless for at least five more weeks, she would have to have care. *Care* was the word they kept using, care that would require a certain degree of intimacy.

Faith was the next of kin.

Stewart had lifted Connie out of the car and carried her up the walk, over the threshold of Faith's house, up the stairs and into the guest room which Faith had prepared with a few things she had picked up from Connie's apartment. They were the wrong things: she'd gone through Connie's closet and dresser drawers with no more than a stranger's notion of what she was looking for. What she found was a green satin bathrobe, all scallops and ruffles, that she'd given Connie for Christmas the year before. Hanging among the plain-cuffed cottons that Connie apparently preferred, it looked garish and silly, the kind of present you made jokes about. Faith took it anyway, because it was the only thing in the closet that looked familiar.

Stewart made jokes all the way up the stairs about brides and grooms as Connie hung grimly in his arms. Faith could see how mortified she was to be helpless, to be an invalid in someone else's house.

It has been only a few days now since Connie arrived, a fragile collection of bones and fiberglass and tape, and already Faith's house is transformed by the chaos she has always suspected of lurking just inside the lining of her life. For the first few hours she and her sons skulked along the stairs and in the hall, stumbling into each other, excusing themselves for taking up space. Things she used to be able to put her hands on turned up in foreign places, as if these alien presences — a sick relative and a visiting nurse — had invaded not only her consciousness but the inanimate soul of the house itself. She is a little surprised to see the same old rooms behind the front door when she comes in after work.

"How's Connie?" Faith asks Nancy, who is packing up her satchel of knitting. Nancy always leaves on the stroke of five.

"Just fine," she answers, showing her chicken teeth. "Not the ideal patient." Nancy said this yesterday and the day before.

Ben is sitting in the living room, changing the strings on his blue guitar. "I've been playing for her," he tells Faith.

Nancy gives Faith a smoldering look, then turns her gloomy gaze on Ben, his guitar, the lethal-looking amp on the floor next to the chair.

"Not too loud, I hope," Faith says.

Ben shakes his head, and the soft, sticking-up part of his hair trembles like some strange species of black milkweed. Since the first awkwardness of Connie's arrival, he's barely left the house except to go to school. It fills Faith to watch his fierce solicitude—taking plates in and out of the room, bringing home school yard riddles—part duty and part care, tenacious and somewhat perplexing. Whatever is going through him is, she believes, a kindness inherited from his father.

Chris, on the other hand, has turned out to be more like her than she thought: for the first time that she can remember, he has receded from the household. He stays late at basketball practice or at work, or else hides in his bedroom or at Tracy's house. He has eaten dinner there for several nights running, indifferent to the swell of well-wishers (his Fuller relatives, whom he loves) that troop into his own house daily, with casseroles and breads to stock Faith's freezer.

Nancy pulls a scrap of paper from the pocket of her uniform. She clears her throat. "A Stewart Hayden called. He's coming in Friday night, late, and will see you Saturday."

"I'd better get over to clean Connie's place," Faith says, half to herself.

"He said not to," Nancy tells her, and Faith gets the impression that she's being judged. " 'No cleaning' were his exact words."

Nancy is waiting for the stroke of five, and though she has only fifteen minutes left Faith decides not to dismiss her. Let her wait. Faith goes upstairs to check on Connie.

From the hall she hears a labored grunting, and at the door she stands watch, mesmerized by Connie's dogged concentration. She's out of bed, teetering on her one good foot, tapping her casts together like a seal on land, trying to catch the edge of the bedspread between them.

"You're supposed to be in bed," Faith says, moving toward her.

Connie looks wretched, angry, in pain. Her hair is plastered against her face in lank strands. She straightens up, teetering still, the green bathrobe shivering at the edges. Faith sees how wrong the bathrobe is, its frills and flutters hanging useless as dead leaves on Connie's slender, branchlike body.

Connie's lower lip pulls away from her teeth, quivering. "She

185

never does this right." Her voice is broken as static. It is a moment before Faith realizes she is crying. Connie beats her casts gently against the blankets, the full outlet of her frustration thwarted by the threat of pain. She cries out, a primitive mutter, then thumps her arms, two useless tubes, at the air.

Faith imagines herself like this, bound and helpless.

"I'll do it," Faith says. She tucks her arm around Connie's waist and helps her back into bed. She pulls off the bedspread, then lifts it like a magic cape, billowing it back down on her sister. She fixes it to the exact edge of the bed. "Like that?" she says.

Connie nods. She starts to wipe her tears and knocks her cheek with her right-hand cast. "Damn!" she says, and rocks her head back, her sweaty hair a blot against the clean pillow.

Faith gives the bedspread another yank. "There."

Connie lifts her head, examines the arrangement of blankets. "Thanks."

Faith sits on the edge of the bed.

"I miss my coma," Connie says.

Faith laughs a little, hoping this is a joke. "Ben says he's been playing for you."

Connie barely moves her head. She seems exhausted from the effort of crying, of standing up. "He's not bad, you know. He wants to be Isadora."

"I hope he's not a bother."

"He's an angel." Connie smiles. "You're so lucky."

At first, Faith can't place it. Something about Connie's face. She has watched this face for weeks now, against various pillows, and the face has changed somehow, in that slow way you recognize all at once. Her bruises are gone except for a mild, yellow-green disk lingering over one temple. The stitches on her forehead have disappeared, a small pink scar materialized in their place. After this healing, Faith expected to see Connie again, but this is not Connie: the darkened hair, the clipped, naked nails, the unprotected face, the eyes defined by nothing but their own color. The feathery eyebrows have grown in, and the lips are dry and peach-colored. What Faith begins to recognize is recognition itself, like the first time she saw her own face in the face of her sons. This is indeed Connie, but it is the Connie she has not looked upon for a long time. Stripped of her makeup, her work, her furious hurry, she looks no more than fourteen. Faith has not looked upon this face for more than twenty years.

"Faith," Connie says. She's whispering, looking into the bedspread.

"Yes?"

"I'd like a drink."

Faith stands up and pats the bedspread down. "You mean water, or apple juice or something?"

"No."

"You mean wine, scotch, something like that?"

"Yes."

"You're on medication."

"Please, Faith." Her eyes are glittering; she might be about to cry again.

"I'm supposed to be taking care of you. They said no alcohol. They even wrote it down."

"Please."

"You don't know how much you've been through."

"You don't know how much I want a drink."

They stare at each other a moment, then Connie backs down, a deeper shadow in the pillow.

"I'll get you some apple juice," Faith says, and turns from the room, the bed, her sister's need.

Downstairs it's five o'clock. Nancy waits by the door with her coat on, watching Joe and Chris come up the walk.

"I'm leaving," she says.

"See you," Faith says. And then: "When you do the bed, would you bring the spread up a few more inches? She likes it to be exactly even with the edge."

Nancy nods grimly. "You two are the limit," she says, then starts out, her galoshes slopping against the snow-damped porch steps. Joe says something to her as they pass on the walk, and Nancy smiles at him, her deep wrinkles jamming against the knitted border of a tied-too-tight pullover hat.

"You've certainly got *her* charmed," Faith says when he gets inside.

"Pity the woman," he says, smiling. "My God, working for Felix Unger and Felix Unger, what a fate." With a dish towel in each hand, he's holding an entire lasagna, another gift from the family. "Will and Sarah," he says, lifting it to show her.

Chris breezes past, wordless, his face ruddy but stern. Ben, who is still tinkering with his guitar strings, says something to his brother, and to Faith's surprise Chris snarls at him.

"'Scuse me for living," Ben says cheerfully, winding a tuning peg with renewed vigor.

"Hold it, pal," Joe says, but Chris ratchets himself past his father, throws his jacket over the newel post, and bolts up the stairs.

"Was that my son?" Faith says, looking up the stairs as if watching the plumy trail of the Roadrunner.

"Her Majesty probably broke up with him again," Ben offers from the living room. "It's either that or his shooting slump." Chris's sudden blackness has somehow made Ben lighter, as if the emotional content of the household ran on a careful ledger, a zero-sum.

"It's all this confusion," Faith mutters, heading into the kitchen for Connie's apple juice. "I thought he'd be better about all this." She pauses. "I suppose he had to figure it out sooner or later."

"Figure what out?" Joe says, setting the lasagna on the stove, removing his jacket, in for the evening.

She waves her hand upward, in the general direction of Connie's room. "That it's not all sing-alongs and holidays."

She senses Joe behind her, then feels his fingers around her elbow. "I think he already knows that," he says into her ear. "His father lives on the other side of the goddamned city." She whirls around to answer, or not answer, and finds Ben standing behind him, his newly strung guitar hung like a baby in his arms. On his face she sees a look she remembers. *Your father and I . . .* she had told him. *Honey, sometimes, even when two people love each other . . .* He had never fought it, neither of them had, they had just accepted the divorce as part of their life, a resignation that had rumbled in Faith's conscience like an aftershock ever since. She never expected them to be docile. By making it easy, they had made it hard.

"Ben?" she says, and Joe grimaces, turns around. "Will you tell Connie I'm on my way up?" Ben regards them suspiciously, then turns to go.

"I'm sorry," Joe says. "I didn't know he was standing there." He leans against the counter while she pours out some juice.

"I just don't like all these—these *people* in my house," she says. She picks up the juice, puts it back down.

He slides his arm around her, tugs her gently, until she lays her face against his shirt. "You're a trouper, Faith."

"I'm not. I'm just putting one foot in front of the other." She relaxes some against him. "Stewart's coming this Saturday."

"Where are you going to put him?"

"He can stay at Connie's." She sighs. "All these people. Greg and Amy were here most of last evening after you left. They brought *two* casseroles, for God's sake, and then stayed, thinking they were helping me, I guess."

Joe chuckles a little. "Brian and Maggie are coming tonight with Mom."

She pulls her head away, looking at him. "Your family is killing me with kindness."

"They're still your family, too."

"I hate making conversation. I just want to hide in a blanket. I don't want to see anybody else."

"Does that include me?"

"No," she says, and because it is not exactly she herself who has said it—rather some exhausted, stripped-away version of herself— she realizes how much she means it.

She relaxes against him once again, fixed in his warm hold. She wonders what others might think of these husbandly attentions in the wake of a divorce. To her they feel natural, and she knows now that Brenda was right: he never left her. They begin to drift into home talk: Ben's guitar-playing, Chris and Tracy.

"What's gotten into him lately?" she says suddenly. "He used to be so easygoing."

"Today's a car problem, Faith."

She closes her eyes. "Do I want to hear this?"

"Nope. He got back-ended by a pickup in the school parking lot."

189

"God, what next. Tell me no one was hurt."

"No one was even there. Some kid left his truck in neutral, and it rolled down the lot and hit the Corvair while Chris sat in some classroom solving for x."

Faith has always suspected cars of having secret lives outside of human sight, and now she knows. A thought strikes her. "Wait a minute, the engine's in the back."

"Right," Joe says grimly. "I haven't taken a look yet. Naturally the other kid is uninsured."

"Poor Chris." She's thinking of Joe's old car, her first ride in it. "He must be heartbroken."

"It feels like it happened to me," Joe says. "I told him I'd tow it back here with the truck tomorrow."

"You're going to fix it yourself, aren't you," she says.

"Probably. I'm a sucker for broken things."

She moves gently away from him. His arms hang like dead branches. "It's not your car, Joe."

"I know that."

"He should fix it himself."

"It'll take him forever."

Faith picks up the juice glass on the counter. "That's how long some things take." The single toll from Connie's bedside bell comes as a relief, for Faith is afraid of the web of Joe's arms, afraid of all it makes her want, all the possibilities for failed hope.

"Wait," he says.

"She doesn't ring unless she's desperate." She moves farther away.

"Faith, I want to come back."

"Don't, please," Faith whispers, her eyes cast down. He begins to set the table, readying the kitchen for dinner as if he had never left. Faith can't bear to watch, and retreats upstairs.

"I have to pee," Connie says from her bed. She is half in, half out, trying to right herself. Faith hurries over and catches her around the waist, setting down the glass with her free hand.

"I thought Ben was up here with you."

Connie hops down on her good foot and leans against Faith, her hard angles pressing into the soft spots on Faith's body. "I told the poor kid to take a break."

They hobble down the hall to the bathroom like one slow-moving creature. In the bathroom Faith props Connie against the wall and lowers the toilet seat. "I *tell* them and *tell* them," she sighs, then turns Connie around. Connie makes the effort to help, but her bound hands are useless as stumps; it is Faith who hikes up the nightgown, pulls down the panties, helps her onto the seat. She pulls a wad of tissue from the holder, and Connie bunches it between the tips of her fingers. Faith steps out to wait beside the door.

On the first day, they had concocted a bathroom routine that would cause the least embarrassment. Connie decided that once she was sitting she could, with effort, tend to herself and with her elbow reach the flush handle behind her. Faith would then return, lift her sister, pull up her underwear and help her stand — as she does now, squaring Connie under the arms as if they were about to have a dance. After a lifetime of not touching, there is suddenly nothing that doesn't require the laying on of hands. Faith knows the knobby wings of Connie's shoulder blades, the tender flesh of her upper arms, the pickets of her ribs, and the hard pucks of vertebrae stacked the length of her back. She knows the disappearing bruises on her face, the dwindling weight, the dry nails, the tiny slits in her earlobes that used to hold small, shiny earrings.

"Would you like me to wash your hair?"

Relief spreads over Connie's face, a buttery glow. "Nancy offered, but I'm so sick of strangers with their hands all over me."

Faith sizes up the tub, the sink. "We'll figure this out." She helps Connie sit on the floor at the side of the tub. Between Connie's neck and the rim of the tub Faith places a folded towel. "That's how they do it at the hairdresser's." She fishes a basin out from under the sink and fills it with warm water. "Tilt your head back," she says, then pours the water over Connie's hair, baptism-style, starting at the forehead.

"Ahh," Connie says.

As Faith's hands work around the hard ridges of her sister's scalp, she is visited by a dim remembrance, not of a time or place, but a *motion*, as if she had washed her sister's hair a thousand times. Perhaps it's the memory of her own hair, her own head, so like Connie's in texture and shape.

191

Faith sits back on her haunches, toweling Connie's wet head. "It feels good," Connie says. "Thanks." She pauses. "If I were in Paris my next stop would be the *bidet*."

Faith pauses. "I could give you a bath." Connie looks at the tub, her foot, her arms. "We can do it," Faith says.

They do. Faith helps Connie off with her clothes and sits her on the edge of the tub. After removing her own shoes and socks and rolling up her slacks, she steps into the water herself, locks her elbows under Connie's armpits, and slides her carefully backwards until Connie is sitting crossways in the tub, her feet dangling over the side, her back against the tiled wall, her arms uplifted, safe from the water. "Oh," Connie says. "Thank you. You can't imagine how good this feels."

Faith soaps a washcloth and begins to wash her sister, careful to avoid the casts. She washes her face, her neck, her back, gently, for there are tender spots, still, all over. She works her way down, looking discreetly away.

They say nothing to each other, do not look at each other, yet Faith's hands are sure, they do what they must, they are taking care in a way that seems to have nothing to do with her. Her fingers tingle with lost sensations: the soap-slicked surface of Delle's thrashing body; the peachy wet contours of her baby boys' scalps; the magnificent ridges of her new husband's back, hot soap bubbling between her hands and his skin. She has not felt or remembered these things since they happened, and recalls them now only as a curious drumming in her fingertips. Her hands drift easily over the bony contours of her sister's body, as if she had repeated these motions every day of her life, as if they were embedded deep in her muscle memory, as if she had an intimate acquaintance with the tender machinations of care.

TWO

THE CARDS CAME FIRST by the bunch, then by the handful, and now two days have gone by without a word from anyone but Stewart. She lies in bed, sits up, looks out the window, listens to the radio, but there is no escaping. She's stuck with her own company. Sometimes she presses her casts to her ears, hoping to hear the bones curing.

Because she can't bear to remember the crash or the people in it, because she can't bear the idea of moving ever again through a cabin full of unsuspecting faces, her thoughts careen far back, before her flying days. When Faith stops in to check on her, feed her, help her into the bathroom, Faith could be seven, or nine, or fourteen, the two of them fending for themselves again, defining a weird, wordless domesticity in the midst of chaos.

They are circling, circling, holding. It is all they have ever done.

When the present does show itself, it is defined by the walls of Faith's house, Faith's life. Connie watches her from the window, planted like a snowman in her yard, flanked by burlap-covered shrubs and flower beds, offering seeds to her restive birds. Where does it come from, this careful tending, this affection for the natural world?

Faith's care is something she did not expect, and yet every detail of it, every slip and hollow of its generous landscape, is familiar as a face. Faith's cool fingers, as she smoothes down the lotion Connie has crudely dolloped onto her own face, are fingers Connie knows. Her dainty tugs, as she coddles the clothing on and off Connie's body, feel practiced and reassuring. And though Connie sometimes

193

yearns to tear herself from her own body, to beat down the front door of her own apartment to be sure it is still there, when she's being ministered to by Faith there is no place else, no other time or inclination, there is simply a tending that she submits to.

But the other times. Alone with Nancy and the dog in the doldrums of a winter day, unwilling to ask for anything, give anything. She has thought of firing Nancy, of taking her chances waiting alone with the dog for the house to fill up, first with Ben home from school, then Faith home from work, then, later, Joe, with the wheelless Chris in tow from basketball practice; but she needs something besides her own confinement to arm herself against, and so she arms herself against Nancy, secretly enjoying the collusion this rebellion fosters between her and Faith.

Faith's care of her is larger than she expected. Joe's family marches in and out, by ones and twos, in predictable shifts throughout the week for short check-ins, like a platoon on maneuvers. Joe Senior, shy and rattled, has come once. Phoebe comes every day. She brings nail polish, magazines, sympathy. Connie remembers her amazement at the first glimpse of Joe's family, at a Sunday dinner so long ago. Their health and benevolence had been curiously forbidding then, but now, in her diminished state, she welcomes them. Joe's brothers, with their heavy shoulders and dark voices, arrive at the door of her room behind their wives, and Connie tells them she's better, and she is, for seeing them there, for these brief appearances that seem designed to show her simply that they exist.

Under the surface of all this care, two things fester.

One, Isadora has not called. Connie slides a little lower into the covers, listening to the quiet house, hoping that the phone will ring and it will be Isadora, out of breath and full of news. Faith placed a call to San Francisco on Connie's first day here, and Isadora had chattered about the show, the show, the show, a sprightly monologue. Since then, Connie has envisioned her baby sister singing in some rehearsal hall by day, riding the trolley with her leading man by night, telling him about her big sister, the one who survived a plane crash, the one who scared her half to death—to death!—by steeping herself in a twelve-day coma. But Isadora has not called.

Two, she wants a drink. Her insides feel scratched and burned.

At first she blamed this feeling on the crash, on thoughts of the crash, but in truth she remembers none of it. She remembers this feeling, though, and the swampiness inside her head, from the other times she stopped drinking just to make sure she could.

Because she wants a drink so badly, because she has so much time on her hands to consider *how* badly, she has thought of sending Ben—her newest friend—in a search through Faith's cupboards. This scheme, which she has very nearly carried out, shames her.

"Do you need anything?" Nancy asks, appearing at the door. Connie feels like the prized spectator in a box seat, watching a play in the hall, the same characters appearing and reappearing. Nancy is straight and starched as always, in the same costume right down to the white running shoes.

"No, thank you." Actually Connie wants urgently to pee, but the thought of Nancy's skeletal fingers peeling down the lace hem of her panties gives her a shudder. She'll wait for Faith. She'll hold out. She'll almost enjoy her discomfort, her stubbornness, for it will give her something to dwell on, a way to measure the rest of the afternoon. It's better than dwelling on her shriveling life.

She thinks of herself now as a thin pink shell. Her years of motion—the swirl of plane trips and colleagues and passers-by and lovers and, more lately, the brand-new sister—seem nothing more than a storm which had happened around her while her only true existence had lain the whole time in its motionless eye. Without the accouterments of her profession, her life came down to long talks with Stewart and twice-monthly dinners with Faith.

During her last days in the hospital, she'd had too much time to think. She knows now why they call it a "battery" of tests, for she had indeed felt battered. And the news was good. "I'm happy to report you've come through this as a reasonable facsimile of yourself," the doctor joked. She remembers the effort of smiling. "I was hoping I'd come through as a reasonable facsimile of someone else." She was only flirting a little, but now she wonders if the weakened speak the truth.

"I don't know why you're paying me," Nancy sighs. "You could train your sister's dog to pull your bedspread down." She glares accusingly at Sammy, who slumbers near the doorway, then she turns, exiting into the wings of the house.

Ben is home, late. Connie knows it even before the dog does, a certain shifting in the timbers of the house. She has lain so long in its shelter she could be part of it, a floorboard or stair tread, and knows its inhabitants the way the house must—their footfalls and handprints, how the door opens, hard or soft.

The dog lifts his head, rises from his late-afternoon torpor, and trots out. She hears his nails scrabbling on the stairs, the door opening (hard), the cheerful punctuations of Ben's voice.

He comes to her with a stack of coffee-table books, huge, colorful, one-subject tomes: wildflowers, birds, houses, and, inexplicably, a book on the first computers. "I got these from school," he tells her. A flame of self-consciousness rises red on his cheeks. "I wasn't sure about the birds." He opens one on her lap. "See? It won't fold up on you like those other books."

She laughs. "Ben, you're a genius." She looks at the books, at his own awkward tending, and puzzles over what he had assumed would interest her. He's over an hour later than usual; he must have taken a long time deciding. She taps her casts together and lifts a page with the tips of her fingers, gingerly turning over the leaf. "It works."

He runs his hand over his forehead the way his father does. She looks at the turned page, a photograph and description of a black-poll warbler. These are books he would have gotten for his mother. "Thanks, Ben."

He's bouncing on the balls of his feet. "I can't stay with you, Aunt Connie, I've got to get over to Rick's house." He thrusts his hands into his pockets and looks at her. "We're starting a band."

Connie grins. "Well, well. Another Spaulding in show biz."

"Don't tell Mom, okay?"

"I won't."

Thus confided in, she watches him go, then elbows the oversized, inappropriate book to one side and hobbles herself out of bed. She hops to the window, propped by her hip against the wall, to watch him trundle down the street with his guitar case swinging from one hand; the dog, tail similarly swaying, wends after him. Already the afternoon is waning, its wintry light low and gleamy on the drifts.

Back in bed she wrestles the book into her lap and, page by page, looks at the birds. She tries to see what Faith sees: their furlike feathers, perhaps, or their stripes and colors. She forgets her confinement, her stripped life, and concentrates on this gift from her nephew, liking it for his sake. She forgets that Nancy is in the house, forgets to count how long before Faith comes, forgets her full bladder. Her nephew's silly secret has left a sweet stain, and she regrets every moment of his life she so purposefully missed.

She took the boys for an afternoon once, an outing she'd offered in a fit of longing. The boys were just children then, and the sight of them together — dark and light, big and small — had filled her with the most inexplicable yearning. Joe had seized upon her offer, Joe the family man, the man of many relatives, and had foisted them on her that very day. She took them back to her apartment and recognized all at once her foolishness. She didn't know the first thing about children, for she herself had never been a child.

They rescued her, after a fashion. After an awkward hour in which the boys sauntered around the apartment, investigating her things, Chris engineered a complicated game of cops and robbers, thrusting Connie into the role of a helpless maiden who'd been tangled somehow in a bank robbery. She was never clear on whether she was a cop or a robber, but she dutifully repeated the lines the boys granted her as they walked her through this game with the plodding patience of caretakers with the afflicted. First you do this, Aunt Connie; then you do that. She hid behind her sofa as instructed; when they pretended to rescue or arrest her — she couldn't tell which — she squeaked *oh, oh* in a woeful monotone, catching the tolerant pity in her nephews' faces. The afternoon was a deep embarrassment, for it was she who played the child, the children playing wizened elders with all the answers.

Ben's small confidence has somehow restored her from that day.

By the time Faith comes home, helps her into the bathroom, brings a snack on a plate, Connie is restless again.

"Has Isadora called?" she asks.

The question makes Faith look tired. Her hair is gathered into a clip at the back of her neck, leaving her face vulnerable to its expressions. She sits on the edge of the bed. As she reaches to cut an apple into pieces, her sleeve rides up on her arm, revealing a small wrist with a sharp button of a wristbone. Connie wonders if to other people she and Faith look frail: though they are tall, like Isadora they are slender and small-boned.

"Did you hear me?" she says, chewing a piece of apple.

"She hasn't called, Connie."

"I just asked. Did you have a bad day?"

"It was good. He was running on time."

"Are you sick of me?"

"I'm sick of your asking if Isadora called."

Connie chews up another piece of apple, thumps her arm on the stack of books. "Ben brought these."

Faith looks them over. She smiles with recognition. "I hope he's not trying to turn you into me."

"Don't you think it's strange that she hasn't called?"

"No."

A swatch of cold, colorless light streaks through the curtain onto Faith's cheek, already fading as she sits there. Her skin brightens and pales at the same time. Her face becomes white, saltlike, rendering her immovable as Lot's wife.

"Do you think everything's all right?" Connie says.

"Yes."

Connie presses. What else is there for her to think about? Two hundred dead people? "I don't understand why she hasn't called. I hope nothing's happened."

Faith blinks, a statue blinking. "Don't worry about Isadora. We'll hear from her when she needs something."

She cuts the rest of the apple into small pieces that Connie manages to maneuver between her fingertips. For a while they sit in silence, the squish of apple between Connie's teeth the only sound.

Connie pushes the rest of the apple away. "Faith, give her a chance."

"To what?"

Connie sighs. "Are you doing this on purpose?"

"Look," Faith says. "I have nothing against her. I *like* her. I believe she's related to us. What more do you want?"

Connie looks away. "I don't know." But something.

Faith takes the plate with the remaining pieces of apple and plunks it unceremoniously on the bedside table. She stands up and looks toward the window, her yard, the street, and beyond that Connie can only guess. She seems to be searching for something. The light is draining rapidly in the way of winter, and Faith's rigid form darkens from the bottom up: her blue skirt deepens to gray, then the folds in her blouse blur into a murky wave, and finally the maddening secret of her face dissolves into shadow.

"Did she do something?" Connie asks. She wants to know and she doesn't. She understands, against her will, that Faith is fighting her out of kindness. "You said she was at my bedside, Faith. You said she was there around the clock."

"She was there. That doesn't make her a saint."

"Did I say she was a saint?"

"All right." Faith takes the plate and heads for the door.

"Wait a minute," Connie says. At the corner of her vision the picture book lies open, a magnificent photograph of birds in a nest, their beaks open, impossibly huge, bigger than their own heads. They look to her like her own life, her own gaping mouth. She filled it with food, wine, the tongues of men, her own bunched fist in her frightened nights. *I want, I want,* a small voice calls.

"I never said she was a saint," Connie says. "All I ever said was she's our sister." She sits up, scuffs her bare foot on the carpet just to feel herself moving. "God, I want a drink."

Faith waits, stolid and unhappy, staring at Connie's jittery foot. She could be nine years old, Connie thinks, mad at me for begging.

"Isadora would get me a drink. It's not so much to ask."

"Isadora isn't here, Connie."

"If she were here she'd get me a drink."

Their words are dropping like beads of hail. Faith's eyes are fixed on Connie's, like the stubborn little beams from the astro-phones that had to line up exactly.

"Isadora would do it," Connie repeats, amazed at herself, at her smallness. She could be five years old, she *wants* to be five years old, demanding what she needs.

It is suddenly dusk. Faith sets the plate on the dresser and presses both hands to her temples. "The things you want, Connie—they're always so impossible."

Connie reaches for the table lamp, the silly green scallops of her robe shimmying down the ridges of her cast, and tries to press the lamp on. She can't quite manage it. "Can you turn this on?" Connie says. She wants to see Faith's face. Faith doesn't move. "Faith, turn on the goddamned light." Faith steps back toward the door, flicks on the overhead light. It sounds like a snapshot and there they are, exposed.

"Was she really at my bedside?" Connie asks. "You said around the clock. Were you lying?"

Faith is squinting in the sudden light. "It wasn't exactly around the clock, now that you mention it."

"Just *tell* me."

"She left after two days, maybe three," Faith says. "She got tired of playing the grieving sister and went back to New York. I believe her exact words were 'the show must go on.' "

Connie can picture Isadora's leaving, the narrow shoulders turning away.

"I'm sorry," Faith says. "Really, Connie."

"Why did you lie?"

"I didn't have anything else to give you." She waits. "When she was there, she was wonderful. She talked to you incessantly, just the way the doctors said to. And then she left."

"Well," Connie says. "She had her commitments. I never expected her to drop her life for me."

"Yes you did."

Connie looks up, startled at the bitter tang in Faith's voice. "No I didn't," she insists, but she feels found out, caught at something not so much shameful as greedy.

"We thought you were dying," Faith says. Her voice is flat and tired.

All at once Connie is angry, angry to be trapped in the stingy silence of Faith's care while Isadora's generous voice gladdens the hearts of a pack of strangers in a theater 3,000 miles away.

"You want to hear something really funny?" Connie says. "I had myself believing you two *argued* about taking me in. That I had two sisters out there vying for the honor." She laughs, a small lonesome sound.

"No," Faith says. "Only one."

Connie sinks back on her pillow, crushed under the weight of disappointment. "I thought I finally had a real sister," she murmurs, then freezes, horrified, but it's too late, her words are zigzagging into the room like a let-go balloon.

Faith says nothing. A few strands of hair have come loose just at the hairline, the fine glinty strands left over from childhood.

"I didn't mean that the way it sounded," Connie says. "Faith, I'm sorry."

"You aren't going to get what you want from her, you know. I don't think either one of us was quite what she was hoping for."

"Faith, I didn't mean to hurt your feelings."

Faith looks fragile and ghostly beneath her undone hair. All this care has taken its toll. "I'm not hurt," she says. She turns to go.

"It's not the same for you, Faith. You have what you need."

Faith lingers at the door but does not turn around. It hurts to look at her.

"I need a drink."

Faith's shoulders drop. "No."

"Will it kill you to get me a drink?" She can only see Faith's back.

"You know who you sound like?" Faith says.

Connie's anger returns as a gulping want. "One drink, Faith. A glass of wine, anything."

She won't turn around. "Listen to yourself."

"Will it kill you?"

Finally Faith wheels around, her face crumpled with disgust. "You sound exactly like Delle."

Connie gasps. "Go to hell."

Faith snaps off the light, her voice cutting a bitter swath in the dark. "Just *listen.*"

"Faith!" Connie bellows into the room. She stumbles out of bed, sliding on the carpet and landing with a thud on her hip. "Ow! God-dammit! Faith!"

She hears the harsh whisper of clothing as Faith moves from the door, the furious lash of footsteps against the stairs, a rustle in the downstairs closet, then the languorous groan of the front door opening and closing. A gravelly crunch of snow under urgent foot-falls that shortly fade away.

Faith is gone. Connie squints into the dark, unable to move. Her foot cast is locked under the bottom edge of the bed, but in the dark she can't quite see it. She rotates her caught foot warily—her anger subsiding, fear surging into its place—until a twinge of pain lances her ankle, straight up through the knee. "Damn!" she mutters. She freezes, not daring to move. The dark is heavy and ominous, the outline of pleasant hunks of furniture gone gray and mean in the wake of Faith's flight.

"Faith!" Connie calls. The house answers, a mild soughing of tree against shingle. Connie drops against the carpet, the rough pile grinding against her cheek. "Faith!" She turns her foot again until the pain stops her. "Faaaith!" Her voice drops to a whisper. "Faith," she murmurs, then gives up and cries like a child.

THE SNOW IN FAITH'S YARD shines silver-blue from the lights of her neighbor's house. Faith does not know this neighbor, though he's lived next door since Ben was born. She waves to him when she drives by in the car or walks the dog, and he waves back. She has never stopped to talk. He has relatives—children and grandchil-dren, she surmises—who visit from time to time, and three or four cats that sleep inside the windows, draped over each other like a pile of clothes. He and Joe have spoken a bit over the years, about lawn mowers and garbage collection and storm windows, and sometimes she has stood by, watching these conversations with a polite smile. She would probably not recognize her neighbor if she ran into him, say, at the office or in a store. The thought fills her with an inexplica-ble dread.

She makes her way to the back yard, lit by the neighbor's rear windows. His entire house is lit, as if he lived there with dozens of people. He must be inside, alone with all those lights. She moves past Chris's car, its back end smashed into a fistlike shape. Though it roosts motionless in the quiet gleam, she gives it wide berth, half afraid it might start up on its own, a stark hiccup in the seamless air. Everything in and around this house today seems poised. Coiled.

Though it has been dark for fifteen minutes, maybe more, Faith thinks she hears the wisp of a chickadee in the branches. She stands still a moment, listening to the winter evening descending upon the neighborhood: the muffled hum of Brighton Avenue traffic a few blocks away, the distant voice of downtown, the faraway whine of a siren. In her head still reverberates the desperate call of her name from Connie's throat. Now she is sure she hears one lisping bird, a smudge of sound. She digs a finger into one of the feeder holes and scoops out a few seeds.

The chickadee is here, she can hear it. She isn't cold, though she shivers. A few striped seeds glint on her hand. Somewhere below this snow-packed ground, spring is already moving, its earthen scent somehow seeping up. She holds out her palm, out of habit, knowing it's past feeding time, when the lone bird swoops out of the dark and lands on her hand. She is so astonished, so thrilled by the pronged feet stabbing her skin, that she whips her hand away and the startled bird disappears into the night.

"Oh," Faith says aloud. Her fingers open, scattering the seeds over the luminous snow. "Oh," she says again. She's staring at her hand, seeing again the scattering of her fingers like the afterimage from a flash bulb. Not her fingers, though; the fingers she sees are pink and gnarled; and not seeds, but jacks, silver-colored jacks rolling off the tips of those fingers and spilling over the hardwood floor of an upstairs room of the house in Connecticut.

The hands must be her grandmother's. She thinks she remembers a ring, a gray braid, and perhaps a song. She bites down on her lip, staring into the snow for the lost seeds.

Suddenly cold, filled with remorse, she remembers Connie lying helpless in the guest room. She slips around the unlighted side of the house to avoid the specter of the damaged Corvair. The house is dark and lifeless. She hangs up her coat, removes her boots, tiptoes up the stairs, heart pounding, turning lights on ahead of her.

Connie is lying on the floor, facing the door. When Faith snaps on the light, Connie flinches, turning her face into the carpet. "I'm stuck," she says. Her voice is a soft croak, as if she has been hollering or crying for a long time.

Faith moves to Connie's side, drops to her knees, and cautiously extricates the cast from the underside of the bed. She's surprised how easy this is.

"Did you hurt yourself?" she asks.

"I don't think so," Connie says, her eyes cast down. "I didn't dare move."

Faith helps her up, front to front, Connie's chin knocking softly against Faith's jaw, their arms entwined, another dance. She sits Connie on the bed, removes the green robe, leaving her in one of the white cotton nightshirts Stewart had fetched from her apartment.

Connie no longer looks fourteen; she looks frail and tired and old.

"I'm really sorry," Faith says. She sits on the bed, nearly paralyzed with remorse.

Connie's breathing is slow and labored. She moves her arm, with heavy effort, and tucks a piece of Faith's skirt between her fingers. "If you weren't here, Faith, who would be?"

Faith stares ahead, into the room she once papered with the help of her new father-in-law. Her hope back then was for a changed and happy life. She senses Connie's upturned face, but can neither look at her nor answer her question. To look into those eyes now, to meet green with green, would be to look into her own howling core.

"Connie," she says. "I think I remember Grammy."

Connie shifts in the bed, but Faith still doesn't look at her.

"Did we play jacks?" Faith asks. "With silver jacks?"

Connie doesn't move. "I think so. Yes, I think we did."

"I remember her braid." She can barely hear herself. "And a ring."

"She was kind to us," Connie says.

Faith nods. "I remember that, too."

She gropes along the ridge of Connie's cast and finds the skinny, sticking-out fingers. She holds them. This is the best she can do.

VII

SILVER MOON

ONE

HER FINGERS HURT in certain weather and she has a slight limp when she is tired. These minor infirmities remind her not of the crash but of Faith's guest room, its furl of white curtains and the dapple of pink flowers on the walls. There are times, alone in her apartment, when she longs to retreat there, to give herself up again.

It is morning, spring, the blue sky and powder-puff clouds surreal as a stage set. Her table is laid out for breakfast, everything matched and proper. A spray of tulips from Faith's garden blooms in a vase, their colors so clamorous they almost have voices. On the window sill sits a sprig of leaf and stem in a pot, a piece of Faith's house that she brought back with her.

Stewart is late. He's due here with Adam, his new lover, a technician at Maine Medical whom he met in her days there. Adam is a nice man, intelligent and gracious, but to Connie his best virtue is keeping Stewart in Portland so much. He doesn't live far away, just a couple of blocks down Brighton Avenue, in fact.

She looks at the set table, the monstrously cheerful tulips, the days on land stretched out before her like a plain.

Stewart knocks jauntily on the door. He never uses the bell, a peculiarity of his, his notion that friends never ring, they knock, as if the door might open on its own for them. "Hi, neighbor," he says.

Adam comes in just behind him and they both follow her into the kitchen. "For our fair hostess," he says, presenting her with an expensive bottle of champagne that she has no intention of drinking. He's a beautiful mixture of obscure ethnic origins, small and wiry with dark skin, a lot of black hair, and pale hazel eyes. Exactly

207

Stewart's type, she thinks, mentally riffing through a deck of relationships, all failures in one way or another. Stewart could say the same of her, of course; they're always her type but they never work out. A petty forecast crosses her mind, a dim notion of Adam's fate.

"Thanks," she says, and puts the bottle in the refrigerator, out of her sight.

Stewart is poking around the apartment as if appraising it for a bank. "The place looks great, Connie," he calls from the living room. "The home of a woman on the mend." He wanders back into the kitchen. "Let's think of this as your welcome back party."

She smiles. "I feel good. It's about damn time."

After she returned from her convalescence at Faith's, AtlanticAir provided her with services she was hardly allowed to refuse. She sat through a mortifying four sessions of a crash survivors' group, most of whose members were already flying again. Healthy, was the implication. And yet she couldn't. They took a field trip into a grounded cabin but she couldn't even bring herself to leave the gate.

She drove four times to Boston for this so-called therapy, and stayed alone at Stewart's, for he was either in flight or in Portland with Adam. She could barely contain herself on the rides back, looking long before she ought to for the subtle jag of the Portland skyline. She would drive by Faith's house to make sure her car was in the driveway, then by Adam's to check for Stewart's car, counting heads the way she used to before takeoff. Thus reassured, she would finally go home, her thoughts fixed on sleep.

"So," Adam says. "What's next?"

Connie scans the counter: vegetables cut into frilly pieces, eggs set out and ready to be beaten.

Adam grins. "No, I mean what's next for *you*, after your accident and all."

Stewart wraps his arm around her. He fashions a microphone out of his free hand. "Adam, we prefer to think of it as Connie's learning experience." She laughs, but catches his eye: it could have been him. Now that she's all better he's spooked. His glibness is just his way of showing off for Adam.

Adam is chuckling now. "And what did you learn?"

Connie moves Stewart's fist and talks into it. "Adam, I learned

208

that I don't want to die. Not in this lifetime, anyway. Back to you, Stewart."

Stewart lets go of her, his smile gone. "You can't ground yourself forever, Connie." He turns to Adam. "Starting Monday she's going to be interviewing nineteen-year-old twits who want to be flight attendants—right here in Portland, Maine."

Adam raises his eyebrows. "Is that what they've got you doing?"

"It's where old flight attendants go to die." Stewart says. "Pardon the expression."

"It'll be a nice change."

"You'll be bored stiff."

"How do you know? Regular hours might do me some good." For weeks she watched Faith leave for work and come back, feed her dog and her kids, tend her birds, her house, her sister. She can imagine living that way, an ordinary life.

Stewart sits down at the table next to Adam. "I think she was at her sister's too long, staring at that pink wallpaper." He puts his fingers to his temples. "You should have seen it, Adam—billions and billions of flowers."

"Why do you put up with him?" Adam asks.

Connie looks straight at Stewart. "Because I've known him forever. Lucky for him, time counts for a lot." Then she blinks him away. "Anyway, things have worked out. AtlanticAir's been good to me."

"They should be," Adam says. "What's it been, twenty years?"

"Not quite. It only seems that long." She checks with Stewart for confirmation, but he's looking at Adam in a way that makes her feel a shade has been shut in her face.

After a moment, Stewart comes to. "So," he says. "You want my news?"

"What is it?" she asks, though she thinks she knows.

"I'm moving in with Adam."

Connie doesn't say anything, until it's too late for anybody to say anything without feeling awkward. Adam excuses himself and heads for the bathroom.

Stewart frowns. "What's with you?"

"Nothing," she says. "What happened to having babies and being a family, close as close?" She's appalled to be bringing this up now, a ludicrous idea in the first place, one she never considered for an instant. She still wouldn't, of course not, but she wants to be asked again.

"You were right, I was raving," he says. "Besides, first things first." She assumes he means Adam.

"And why did you bring champagne, for Christ's sake?"

"Adam bought it. I didn't have the heart to say anything."

"You two can drink it, then."

Stewart cups his hands under her elbows, a gesture she has always found endearing. Of all the men she has ever known, his affections touch her the most. "I thought you'd be happy for me."

She snakes her arms around his waist. "We can't both be happy at the same time," she says. "It's not allowed."

He laughs. "Does the world have rules?"

"Yes." She looks up. "You can love him all you want, Stewart, but you can't *like* him better than me."

He gives her a squeeze. "Not a chance, sweetheart."

She reaches down into their history, reeling back through her illness, his ghostly face next to Faith's at her bedside; back through endless conversations about their love lives or their families or their friends; back through their parallel careers, their gossip about the infuriating little soldiers in the New Guard; back through their first days of training when Stewart taught her how to pour a proper glass of wine, one of the many lessons of polite society she had never had occasion to learn.

"Do you miss Faith?" Stewart asks. "Is that it?"

She grimaces. "Maybe I do. Isn't that ridiculous?"

"You tell me."

"She was good to me, Stewart. Really, I couldn't have asked for more. But we're back to the same old silence. Nothing's changed."

"Nothing?"

She thinks a minute. "I can stop by without calling first."

"Well, there you go. Next thing you know you'll be borrowing each other's clothes."

She can't help smiling. Stewart knows her better than anybody, and sometimes she thinks of him as her real family. The only thing missing between them is blood.

210

Now THAT CONNIE'S BETTER, Isadora is calling again. As Stewart and Adam are drinking champagne in the kitchen by themselves, she calls from a hotel in Philadelphia, agonizing about the show.

"We can't get the music right, Connie. *Everyone's* an expert. The director's a maniac, Garrett's insufferable, and *nobody's* listening to me! Who's the musician in this crowd, I ask you? Everybody has two cents to put in, and believe me that's just about what it's worth." She groans. "*Especially* the critics—there must be a special place in hell for them, Connie, some extra-flamey corner where specially trained devils take turns pinching off pieces of skin." She's been talking so fast she has to gulp for breath. "In San Francisco they called the show *weird*. That's San Francisco, as in California? The weird capital of the universe? God help me, I swear. They hated it in Denver, too, even though they loved *me*. They said I was refreshing." Connie already knows this from the reviews Isadora has sent from each city, with certain sentences, and sometimes entire paragraphs, blacked out. Billy and Delle used to do this.

"Garrett keeps putting more and more of the original songs back in," she complains. "He's ruining the whole concept. Doesn't the poster say 'The Moon Is Blue'? Doesn't that mean blue as in *blues*? It's my professional *identity*, for God's sake, what does he think this is?"

"His show," Connie says. This all sounds wearily familiar.

"I can't sing that shit, Connie, that twitter-jitter shit, how does he expect me to keep from throwing up? God, what a mess. We won't have a show left by the time it gets to New York. *If* it gets to New York."

"It'll be all right, Isadora," Connie croons. She likes this part. "You'll be fine. You'll go to Broadway and be a big hit."

"You really think so?"

"It happened once, didn't it?" She pauses. "You can sing twitter-jitter as well as anyone. It's in your genes."

Isadora laughs, a spirited cackle over the phone line. "That's true. You know, I've had the feeling since the first rehearsal that Billy's somehow right beside me, his big hand resting on my shoulder."

Billy's hands were actually quite small for a man his height, small

211

and slim, delicate as a woman's. Connie doesn't answer. She's surprised to see she's willing to go only so far.

Isadora lets out a long sigh. "Anyway, how are *you?*"

"Me? I start my new job Monday."

"What new job?"

"Interviewing. I think I told you."

"Oh, right, right." Isadora groans. "I'm so *preoccupied*. Connie,
you wouldn't believe what this takes out of you."

"No."

"By the way, one of the reasons I called is—don't say no yet!—I
wondered if you might take Bob."

"Bob who?"

"My *cat*. Bob, you know Bob."

"Oh, the cat. Right."

"My roommates are threatening to turn him out on the *street*. He
misses me so much he's clawing all the furniture."

From what Connie remembers of Isadora's furniture, this doesn't
seem like much of a tragedy. She glances furtively at her own furniture, clean and white. "Gee, I . . ."

"He'll behave for you, I *know*," Isadora says. She's running out
of breath again. "He'll know we're sisters. You might as well be me,
as far as he's concerned. Cats are very sensitive to things like that."

"I'm sure they are, Isadora, but—"

"I'm not kidding. He'll pick up on your DNA or something. He'll
behave like an angel because he'll think I'm home."

"I don't know . . ." She does not want a cat.

"*Please* Connie, you can't imagine what I've been going through,
worrying about him all these weeks. After my mother died he was
my only family till I met you."

Connie already knows she won't repeat a word of this conversation to Faith. "How would I get him?" she asks.

"Oh, Connie, thank you! I'm having him shipped by plane. My
roommate Rosie will bring him to La Guardia and it's a direct flight
from there." She giggles. "I booked AtlanticAir." Connie laughs,
then stops when she realizes the arrangements are already made.

When she returns to Stewart and Adam they are getting ready to
leave. "What was that?" Stewart asks.

"I'm taking Isadcra's cat."

"Cats are evil."

Adam scrunches up his nose. "I hope it doesn't have claws."

All this sounds terribly ominous. She wonders if part of her new life is a willingness to be taken advantage of.

BY AFTERNOON the weather is almost unbearably beautiful. Connie decides to walk, something she has rarely done until recently, when both her physical therapist and the woman who ran the crash group suggested it. *Get out*, they had said, which Connie believes could mean a lot of things. She dutifully "gets out" because she wants to be all better and because she has nothing else to do. Being earthbound has startled her into the sudden recognition of how little she has filled her life with. Without a plane to catch she is bereft. She can't wait for Monday to come, to have a place to go.

Connie is wary of these walks, this acquaintance with springtime. They remind her of her thorough disconnection with the address on her driver's license. Though she has inhabited this city for years, she has never really lived here, has never strolled the mazelike neighborhood that starts at the back wall of her condominium complex. The houses are old, modest, and well kept, with porches and clipped lawns and elderly clumps of rhododendrons. The tipped-over tricycles and tethered dogs in many of the yards remind her of the unease of her childhood, her boundless wanting. She winds her way through the neat curving streets, heading away from the noise of Brighton Avenue, her sneakers padding against the road. Eventually she turns up at Faith's.

No one is home. Faith's house has the same domestic cast as the others, though the Corvair in the driveway, still unhealed, tempers the effect considerably. The front yard is wild with tulips. Connie moves to the back, under the bird feeders, wanting simply to stand on Faith's ground. Flower beds, black and furrowed, lie open like small graves. Near them, pots of frilly pink and yellow flowers sit on the grass. All through the back yard, in tidy clusters, shrubby plants of different sizes are sited like landmarks on a map, and she tries to remember whether or not they will eventually turn up with

213

flowers. She has never paid much attention and regrets now that she doesn't know what to anticipate.

Faith's yard reminds Connie of the way people in big houses sometimes arrange furniture. The bushes and flower beds and rectangles of winter-bleached grass make a careful, deliberate pattern that must be moved through in a certain, predetermined way. It would be impossible to run through this yard; Faith has created an ironic order out of wild, wild things. But it's early, Connie thinks; it could still snow, an ice-blue mantle spreading itself over the leafy shape of all this hope.

Connie gradually notices a high, incessant cheeping all through the trees next to the house. The birds are far from orderly, squabbling in loose bunches around the feeders, not seeming to mind her presence. She wonders if the birds think they know her, if they think she's the one who puts out their seeds, the one who stood here like a statue all winter trying to lure them to her hand. They become bolder, several at once now flying right past her. They think I'm Faith, she decides, pleasing herself with the notion. Perhaps she and Faith have a common scent detectable only by birds, or perhaps a similar way of standing, or breathing; or something less visible, a way of existing in the world, a vibration earned in the womb.

TWO

FAITH FEELS MORE COMFORTABLE behind her desk at Dr. Howe's than anyplace else. Except for time out for babies, she has worked here all of her adult life. Her desk has a long-lived look, though this is not the desk she began with. Her first desk was wooden, schoolish, with heavy drawers and thick feet, and still smelled faintly of pencil shavings. She liked that desk, and the history she imagined it possessed. The new one is sleek and trim, with niches and gullies for computer supplies. Still, it has the appearance of an old friend, for it hosts a framed photograph of Joe and the boys that Joe Senior once took at the beach; a clay turtle that Ben made for her in kindergarten and a wooden candleholder that Chris made for her in Boy Scouts; a stash of hard candies in a glass bowl; two African violets in small red pots; and in a vase one perfect pheasant feather she found eight years ago at the far end of her back yard.

The items on her desk and in the drawers could have been placed according to blueprints. Marion likes to tease her, but Faith doesn't mind; she likes knowing exactly where these things are: the beach stone on the top shelf of her desk hutch, a ceramic box for loose change. And for reasons she has yet to understand, she has for nearly twenty years kept an orange chip from the beak of one of the lawn ducks from her mother's trailer, hidden in a thumb-sized pillbox at the right rear corner of her desk.

It's closing time, her favorite time of day. Marion and Dr. Howe have gone home, leaving Faith here, musing at her desk. She looks around, at the neat stack of paper to tend to first thing on Monday, the watered plants, the put-away files and books. The rose-colored chairs in the waiting room are neatly pushed against the wall, the prints of flowers and birds shiny and silent in their frames. Lately the place has looked too tidy, even to her, at the end of the work week. Her own house looks this way since Connie left: its blissful order has the glossy look of a packed-up place, a place somebody is about to move away from.

It is six o'clock and still light. The days are getting longer, and Faith cheers herself with the thought of digging in her garden until after dusk. The boys are gone tonight, at a Celtics game in Boston with their uncle Brian, a playoff game, one of the last of the season. She pictures them all hollering together in the stands, punching one another on the arm.

When she steps into the crisp, blue evening, she discovers Joe's truck in the parking lot, Joe himself leaning against it, exactly the way he used to lean against the red Corvair to drive her home. This lonesome sight, instead of taking her back, takes her forward: she finds herself aching for something that has not yet happened.

His face is expectant but wary, as it has been for weeks. His having asked to come back looms above them like a lightning-struck tree about to fall.

"Hi, lady."

She smiles. "Hi."

"I came to ask you out for dinner." Deep lines have worked their way into his skin, and she notices for the first time a speckle of gray at his temples. It sometimes astonishes her that they could be any more than twenty. "Will you come out with me?" he asks. "I happen to know you're free."

"No," she says. "Let's go home." He opens the door. She gathers her skirt and slides across the seat as easily as an unrolling ribbon, as if she had been preparing for this very motion all day long.

THEY FACE EACH OTHER across the kitchen table. A swirl of steam billows out of their coffee cups, warm as the years between them now seem. They have been talking about the usual things, the family.

After they run out of talk, Joe says, "Do you think we just did the easiest thing?" By the time she realizes what he means, he speaks again. "I can't remember why we ever—looking at you now, I mean."

The room goes quiet, like twilight falling.

"It's funny," he continues, "but I don't think I've once in the last five years felt not married to you."

If pressed, she would have to admit the same. In some peculiar way she'd felt even more married after the divorce, as if divorce were nothing more than the second stage of marriage. They'd talked easier, somehow, divested of the burden of daily life.

"You know how I used to picture us?" she says softly.

"How?"

"Facing each other over a fence." She squints a little, trying to see it. "Your side was a big lawn party, a real bash, lots of music and kids and party hats and the volleyball net set up and the barbecue ready to go. 'Come on over,' you kept saying. 'Hurry up.'" He is listening, hard, so she goes on. "My side was just a yard. An ordinary square of grass with nobody in it but me. A few flowers, a couple of trees."

"Doesn't sound so bad," he says, his eyes steady on her.

She nods. "It was a hell of a party."

"I should have left you in your own yard." He looks weary. "Maybe we could've lived like that for a lifetime, Faith, just holding hands over a fence."

"Maybe." She rubs the spot on her hand where her wedding ring used to be. "I'm sorry I didn't talk to you more. I was sorry then."

"Talk to me now."

She looks up. "It had nothing to do with—that woman. You thought I couldn't forgive you, Joe, but it was myself I couldn't forgive, for knowing what was going to happen to us, for not having enough—enough faith—to stop it." Her voice coils into a near whisper. "When you told me about her, it was almost a relief. Finally you found the person you'd been hoping I might turn into."

"No," he says. He puts his hands out for her to hold. "It was you I wanted."

"I couldn't believe that." His fingers are dented and hard from years of making solid, identifiable objects. "I didn't have it in me to believe it."

"Why not?" he murmurs. "Why?"

"It was *you*, Joe," she says. "Who you were. Are." She shakes her head, astonished by regret, confounded by the same nameless sorrows she'd felt at Connie's bedside. "You and your traditions, your big heart, your perfect family."

"Faith—"

"I know. But it felt that way to me." She hears in her own voice something akin to awe. "From the first day I met you, I felt I'd been taken in, given safe harbor, a home. But it always felt temporary, no matter what you said, no matter how many times you said you loved me. At first I felt rescued, even whole—but as time went on, as I watched you with the family, with our sons, even with friends and neighbors, I came to understand how broken I was."

She falters now. Where is this torrent of words coming from? She is speaking of two people she hardly knows, people from long ago: one of them young and fearless, the other younger, and scared. Isn't she someone else now? Isn't he? Didn't she herself offer safe harbor, however temporary, to Connie after the crash?

Joe presses her fingers. "I'm still listening."

She keeps his hands. "When Chris was born I was terrified. I mean a real, physical terror, just like someone was chasing me with an ax. I was so sure I'd turn into Billy and Delle now that I had a baby. I wanted that baby, both babies, and I knew there would be nothing temporary about it. I'd have these sons all my life, yet I didn't have one thing of my own to give them, not one tradition, not one hunch or intuition I could trust." She is talking about her children but it's Connie who materializes in her mind, a two-year-old with grimy feet, tottering through the Connecticut house in a wet diaper.

"You carried them around for months, Faith. They never cried. You were a beautiful mother. You *are*."

"I was watching you the whole time, how you did it. How your instincts worked." Felled by these memories, she draws her hands away, hiding her face. "I had no instincts," she says, her voice wavering. "Joe, I was so lonely."

She hears the scrape of his chair, his step, the rustle of his shirt when he reaches for her. She rises, presses herself to him and runs her fingers through the gray part of his hair, along the creases near his eyes, as if she were blind.

His voice drifts out of the silence. "Instinct is *all* you had," he says. "It's what I loved most about you. You knew when it was going to *rain*. You were up ten minutes before Ben woke with a nightmare." The hall clock sounds behind them, a lonesome tolling. "Listen to me, Faith. You don't escape from a family like mine without a written prescription for how your life is going to go. If Plan A doesn't work—say your brother gets killed in Vietnam—then Plan B kicks in. And then there's a Plan C, and D, and forever."

She smiles, remembering. "Always another rabbit in the hat."

"That's right," he says. "It doesn't leave much room for following your nose." He stands away, still touching her, his hands cupped over her shoulders. "Faith, everything I am was *given* to me. But you were different, you had to make it up as you went along." His fingers tighten on her. "Can't you see why you fascinated me? Why you still do? I was supposed to marry somebody like Maggie or Sarah or Amy. A woman like you was definitely not in the plan."

"I didn't exactly fit." She's thinking of her first time at his house, the barrage of questions.

"No," he says, moving to hold her again. "You were a *good* thing. It was my mistake, trying to make you fit." It seems to Faith a long, long time since he has looked so calm, so willing to understand her. He bends his head, holding her, his voice low in her ear. "Faith, you're the only mystery in my life. Listen. This is instinct talking. I need you. I do."

When she kisses him it feels exactly like old times, the oldest times, before their babies, before their wedding, when Joseph Fuller Junior had startled her out of the coma that had been her growing up. She had been moved by him once, had given in to love with imaginary angels smiling over her bed; she had given in and stayed happy as long as she could stand it. Happiness had been such terrible work; there was so much you had to pay attention to. It seems to her now, moving up the stairs of the only place she has ever called home, that she needn't have tried so hard. Can she not, after all these years, understand how his world works, his capacity for care, his belief in love?

At the door of her room, their old room, Joe stops, bringing his arms around her. The years are falling from her like feathers, her lips touching the weary lines of Joseph Fuller Junior's face.

She wishes she could have it back now, their first time, knowing what would come later. Good things: two sons, well-lighted holidays, a home of their own. He crushes her against his chest and her breath comes out as a cry.

"Did I hurt you?" His hair is sticking up like Ben's.

"No." She hugs him. "No."

Their bed is still covered by the quilt she once tore from it. Joe sits on it, pulling her down next to him. He unbuttons her shirt and slips it from her shoulders.

"Joe," she says, suddenly shy.

He runs his hands over her skin. "I love you."

She crosses her arms, gathering her shirt at her chest.

"Faith?"

She gets up and wanders to the other side of the bed, a safe distance away. "This isn't just for now, is it?" she says. "It's not just tonight? Joe, I don't think I can turn back from here."

His eyes are locked on her as if she might disappear. "I *know* I can't," he whispers. She can see that he loves her, she has always seen it; she has only to believe it.

"What I mean is," she says, "I'm still me."

"I'm counting on it."

She closes her eyes, not believing how she feels. There is nothing now but this room, this bed, this sweet man.

"Joe," she says. "Can you hear my heart?"

He tears back the quilt, his eyes bright with desire. "I hear it." The way he is looking at her makes her feel beautiful.

They stare at each other from opposite sides of the bed as the haze of years between them dissolves into this one clear moment. Everything stops. She waits, looking at him through layers of hope and memory, until, after a lifetime of standing still, she is the first one to move.

THREE

IF DIVORCE IS the second stage of marriage, peace is the third. The days go by much as they always have, except that Joe is at the table every evening now and next to her in bed at night. She feels, God help her, like one of the peonies at the back of the yard, a big, ragged, hollering bloom. A simple living thing.

Through the kitchen window she watches Joe working alone on the Corvair that Chris has inexplicably left idle since winter. His stomach, once flat, softens at the middle, a tender ridge over his belt. It pleases her to see these gentle ravages of time. They have a history.

"Looks like slow going," she says to Chris, who sits at the table, sullen, turned away from the window. He still has his name tag, CHRIS, PRODUCE DEPT, pinned to his shirt. He looks pale and sleepless, and the green shadow of wet vegetables shows on his palms. "You could go out there and help him."

"Nah." He shrugs. "It was never really my car." He glances out the window. "He can have it."

"Bad day?" she asks him.

Chris shakes his head, rubbing the stains on his hands. Lately everything she says to him must be measured first by the teaspoon. It always amazed her that, through the transmutations of adolescence, he still liked her. Now she's not so sure.

"You've picked a fine time to turn into me," she says cheerfully, but he chooses not to hear her. Joe's coming back must surely please Chris (Ben, for his part, literally jumped for joy) but he seems bent on making them guess. His silence is eerie, and maddening. In the

221

balance that has always marked this household, they might be exchanging skins.

Outside she hears the clink-clink of Joe pawing through his socket set. She can see only the top of his head now, over the murky engine hold of the Corvair. Her eyes drift once again to Chris, who startles her by staring straight at her, his eyes just a faint wash of green in this light.

"Mom," he says. He takes a breath. "Tracy's pregnant."

Her mouth opens. "Oh my God."

"We're getting married."

A blizzard of ruined images falls before her. "Chris. Oh—" The table top seems to be turning under her hands; the floor shifts viciously. "Chris, you just turned eighteen."

He won't look at her. "Her mother said we can live in one of their apartments for a while. Rent free, while we get on our feet." Numb, Faith listens. "I figure I can work during the day and go to school at night."

"Chris. Honey, there must be some other—"

"No," he says. "No abortion. No adoption. This is my baby we're talking about, Mom."

She freezes, stunned into silence, as if caught in headlights. His eyes shine back at her, sincere and resolute. Helpless, she watches the baby who once frightened her witless make his final transformation into a man. "How long—"

"She's due in November."

"November." She tries to make the word mean something. This is June, his high school graduation days away. "How long have you known?"

"A while." He grimaces. "I didn't have the guts to tell you."

A grandchild.

She stands at the sink, drinking a glass of water. How did she get here? She finds her son standing near her and gathers him, big and loose-limbed, into her arms.

"Mom." She hears the gritted teeth. "I'm scared." She knows exactly how his life must look to him, a vast cavern with nothing in it but things he doesn't know. His big hands grip her around the waist and she thinks of those hands on a basketball, the graceful arc on release.

"You know a lot more than you think you do, Chris," she tells him. She pets his soft hair. "Believe it." He drapes his arms across the back of her shoulders. He is tall, but it's clear this time who is doing the holding. "When you were a baby I was scared to death," she tells him. "I thought the whole world knew a big secret." She presses on his back. "But there's no secret, honey. It's just one foot in front of the other, that's all it is."

"I'm sorry, Mom," he whispers. His need is a palpable thing.

By the time Joe comes in, wiping his hands on a rag, Chris is deep in his room and Faith has grown accustomed to the thought of a grandchild, even as she grieves for her son's lost chances. She imagines a little girl with her grandfather's black hair.

"Chris needs you," is all she says, and Joe disappears up the stairs.

She decides to give them time. She gazes out at the convalescing Corvair, its body repaired, parts of the engine still broken. The phone rings.

"Broadway, Broadway, here I come!"

Faith puts her fingers to her forehead. "Isadora, this isn't a good time."

"Didn't you hear me? Faith! August twenty-fifth at the Palace Theater. We did it!"

"That's great, Isadora. Congratulations."

"Will you come to the opening?"

"I—"

"August twenty-fifth, are you free?"

"Isadora, this isn't the best—"

"I need an answer. Connie won't fly, so I thought you could drive down together. All of you."

"I don't know. Ben has baseball camp that week."

"So?"

"Chris is working."

"You and Joe can come, then."

"We have to be around, Isadora. If we have to go get Ben, if something happens . . ."

"Then come alone. With Connie, I mean."

"Isadora, this really isn't a good—"

"Faith, you *have* to come."

Faith sighs.

"So you'll come? Faith, I don't have anybody else. Believe me, you find out who your friends are when you make it to the top."

"I'll think about it."

"Think hard, okay?"

After they hang up Faith goes upstairs. From Chris's room comes the chop of Joe's voice and Chris's stark retorts. She opens the door. They are facing each other, two men: their bodies rigid, planted, as if they'd each been struck. Joe turns to her.

"It's goddamned *raining* condoms in here and Tracy's pregnant."

"I know."

"He's goddamned eighteen years old."

"Shh. I know."

He turns back to his son. "Do you have any idea how much responsibility you're taking on here, pal?" His pupils are big and black. "Do you have any idea how much work, how much time, how much of your goddamned *soul* you're about to give over?"

"Joe—"

"A goddamned avalanche, that's how much. And sometimes no matter how hard you try, no matter how hard you work and pray, sometimes no matter what the goddamned hell you do, it doesn't *work*. Do you have any idea—"

"Shut up!" Chris says. His face is red and tight and shaking. "I haven't got a clue, are you happy now? I'm not like you, Dad, I don't have a fucking road map for everything!" He makes a sound, a deep, manly groan, and slams out of the room.

Joe sinks to the bed and slumps forward, elbows on knees, hands dangling like mittens on a string. Faith sits next to him and lays her arm across his shoulders. "You're missing a part," she tells him.

He closes his eyes, shaking his head gently. "What's that?"

"Sometimes no matter what the hell you do, it works out anyway."

He gropes for her hand. "Aw, Christ." He lies back on the bed, taking her with him. "I had such hopes for him."

"You still do," she says. "You know it."

They lie there, holding hands, staring up at the ceiling. It is marred by old tape marks from the days when Chris used to hang big, black posters of rock bands named after reptiles. Faith's first thought is to paint it over, a fresh white start. For whom? This room will soon be empty. Her hand is warm and moist where Joe holds it. She decides to leave the ceiling as it is, scars and all.

FOUR

ISADORA'S CAT has ripped the white chair, the one near the window, to smithereens. "No!" Connie yells, and swats the cat on the nose, but Bob doesn't flinch. He simply stares at her, a silent, smarmy, yellow-eyed pronouncement on her life.

Ben gives her pointers. "Pick him up like this, Aunt Connie," he says, showing her. He puts Bob down again, petting his brown head. "Now you."

She imitates him, scooping her hand under the cat's big feet, lifting him under the chest with the other. He stays in her arms.

"There," Ben says. "See?"

Ben has a way of surprising her with all kinds of knowledge. He has taken to stopping by for short visits, usually on his way home from somewhere: school, his friend Rick's house, or Phoebe and Joe Senior's, where he and Rick practice with their band in the garage. She's always glad to see him, and it seems he arrives each time with information of some kind: how many men on a hockey team, the difference between a country scale and a blues scale, Reggie Lewis's field goal percentage, how to pick up a cat. She listens to him, considering his company a gift she has done nothing to deserve but doesn't mind taking. After her long convalescence, Ben is her best sign of life.

"I wouldn't mind getting a cat," he says. "I think Mom and Dad are weakening." He says "Mom and Dad" with a certain intonation, a mixture of surprise and satisfaction that implies a mom and dad who sleep in the same bed.

"How's the band?" she asks.

226

He sits heavily on the ruined chair. "We sort of broke up." He sighs like an old man. "Nobody likes the blues."

Connie smiles. The broken-up band notwithstanding, Ben's body seems to pitch forward with the anticipation of a school year winding down, a summer ahead, the whirl of high school waiting beyond that. She envies him his forward motion, even though she likes her new job, its daily-ness, its distance from danger. At noon every day she leaves the office and walks to Monument Square, where she sits under Lady Victory with a sandwich and a couple of colleagues, watching the homey, noontime bustle. One of the women in the office also used to fly, and Connie thinks they might become friends. She feels young, but not in the way of the youngsters who come to her to be interviewed, their hair done in certain identical ways, a certain collective knowing in their carefully made-up eyes. She feels young in the way of a having a second chance, young in the way of learning a new neighborhood, young in the way of acquainting herself with the landmarks of life on the ground.

"How about I give you a ride home," she says to Ben. "I haven't seen your mother in a while."

They leave Bob to wreak havoc in private, closing the door on his willful face.

"Wanna hear a joke, Aunt Connie?" Ben asks as Connie pulls her car onto Brighton Avenue.

"I love your jokes."

"It's about the Patriots."

"Baseball, right?"

He looks to the car roof for mercy. "Scratch this one, Aunt Connie. Guaranteed you won't get it."

Connie reaches over and cuffs his hair. "You should've known better."

When they get to Faith's, the house is quiet except for the murmur of the television in the den. Faith appears in the hall when Ben calls out.

"Isadora's on TV," she says dryly.

"You're kidding!" Ben shouts, and races into the den. Faith follows him, and Connie follows Faith without a word. Chris and Tracy are sprawled on the rug, close to the screen. They look tragically young, Connie thinks, stripped of their adolescent hardiness. Ben stretches out next to them on his stomach, one fist tucked under his chin, the other arm slung over the dog.

Connie recognizes the show: "Heart to Heart," an entertainment program that comes on before the news: gossipy stories about TV and movie stars, and once a week a live interview with a New York stage actor to spruce up its image.

A statuesque brunette sits in one of those slate-blue interview swivel chairs, chatting with Isadora, who is perched in a matching chair that's too large for her. She's wearing a small black dress, the familiar glossies of *Silver Moon* spread out on her lap. Connie misses her. She hasn't seen her in months.

"What's—"

"Shh!" Ben says, without turning.

" . . . the same show where my mother met Billy Spaulding," Isadora is saying. "I can't tell you what a thrill it is to bring this show back, just the way it was." She looks directly at the brunette in a way the woman seems to find endearing. On television Isadora's eyes look unnaturally green.

"They've restored all the original songs," Faith whispers. "The moon is silver again."

"Isadora said that?" Connie whispers back.

Faith nods. "When all was said and done they couldn't bear to alter a classic." The corner of her mouth flickers in the blue light of the TV screen, and it takes Connie a minute to realize they're sharing a family joke. She remembers Billy and Delle, suddenly fired, lamenting their "classic" being ruined by Garrett and a new director and a brace of understudies who had the temerity to show up sober for every curtain.

The brunette swivels her chair toward the camera. "Theater buffs will remember him as one half of Billy and Delle Spaulding, the acting duo whose career was cut short by personal turmoil, alcohol, and premature death." She begins to quote from reviews of the original *Silver Moon*, asking Isadora how she thinks the revival will compare. Each snippet rustles in Connie some half-formed memory, and she can feel Faith tensing next to her. They could be standing

228

under a marquee somewhere, side by side and not touching, nine and eleven years old.

The camera flits back and forth from the interviewer to the interviewee. Something is happening in Isadora's face. Her eyes take on a ferocious wanting, her whole body seems to swell. Connie finds this physical attitude unsettling, for it is reminiscent of Billy and Delle at their worst, so stuffed with themselves she feared they might literally burst. Connie turns, begins to say something to Faith's implacable profile.

"Shhh!" comes a voice from the floor. Chris this time. "They're talking about you guys."

" . . . as if the fates brought you face to face with your heritage and your destiny at the same time," the woman says, tapping Isadora's wrist for emphasis.

"Wow," Chris murmurs. He moves even closer to Tracy.

Isadora lifts her eyes slowly. For the first time it crosses Connie's mind that Isadora can probably act.

Joe has slipped into the room. He smells of machinery, though he has shed his coveralls and his hands are more or less clean. He touches Connie's shoulder, whispers hello, then stands behind Faith, twining his arms around her waist. She tilts her head back and says something to him.

"Sh-shhhhh!"

"And then when I met my sisters, we *literally* fell into each other's arms and cried," Isadora is saying. Her fingers are moving like butterflies. "They'd been looking for me for *years*."

Ben and Chris turn as one face, their mouths half open, but before Connie or Faith can say anything they are all riveted back to the set by Isadora's voice.

"Billy told them about me the night he died." Isadora casts her eyes down. "It was just like he . . . knew . . . he wouldn't be coming back."

"Oh, for God's sake," Faith says.

The camera moves in tight on Isadora's face. "For some reason, though, he never told me about them."

"You *knew* him?" the interviewer asks, her eyes flickering over her notes.

"Oh, yes. It was a secret, of course. He used to call me a couple of times a week, at night." She smiles. "Sort of like tucking me in."

Tracy's head swivels back. "Is that true?"

"No," Connie says, bewildered. "She never even knew he existed."

"You can't imagine how I felt, finally meeting my sisters! To finally see them in person! It was like we'd known each other forever." Isadora touches the woman's hand. "We're *very* close."

"Well of *course*," the woman says, her hair swaying. "It's the most natural bond in the world."

"Exactly," Isadora says. "When I was laid up for a while over the winter with a broken leg, they took me in and nursed me back to health." A palpable silence descends upon the room. For a moment the sound blinks off, leaving Isadora's lips moving desperately. When it returns she's still going. ". . . while I was healing it gave me a chance to teach my nephew how to play blues guitar." The woman murmurs something, then Isadora plunges on. "Yes, oh my God, he's unbelievable. An absolute natural."

Chris howls with laughter.

"Shut up," Ben says, his face flaming.

"Save it, guys," Joe warns them.

"It's in the blood," Isadora says. She twists her hands together like a child. The camera holds her a moment, then closes in on the brunette.

"Thank you, Isadora James." She turns to the camera. "Isadora will appear later this summer in the Broadway revival of *Silver Moon*, a show that originated almost thirty years ago with her father, actor Billy Spaulding,"—she falters slightly—"the father she knew only as a voice on the line."

The show is over. As the credits roll, the camera lingers on a long shot of Isadora and her interviewer, just shadows now in a darkened studio.

Connie is afraid to look anywhere. On the floor Ben is sitting up, stunned as a bird that has just hit a window. Chris is whispering explanations to Tracy. Finally, Connie steals a look at Faith. She's leaning against Joe, who still holds her around the waist. Her fingers are gathered loosely over her mouth and her eyes are riveted to the screen as if she were watching one of her sons perform dismally in a big game.

Chris snaps off the television but the room does not come to life. Ben looks miserable, having been falsely exposed as an eighth-grade blues prodigy.

"She wasn't so far off about you, Ben," Connie says, but she sees that her lie is worse than Isadora's.

"None of your friends watch this, anyway," Chris says.

"How do you know?" Ben snarls.

Chris shrugs. He did his best.

"Let's get out of this room," Faith says. "Connie, are you staying for supper?"

"Thanks," Connie says quickly. She doesn't want to be anyplace else tonight, least of all alone in her apartment.

Faith turns politely to Tracy. "Tracy?"

"Gee . . . no, thanks," Tracy mumbles, as if aware of being caught inside some family business she's not quite ready for. "I have to get home," she says.

"Are you sure?"

Tracy nods. "I'll be back later."

She gets up quickly and Chris trails her to the door, where they kiss furtively for a few minutes before she leaves. A resigned look passes silently between Faith and Joe. He winks at Connie. "We're getting there," he says.

They all file into the kitchen, and the mechanism of dinnertime clacks into motion. Water hisses on the stove, the refrigerator groans open and closed. Ben is muttering to himself.

"Isadora only said that because she likes you, Ben," Faith says.

"Think if she *didn't*," he grunts. "Boy, can't she tell some whoppers."

"Remember when we first met her?" Chris says. "All that stuff she supposedly knew about baseball?"

"What about it?" Joe says.

Ben shakes his head. "She didn't know beans, Dad. She had the names all mixed up."

"I don't know what to say to her after this," Connie says.

231

Faith turns from the stove. "I don't think it makes much difference. She's not what I'd call a good listener."

Connie pauses. "I suppose not."

"Why'd she make up all those stories?" Ben asks.

"I don't know," Faith says. "At least she didn't mention us by name."

The phone rings.

"Hello," Faith says. She looks at Connie. "Yes, we saw it . . . No, Isadora, it's all right— No, I understa— Isadora, it's all—" She hands the receiver to Connie. "I'm sorry, she just exhausts me."

Connie takes the phone. Isadora is still talking. "Isadora, it's Connie."

"Connie! You're there, too? Did you see me on TV?"

"Yes. Where are you?"

"I'm standing right here in the studio. You should see this place! Listen, are you mad about what I said? The part about me and Billy, that's just publicity. Garrett thought of it, it wasn't my idea. Are you mad?"

"No. No harm done, I guess."

"I don't blame you if you're mad. I didn't even know what I was saying, it just came out on automatic."

"It's all right."

"Are you sure? Are you still coming to the opening?"

"I don't know about opening night. I'd rather wait until Faith can drive down with me."

"No! You have to come to the opening, Connie, both of you!" She pauses for breath. "You're mad, aren't you? It was the broken leg, wasn't it. Was that it?"

Connie closes her eyes. "Isadora, I'll call you back tonight."

"You're not mad?"

"No."

"Is Bob all right?"

"He's fine."

"Does he miss me?"

"I'm sure he does." How is she supposed to tell?

"Promise you're not mad?"

"Promise."

She hangs up to find everyone looking at her. She sits down. "Isadora thought we might be mad," she tells them.

They stay quiet, all of them, all through dinner. Down the street someone is calling a dog. The distant drone of a lawn mower drifts in and out of hearing. It seems to Connie they sit closer to the table than usual, and closer to each other. It seems to her they stay longer, and eat more heartily, as if to fortify themselves against Isadora's version of the truth.

FIVE

BOB HAS BEEN MISSING for a day and a half. First Connie looked around the tidy grounds of her condominium complex, under the boxy hedges and behind the dumpster, then along the white paths of gravel that connect the squares of rear patios. She enlisted Stewart and Adam, who made a grim pilgrimage to the frog pond at the center of the complex in case Bob had drowned. Ben checked both sides of Brighton Avenue in case Bob had gotten hit. Faith and Joe walked the length of their street and the curving roads leading back to Connie's in case Bob had gotten lost. Tracy drew a picture of Bob that Chris hung up at the Shop 'n' Save in case Bob had gotten far lost. Phoebe and Joe Senior stopped over to walk the complex again, check the hedges again, peer around patio fences again, in case Bob was just hiding.

But the cat is gone.

Connie wakes late on Sunday and in her bathrobe goes out to check around the door, the walk, the little bush at the foot of the lamppost. She slams back into the house and calls Stewart.

"He's still missing."

"Don't worry," Stewart says. "Cats always find their way back home."

A horrifying thought seizes her. "Oh my God, he's probably walking to Brooklyn."

"Take a bath, Connie. Drink some tea."

The knot keeps its grip on her stomach. "She'll never forgive me, Stewart." She fiddles with the broken screen on the window through

234

which Bob escaped, cringing at the ragged edges. Had he wanted out that badly?

"That's what she gets for palming the critter off in the first place," Stewart says.

"She loves that stupid cat, Stewart. 'How's Bob,' she asks me, the second I pick up the phone. She doesn't even say hello."

"Take a bath."

She laughs a little. It sounds like old times. "I'm going out to look. At least I won't be home if she calls."

Connie has gotten used to walking, and knows all the turns of the neighborhood now. She walks slowly, calling "Bob . . . Bob . . ." in a self-conscious stage whisper. She has no real thought of finding him; he has never been outside, either here or in Brooklyn.

"Lose your dog?" someone asks, an old man standing in his yard with a pair of pruning shears.

"Cat," she says. "Big brown cat, no tail."

"I'll let you know," he says, and she knows he will, for she sees him out in his yard every time she comes this way.

She trudges on, trying to appear nonchalant while she rubbernecks back yards and half-open garages, hoping to see a pair of haughty yellow eyes. Ahead of her looms the specter of loss: not of the cat, but of Isadora somehow. The creature entrusted to her has disappeared. She's not sure what the protocol is about losing your sister's cat. Say you're sorry? Buy a kitten? Say he turned up dead on the bedroom rug? In any case, she has bungled her sisterly duty. She stops calling for the cat and makes the rest of the circuit to Faith's house.

The front door is open. "Faith?" Connie calls, but no one answers. She sticks her head inside but the house is silent. She knows this silence, its hidden comforts.

"Faith?" she calls again. She mounts the stairs and spots the attic ladder hanging down like a prop in a funhouse. She hears a faint scuffing above her.

When Connie pokes her head through the opening, she has to blink back a gauzy beam of sunlight coming through the south window. Faith is there, her pink blouse the only identifiable color in the dusty, unpainted room. Among the ordinary odds and ends of a household stands an extraordinary object: a great, gilded traveling trunk with a rounded top, ornate as a treasure chest. Faith is on her knees, rummaging through it.

"I'm looking for something to give Chris," she says. "I thought the baby should have something."

Connie gazes into the trunk's vast opening. "I'd almost forgotten this thing existed." She remembers hauling it out of the trailer with the help of Faith's new family.

"He's been asking about Billy and Delle," Faith says. "His upcoming fatherhood has put all sorts of notions in his head. Not to mention Isadora's performance on that talk show." She grimaces. "Heritage and destiny are his new favorite words."

"Look at all this," Connie murmurs. Although Faith has already removed one layer of things and stacked them on the floor, the trunk is still full.

"I know. I can't imagine what he might want. I was hoping I'd find something of Grammy's in here."

Connie's mouth opens. A thought streaks across her consciousness like a riff of music. "It just dawned on me, Faith. This baby's going to make you a grandmother."

Faith laughs, her eyes crinkling at the corners. "How does 'Great Aunt Connie' sound to you?"

"It sounds old," she says, "but I guess I don't mind."

"God knows they aren't ready," Faith says, "but I can't help feeling happy." She begins to sift idly through the trunk. "I'd never mention this to Chris and Tracy, of course, but I feel like I've got some kind of claim on her."

"Her?"

"I'm hoping for a girl."

"A baby girl," Connie says. She crouches down to help Faith look for this baby girl's present. The backstage scent of costumes and old wood permeates the room, rising like steam from the heap of belongings. Connie watches Faith extract one item after another from the chest, stunned by the clarity with which they return to her.

Faith holds up a pink feather boa. "*Mister Mistake*," she says.

Connie nods. "That's the one that closed in Seattle. Aptly named, as I remember it." She pulls a red velveteen cape from underneath a nest of photographs. "This is from *Count Your Change*."

"*Smythe and Smythe*, the courtroom scene," Faith says, lifting a pink gavel and laying it on the floor.

"It was endless, wasn't it?" Connie says. "Always one more show." She picks up the yellow bowler hat from *Same Old Song* and plucks a thread off its rim. The hush of the attic settles like hands on her shoulders. She takes a stack of photographs from a fat envelope and lays them down, one on top of another, exchanging brief, wordless glances with her sister as the chameleons that were her parents mug and preen from old glossy squares.

On and on, through the layers of the great trunk: newspaper reviews with lines blacked out and superlatives underlined in red ink; playbills and smeared musical scores and parts of scripts and pressed roses and small props; dozens and dozens of photographs, most of them publicity shots, including the one Isadora presented a year ago in Armand's office, the gold heart laid flat against Marie Lazarro's chest.

"Look at this one," Faith says. She hands Connie another photograph. An ordinary snapshot, probably from Armand's camera, of Billy and Delle under the marquee of *Silver Moon*, their hands elegantly poised on the shoulders of two stiff little girls. Their frilly white dresses look foolish as frosting on their stalwart postures. They are already tall.

"There we are," Faith murmurs.

"We don't look very happy," Connie says. She stares into the picture, remembering that white dress, its prickly constrictions. Billy and Delle look shorter than she remembers, and not as mean. "I hated those dresses," she says. "Those stupid shoes. Even back then I knew a prop when I saw one." Faith's breath is cool on her neck as she leans in to see the picture again.

"We were sort of pretty, don't you think?" Faith says.

Connie places her hand on her heart, staring at the two little girls as if they were strangers she might once have tried to help. "But Faith, we were so unhappy."

Faith takes the photograph in both hands. "You wanted everything to be different," she says softly. She's holding the picture close

237

to her face, her head bent down, her voice a small and distant thing. "My God, you were heartbreaking." She seems to be speaking directly to the child in the photograph. "They should have named you Hope."

Connie hugs herself. "It feels like they're here."

Faith looks furtively around. "I don't believe in ghosts."

"I do," Connie says. "I believe in anything that can hurt me." A timid, curiously intimate smile from Faith, which Connie takes as understanding, calms her.

Faith sets the photograph down on the floor, so precisely that Connie realizes that she means to sort in earnest, to lay these things out as if laying out bones. Within a few minutes they have three careful piles: one for Chris, one for Ben, one for Isadora. Still no present for the baby.

"Do you want anything?" Faith asks.

"No." Connie looks at all they've unearthed and recognizes that she already has the only things she wants that are connected to Billy and Delle: Grammy Spaulding's lace doily, and Isadora.

Faith curls her fingers over the lip of the trunk. "I kept them from my children all their lives," she says. "Until Isadora showed up they never asked a single question."

"They had Phoebe and Joe Senior. Why would it even occur to them to ask about Billy and Delle?"

Faith looks up. "They had a right to know where they came from."

"They came from you, Faith. You and Joe. What more did they need to know?"

Connie waits, but Faith does not answer. Instead she is still, listening, waiting for more. Is this what it is to be sisters? Isadora never listens and Faith never talks—how can Connie figure out how it's supposed to go?

"You brought them luck, Faith," Connie says finally. "That's what I think. You've got two lucky boys." She falls silent herself now.

Faith smiles faintly, a thank you. "There's no harm in the truth, I guess," she says. She lifts the dog-eared remains of a written-over script from the depths of the trunk, yellow and sick-looking. "They were good actors. They sang like angels. Maybe the other things they were will eventually fade away."

They paw through more musty items—costumes and posters, even some pots of congealed greasepaint—until the trunk stands empty. Then they begin on the boxes. As Connie strips the tape from their tops, she remembers the vengeance with which she had once taped them shut, and her mother's dreary trailer reappears: the heavy, autographed pictures that once hung on its dim walls, the trophies and framed awards, trinkets large and small whose significance has long been lost. One by one she removes them, placing them on the floor with the rest.

They are done, sitting amidst the wreckage of cloth and paper and glass and wood, the leftovers of a life. The trunk and boxes stand empty. Stripped of their contents, they are no more than harmless empty spaces.

"Look at this," Faith says.

Connie looks up. Faith is holding a small marble box, the one that sat for years on Delle's dresser, the little gift from Helen Hayes that they had swept into the trunk on their last day in the trailer. The lid is flipped up, Faith staring hard into it. Connie leans over, peers in, and finds, pinned to a tiny satin cushion, two faded but unmistakable locks of hair: Billy's fine, golden blonde, and next to it Delle's chestnut-colored curl.

"Oh!" Connie shrinks from it, as startled as if she had just seen her parents' dead bodies.

Faith lowers the lid. "They thought they were so romantic." Her voice is bitter, but she lays the box down carefully, as if it contained a living thing.

"What should we do with it?" Connie says.

"Pretend it's not there." Faith pushes it a few feet away, its delicate legs scratching painfully against the floor.

Connie eyes the box for a few minutes to make sure it can't move, then she begins to riffle through some more photographs. At the edge of her vision she senses Faith moving once again through the piles, lingering over the ashes of their childhood; and at the center of her vision she sees herself, a little girl in a white dress with a terrible throbbing at her throat.

239

For a long while there is no sound but the occasional click of an object being moved from one place to another. It is so quiet, Connie can hear Faith's breathing, and then the sudden change in it.

Faith's skin has gone dust-white. In her hands is a sheaf of papers she has taken from a large brown envelope. Something about them looks official and dangerous.

"What is it?" Connie asks.

"It's—" She takes a breath, and another. "It's a court document. State of Connecticut." Her lips form a thin line. "It's about us."

Faith holds out the papers, but Connie doesn't move. Whatever it is, she knows it can't be good. "Read it to me," she says.

Faith reads it over silently. "It's a petition," she says. Connie can almost see through her skin, the delicate network of veins pulsing beneath the white. "It's"— she is reading directly now—"a release of parental rights." She doesn't look up. Her eyes are huge with wonder, translucent as sea glass. "A bunch of forswears and whereases, but the gist of it is that Grammy Spaulding was planning to adopt us."

Her heart thundering in her ears, Connie takes the document from Faith. "Faith Spaulding, age three years, seven months," she reads. "Constance Spaulding, age twenty-six months." She looks up. "It's dated August."

"Grammy died in October, two months later."

Connie scans the second page, the third, unwilling to make the words mean what she knows they mean. The fourth page is decorated by the exuberant signatures of Billy and Delle Spaulding, the prim hand of Mary Elizabeth Spaulding, and another name, equally familiar.

"Faith," Connie says. "The lawyer of record—"

"I saw it."

"Why didn't he tell us?"

"Would *you*? How would you tell two girls their parents tried to give them away?" Faith's voice is worn out. "How on earth would you tell somebody that?"

"You wouldn't," Connie says. "Armand especially wouldn't." She tosses the papers into the middle of Billy and Delle's things, half expecting them to ignite.

Faith is stone still, her hands loose and open in her lap. "I don't know why I'm finding this so hard to believe."

"All this—junk," Connie says. Her throat is a bunched fist. She moves to the trunk to make sure it's still empty. "That's it," she says, running her hand along the trunk's smooth sides. "Here's their whole life, and there's only one snapshot and that sickening document to prove we were ever born." She closes her eyes. "There's nothing here. Nothing. No birth announcements, no baby booties, none of those cards we used to make for them . . ." When she opens her eyes Faith is staring at her, steadfast as a statue, listening. "Where *are* we?" Connie demands, her voice thickening. "Where are the report cards, the school pictures? There's nothing here, not one stupid little kid treasure, not a goddamned stick man or paper doll, not one pot holder or paint-by-number, not one, couldn't they have saved just one goddamned fucking *anything* from their own kid?" Faith is moving toward her now, crawling over the bumpy dross of Billy and Delle's small, mean life, short cries escaping her lips. Connie's own voice is rising, sailing, a tether thrown loose at her throat. "It's all erased! It's like I never even existed! There's nothing here, Faith, nothing! Why didn't you *help* me? Why didn't you *help* me?"

Connie is shrieking now, crying, the room is tilting, her fingers are caught in the collar of Faith's blouse. She can hear Faith calling to her, can see her mouth opening and closing, her hair flying out from the sides of her face, all of this a blur as she twines her fingers through Faith's buttonholes and pulls hard, tries to shake her, make her answer in words she can understand, until she does understand, "It's all right, it's all right," Faith is saying, and "Shhh, stop now, stop now," the words forming like bubbles in the air, but Connie can't stop, she's pushing Faith away, fighting her sorry comfort, until she feels herself reeling forward, feels Faith pulling her in, her strength a shock, her body warm and enveloping, shuddering against her, holding on until Connie is finally still.

The house settles.

"Look at me," Faith says quietly. Connie lifts her head. "I was just a little girl. I couldn't save you any better than I could save myself."

Connie nods, her face hot and wet. Faith's blouse is torn at the neck, exposing a delicate collarbone and its deep hollow, one more way they look alike. Faith loosens her hold and slides her hands down to Connie's wrists, gathering them. "It's not erased," she says, "not for me, not as long as I can look at you." Thin tears run down her cheeks. "You're my proof, Connie. You were there. God knows they were miserable years, but imagine if we'd each been there alone."

Connie looks away, her wrists warming where Faith holds them. "Sometimes I think we *were* there alone, nothing more to do with each other than two little hamsters in a cage."

Faith drags her palms over her wet cheeks. "But Connie, imagine being *one* little hamster in a cage."

All at once, the memory of a high-up room: a hotel room, with flimsy carpets and vinyl chairs and a strange city throbbing outside the windows. Connie tries to picture this room without Faith in it—Faith, slung over the couch reading a book, or standing by the window gazing into the street, or examining the directions for a toy from Armand. She sees herself alone with the avocado drapes, the pale food from the next-door restaurant, the paintings of daisies, the sounds in the hall. For a moment she longs to go all the way back there, to feel herself a child again with a sister who accompanied her, silent but steadfast, through the steely corridor of childhood; she longs to go back for the click of time it would take to thank Faith for existing. For bearing witness.

Exhausted, she slides into Faith's lap, soothed by the gentle pressure of her sister's cool hand on her forehead. "Faith," she murmurs. "You're my one decent memory." Within her reach lies the marble box. She tucks it into her hand and brings it close, cuddling it like a doll to her chest.

It is a long time before she speaks again. The room has fallen utterly silent, their shadows have shortened with midday. She thinks she might have slept some, but her hand is still curled around the box, and Faith is still holding her.

Connie blinks in the sun streaking in at a new angle. "Faith, how old was Grammy?"

"I don't know. About sixty, I'd guess. Sixty-five, maybe."

"Can you imagine a sixty-five-year-old woman wanting to adopt two babies?"

"No." Faith shifts position, stretching one leg out, the scent of laundry soap whiffing off the sleeve of her blouse. "I'm not even sure it was legal."

"Probably Armand got around it somehow."

"It might not have gone through anyway," Faith says. "When all was said and done."

"Maybe not." Connie slides her finger over the sleek marble surface of the box, damp from her grip. "But she must have wanted us." She turns her head, looks up into Faith's green eyes. "She must have really, really wanted us."

"That's just what I was thinking," Faith says. She shifts her leg again.

"Are you stiff?"

"It's all right."

"I'm sorry I tore your blouse."

"It's just a blouse."

"We didn't find anything for the baby."

"No, we didn't," Faith says. "I guess I'll have to give her something of mine."

Connie has lain in Faith's lap a long time by now, but she can't bear to move. Their touching seems like the most natural thing in the world, less a touching than a fitting together, as though, stationed among the ruins of their parents' life, they could be two parts of the same person.

IT IS MID-AFTERNOON by the time they get into the car. Faith steers them out of town, into the country. The midsummer flowers that Faith would know all the names of fly by outside the open windows in a violent streak of color.

"Faith, what are you doing?"

Her profile is serene. "I'm helping you."

Connie decides not to ask anything else. She settles back in her seat, content to trust that Faith is telling the truth. A few more miles churn behind them. The shell inlay of the marble box on the seat between them shoots sunlight back through the windshield as the city disappears from view.

"Did you ever find the cat?" Faith asks.

Connie grimaces. "No. She'll never forgive me, Faith."

"She'll forgive you," Faith says. "What choice does she have?"

The rural scent of distant barns begins to waft through the windows. They pass Fuller Machine Company, a forlorn-looking outpost with its Sunday-empty lot. The trees come thicker on the side of the road. Faith slows the car and turns into a wide dirt path, deeply rutted, steaming with dust. She rolls up her window. "We're almost there."

The path winds around a dense ridge of trees, and they bump over it for another few minutes before it opens into a summer field dotted with orange flowers.

Faith stops the car and looks out the window for a few minutes. Connie follows her gaze beyond the field into a grim stand of evergreens.

"I've always liked this place," Faith says. She opens the lid of the marble box and plucks the two locks of hair from the satin cushion. She works the hair into one thick piece, red and gold, then divides it. Connie takes her half gravely, as if she's being given a medal. The hair feels raw, unseemly, in her hands. She can't remember touching this hair when it was alive.

They get out of the car. The grass is upright and waving, families of flowers poking up in random clumps. The burdensome odor of new growth comes to Connie in a sultry gust of wind, with the loftier scent of new leaves and the roiling ocean somewhere beyond the farthest trees.

"Joe and I saw a snowy owl here once," Faith says. "Right over there." Connie looks toward a snag in the middle of the field. "Listen," Faith says. Connie listens: a faint teeming of birds, high calls and warbles from deep within the trees. The hair pinched between her fingers begins to feel alive.

Faith lifts her tuft of hair. "It'll end up in a bird's nest," she says. "It's not exactly like throwing it away." She scans the trees as if she can see each bird, each nest. The field unrolls from all sides, the far trees dissolved into a downy wash of green.

244

"Say goodbye," Faith says gently. She backs into the breeze, tearing a few strands from the lock and letting go. Connie follows, walking next to her, shoulder to shoulder, strewing hair like petals in a wedding.

"Goodbye," Connie whispers. The strands flare briefly, then disappear, into air, grass, trees, seasons, time.

THEY DO NOT SPEAK at all on the ride home, but their hands lie next to each other on the seat. The sun is low but the sky is still light, and will be for some time.

When Faith eases the car into Connie's driveway, Connie doesn't move, not wanting to abandon her sister's company.

"Are you okay?" Faith says.

"I think so."

She moves her hand and Faith takes it up. "Good." Their fingers twine around each other, the same fingers.

Suddenly Faith laughs. "You've got company." Connie looks toward her front door, painted gray like all the other units in the complex. Plumped beneath it, with the self-possession of a visiting prince, sits a big brown cat.

"I don't believe it," Connie says. She slips out of the car and tiptoes down the walk, clucking softly, afraid of startling Bob into disappearing again. But the cat clearly has no such plan. He settles deeper into his own fur, plump as a tea cozy, staring. Connie reaches for him, picking him up exactly the way her nephew taught her.

"See?" she says, holding up the cat to Faith like a sign: this remarkable animal who, having never once seen this place from the outside, somehow found the way home.

VIII

OPENING NIGHT

IT IS A NIGHT like so many she remembers, the marquee lit up like a merry-go-round, a whirl of showy dresses sweeping through the theater doors. Armand is waiting just inside, fussily dressed—for *them*, Faith is pleased to recognize—in a silk suit with a hand-kerchief fluffed out of the breast pocket. Connie reaches him first, wending through the crowd easily from years of maneuvering through airports. Faith arrives in time to catch the powdery scent of Connie's perfume on Armand's wrinkled cheek.

"How was the drive?" he asks.

"It didn't seem long," Faith says. She glances at Connie, who raises her eyebrows good-naturedly. Seven hours in a car, miles of highway landscape, conversation patterned after the monks' in Ben's favorite joke. And yet she can see Connie agrees with her: It didn't seem long.

"Have you seen Isadora?" Connie asks.

"No," Armand says. "She had some notion it would be bad luck." He squints up at the ceiling. "It's crossed my mind that it might not be an altogether marvelous evening." He pauses. "Things in the air, you know. A few ghosts."

He looks different to Faith now—his Santa Claus face seems bur-dened by kindness, lined with a trail of wrongs he could not right. She pats his arm. "It's all right," she says. "Let's go in."

Armand shepherds them to the front row. Faith looks around self-consciously, suddenly aware of being gawked at.

"People are looking at us," she whispers to Connie. "Why on earth would anybody care?"

Connie turns her head, scanning the crowd. "Garrett must have put out the word."

Faith sighs. "God only knows what he said."

"Brace yourself, here he comes."

Faith is surprised to find Garrett so little changed. He's wearing a handsome tuxedo that doesn't quite fit. He kisses her hand, his thin lips dry on her skin. She remembers suddenly that Billy used to kiss ladies' hands, an affectation he took on after playing an archduke.

"We've got a hit on our hands, friends," Garrett says to them. "A hit like you wouldn't believe."

"Is that so," Armand says genially.

"We got the last of the bugs worked out in Pittsburgh. It's a gold mine, mark my words."

"So marked."

"You ladies will want to pose for some shots backstage," Garrett says. "The three sisters and all that jazz." He moves his shoulders inside his tux and pulls down the sleeves. "The press is hot for it."

Faith blinks. "I don't think so."

"You'll change your mind," he says, rapping on her chair arm. "Enjoy!" The house lights begin to dim and he disappears into the hush of the crowd.

After a sluggish, meandering overture and the requisite applause, the curtain rises. The set is thrillingly huge, a seemingly endless expanse of sky and field. At the fading edge of the applause enters Isadora, stranded stage left in pink gingham, no bigger than a locust against these tricks of the eye, miles and miles of waving, sunglinted corn stalks. Already Faith can see that the show is a failure. Next to her Connie's breathing stutters, as if this recognition has passed like a current from one sister to the other.

Oblivious, Isadora propels herself through each scene, hurling her lines over the footlights as if she were begging for mercy. When the leading man appears out of the burnished corn rows—a dark-haired, six-foot bear of a boy—Isadora seems to shrink even further into the scenery, nothing but a husky voice to prove her presence. They look strange together, stranger still when they sing: the boy's notes float from his thick throat in a delicate, incongruous tenor, while Isadora's warm, whiskey-soaked tones give her farm girl a disquieting air of the street.

Faith can't bear to watch. She turns away, focusing instead on Connie, whose profile shimmers in the creamy light coming off the stage, her eyelashes casting a spidery shadow on her cheek.

"Faith," Connie whispers, staring straight ahead.

Faith turns back to the stage. "I know." She closes her eyes, letting the show wash over her—the familiar score, the remembered melodies, the flurry of dialogue. Listening, but not seeing, she allows herself to spiral back into time. Even then, *Silver Moon* was just another silly musical, yet Billy and Delle had possessed enough talent, heart—*something*—to transform it. She remembers their faces, ruddy with joy, singing their plain intentions, two kids trying to save the farm. How did they do it? From what pocket of their exhausted souls did they retrieve this sweetness, this simple yearning? She remembers watching in wonder, remembers her fleeting belief that these wholesome lovers were the real Billy and Delle.

It is possible to live an imagined life. This Faith knows. She begins to believe Billy and Delle could have had a cache of sweetness stored somewhere, held in reserve for their life on stage. And what might she herself have hidden, in her own reserves? *Willingness* is the word that comes to her; a virtue far short of courage, but, in the business of ordinary living, more practical. She holds to this thought, suddenly missing Joe.

The show is over. The audience, irritable from suffering ninety minutes with no intermission, offers a halfhearted rumble of applause. Isadora takes the final bow, a bouquet of roses bunched in her arms, her eyes flickering over the front row, full of questions. By the time the house lights begin to come up, most of the audience is already moving, gathering wraps and purses, a steady, querulous murmur circling through the rows. "Ill-bred bunch," Armand says. The curtain is not quite down, the house lights not quite up.

An instinct for escape seizes Faith as she looks frantically for the exits, but the doors are clogged with theatergoers making their way out. At the back of the crowd she spots two tiny women, each with identical rolls of silver-blue curls arranged like hats on their heads. They are ancient, stooped, obviously sisters, decrepit in exactly the same way, walking deliberately, cautiously, arms hooked together for purchase. Faith watches their slow progress, resisting the inclination to help them. All evening she's thought of nothing but thirty years past, yet here before her is a glimpse of thirty years hence. Two sisters left after a spate of sorrows, the inevitable string of losses: Phoebe and Joe Senior; Armand; one of the brothers, perhaps, or two; one of the wives, a child, a grandchild—all of this unthinkable, yet she thinks it—perhaps even Joe himself, or one of her own sons.

In this view of the future, she and Connie remain. She can imagine a front door, not the front door of the house she lives in now, but another house, one like the Connecticut house before her grandmother left it. She can imagine the doorstep of that house on an ordinary day, a visit from her sons and their children. They will be standing at the door in a cluster—Isadora is there, too, she's surprised to see—all of them holding something: a baby, a round of bread or some flowers, a birthday present. The sky will be streaming down on them, lighting the tops of their heads as they wait for Faith and Constance to open the door.

"Do you think we can do this?" Connie says. Faith turns, startled, and sees that Connie intends to go backstage. "She'll be looking for us, Faith. We have to go."

Armand hangs back, leaving it all to her. Faith lets out her breath. "We'll just tell her she was wonderful." All at once it seems easy. "We can say she lit up the stage."

Connie nods solemnly. "That's just what I was thinking."

Faith glances back at Armand. "You coming?"

He shakes his head. "I'm not a brave man."

"Wait for us, then," Faith says, and begins to move up the aisle, Connie at her elbow.

Backstage the air is sparked with a current of recrimination, but this is Broadway: the room is filling anyway, with cast members and friends from the new and original *Silver Moon*. To Faith some of these people look familiar, but she cannot recall what they might once have meant to her. She stands still, trying to orient herself to the blur of faces, feeling for the nearness of Connie, whose shoulder bumps against hers. She sights the yellow top of Isadora's head flitting through the crowd. "There you are!" Isadora calls, moving through the thicket of bodies.

Faith lifts her hand just as Connie lifts hers, in the same shallow arc. The gesture is involuntary, precise: an offering they are making together. Faith watches, fully present, as Isadora reaches for them, flattens herself against them, holding on as if they were the last living things.

The crowd presses in: warm, insistent, curious. Faith allows it, she is willing; the rush of voices wheels around her, a cloud of sound. Already she can see the way home, the seven-hour drive, the hushed capsule of space, the peaceful drone of the engine, the quiet of Connie's company. Their silence is a mystery they need not solve. It is simply a way of being together, the way birds fall silent in autumn, their work done, nothing to do but leave one place for another. They lift themselves from the earth, their destination a secret they know without knowing, the blue distance before them a pure and perilous thing.

Secret Language

Monica Wood

A Reader's Guide

A Conversation with Monica Wood

Debra Spark *is the author of the novels* Coconuts for the Saint *and* The Ghost of Bridgetown. *She teaches fiction writing at Colby College and Warren Wilson College's MFA Program for Writers.*

Debra Spark: You dedicate this book, your first novel, to Anne Wood, your sister, and, you write in the dedication, your "guardian angel." I know that two of your siblings (a brother and a sister) are quite a bit older than you (and your other two siblings). Indeed, Anne was your high school English teacher. Can you tell me a bit about her and her influence on your writing?

Monica Wood: You just asked me about one of my favorite subjects! Anne *was* my high school English teacher. She was—and is—the center of our family.

Let me tell you a story about Anne, an emblematic story.

I grew up thinking I was some kind of child prodigy, and the evidence for this was some letters I wrote to Anne, when I was five or six years old, and she was in college. Over the years, Anne mentioned these letters as proof positive of my talents. Recently, I was going through my mother's cedar chest and found the letters. They said things like, "Hi, Anne. How are you? I am fine. I miss you." That was basically it. All of them were pretty much the same.

"Are these the letters you've been telling me about?" I asked her.

She said, "Oh, yes," all misty-eyed, and I'm saying, "Are these ALL the letters?" I kept hoping there was a secret stash somewhere.

DS: Could you tell me a bit more about the rest of your family?

MW: It's an Irish-Catholic mill family from Mexico, Maine. My grandfather, father, and brother worked all their lives in the paper mill. My father was born and raised on Prince Edward Island, and my mother's family also came from there, so there's a strong Canadian influence. For example, we didn't grow up with strong Maine accents—you can hear maritime Canada as much as western Maine in our speech. Also, my family is kind of unusual in that there are two generations of kids with the same parents. Anne and my brother Barry are fourteen and nineteen years older than Cathe, Betty, and me.

DS: One of the reasons I'm curious about your family has to do with what your novel seems to say about families, about how we are shaped—irrevocably—by who we come from. This seems as much an issue of nurture as nature, since Isadora has inherited so many traits from the father she never knew, and since both Faith and Connie have been damaged by their parents and saved—to a degree—by their childhood coping mechanisms which continue into adulthood.

MW: The central notion in *Secret Language* is that we're shaped more by shared experience than by blood. Isadora's never going to fit in the way she wants to, because she didn't share a childhood with Faith and Connie. They're going to take her in, but that's not the same as absorbing her into their experience. Not surprisingly, sibling dynamics have always fascinated me. For example, I love my older brother, but because he joined the air force the year I was born, I have a different relationship with him than with my sister Cathe, with whom I shared a bed for eighteen years. Because I never lived with my brother, he was always more of an uncle figure than a brother figure. He has children my age. On the other hand, because my brother and I are the musicians in the family, we share something unique.

DS: You strike me—you'll excuse me for being personal—as a very loving person.

MW: Oh, thank you.

DS: And yet your novel is about people who need to learn how to love, who can't quite articulate either their needs or their affections. I wondered where that came from, the interest in that subject.

MW: As I look at my work over time, I realize that a recurring theme for me is of replacing things that have been lost. People assemble families out of scraps sometimes, since everybody needs some kind of family. For some people, family is the family they were born into and never manage to shake. For others, it is a family that they later assemble. Or a work environment that is somewhat circumscribed.

DS: Connie creates a family with Stewart.

MW: And Isadora, who is trying to collect on something she thinks she missed out on. Life is a series of losses for everybody, and we just keep filling up holes as we get older. Some people have to start at a very early age.

DS: I happened to read your second novel, *My Only Story*, before I read your first novel, *Secret Language*. They're very different books, though I'm struck by one rather profound similarity. In both books, there is a woman who is an observer of a very connected, noisy family. In the case of *My Only Story*, it's Rita, the hairdresser/narrator who wants very much to claim the Dohertys as her own. In *Secret Language*, Faith marries into a family very much like the Dohertys, and yet she's overwhelmed by them. It all makes me think of the famous Tolstoy quote about how happy families are all alike, but unhappy families are each unhappy in their own special way. Do you agree with Tolstoy?

MW: Oh, no. I think happy families are happy in infinitely varied ways and that happy families are not happy all the time. Although I wouldn't want to write a novel in which a happy family takes center stage, I love them as a counterpoint or backdrop to the main character's struggle. A happy family can feel burdensome if you're not happy yourself. No matter who you are, you think of the world at some point in terms of insiders and outsiders, and people rarely cast themselves as insiders. Feeling like an outsider is a common human theme, and in my novels, it seems to show up in the guise of a big family that's hard to penetrate.

DS: I wonder if you could say something about your title. It refers, of course, to the secret language that Stewart mentions on p. 154, the supposed secret language that indicates the special understanding of siblings. It seems to me that many people in your book speak a secret language. Connie and Faith. Connie and Stewart. Even Billy and Delle, to a degree.

MW: My original title for this book was *Muscle Memory*. My editor said, "You can't call this book *Muscle Memory*. It's just stupid." But I actually think the original title describes some aspects of the novel more precisely than *Secret Language*. When you do something often enough for long enough, your muscle retains the motion. Emotionally, that's what Faith is up against; she's been closed off for so long it's almost impossible for her to exist any other way. But *Secret Language* is a decent title, too, because the notion of a secret language filters down to all the characters in one way or another. Joe and Faith have their married way of speaking long after the divorce; Connie and Stewart have the banter of exhausted singles on the prowl; Billy and Delle have their scripts and song lyrics—the only thing that seems to satisfy them at all.

DS: I read somewhere that you feel your fiction is getting more, rather than less, autobiographical, and yet I do notice a significant autobiographical detail in this novel. So let's talk birds, for just a second. Faith is an avid birder. She can even do that trick of getting a black-capped chickadee to land on her finger. I've seen your house. I've seen the bird feeders outside and all those ornithology books inside. So, first, a personal question. Can you do that chickadee trick?

MW: Yes.

DS: You can?

MW: I do it exactly the way I describe it in the book. The first time I did it I was in the woods in New Hampshire, on a beautiful fall day. This chickadee—well, they're fairly tame anyway, not that you can reach up and pluck them off a branch or anything—this chickadee perched just over my head and

I thought: "He's tame." I put up my hand and he landed briefly. I silently thanked the woman—I was sure it was a woman—who had tamed this guy at her feeder in Maine or Massachusetts or Quebec, who knows where.

DS: A simple read of the birds in your book would be that they demonstrate Faith's ability to love. She's sufficiently damaged by her parents that she can't articulate her emotions very well, even when Joe, her husband, needs her so desperately to *say* what she feels. But what else do you think Faith's birding reveals about her?

MW: Well, for her, I think all the birding—and the flowers that she tends and her house—exhibits her natural instinct for connection that has been blunted by other circumstances in her life. I don't want to get too heavily symbolic with the birds. They arrived in the book because I love birds. And they stayed in there because I wanted to give this poor woman something to animate her. After all, she's a tough character in a lot of ways.

DS: Three of your characters—Billy, Delle, and Isadora—are all performers. They are also narcissistic, rather manipulative people. Do they strike you as incapable of love?

MW: I think Billy and Delle really are. They're in love with the idea of themselves like . . . I hate to say it . . . a lot of people in that profession. They're also in love with the idea of themselves with two perfectly beautiful children. But I do have affection for them. They're talented. They're emotionally outsized. There's something perversely attractive about them. Isadora is a whole other problem, though. She's willing, she's capable, but she is also . . . to say self-involved would be putting it mildly. But she's not *just* a user. Her motivations are more complicated than that. There's something really appealing to her about having instant sisters.

DS: You're a singer yourself. Can you say a little about your performing experience? Is there a reason you never pursued a career more seriously?

MW: Well, let me tell you something . . . singing in bars at night gets old really fast. You're breathing smoke all night long. You're lugging equipment around. I did it for a few years. Now I don't really do much performing to speak of.

DS: For eight years, you were a high school guidance counselor. For me, some of your novel's most affecting material concerns the years when Faith and Connie are in high school, surviving as virtual orphans. I wonder if the characters of Faith and Connie were drawn from something you came to understand about adolescents when you were still working at Westbrook High School.

MW: I was still at Westbrook when I started the early versions of this book. Or it was right after I left. It's hard to remember how a book starts. One thing about being a high school guidance counselor is you see every kind of kid there is, and you see kids in groups, which is different from interacting with your own kid and your own kid's friends. You learn different things about kids' hungers and fears. I did have kids who seemed to have been born forty, like Faith. They broke my heart, but I admired them deeply. They were able to somehow manage in the most gruesome situations.

DS: Could you tell me a bit about the storytelling tradition in your own family?

MW: I learned early on that if you were going to tell a story, you had to do it in a certain way. It had to be suspenseful or funny or compelling or flat-out eye-popping or nobody would bother repeating it. When someone starts to tell a big story in my family, we all sigh, "Oh, here goes Mrs. McCarn," referring to one of the many Prince Edward Island eccentrics we grew up hearing about. Apparently this woman couldn't tell a story without grabbing a coat off a rack or a pan off the stove, roaming the room to act out all the parts. We make fun of this storytelling method, but we all do it. My mother was the champion, but my sister Cathe and brother Barry are right on her heels. They can tell a hell of a story.

DS: One thing I admire about your novel is how you handle time. Both how you move forward in time, and how you make time itself (memory and the past) part of your story. When I finished your novel, I thought of the optimistic Grace Paley quote about how characters should be allowed "the open destiny of life." I have a rather happy sense of what may happen next to your characters, though I realize there are questions left up in the air. Certainly your novel feels done, and yet I wouldn't mind re-meeting these characters in another novel or story. Have you ever felt tempted to go back to them? Or indeed to return to any of the characters in your finished work?

MW: Never Never. By the time I finish with a novel, I have spent so much time with these people that I love them dearly, but I never want to see them again.

DS: Your own formal education in writing was relatively brief—you attended a month's worth of writing workshops with George Garrett—and yet you yourself are a rather famous writing teacher in Maine. Your students speak of you with great affection and admiration, and you've written several books about writing. How does teaching writing influence your own writing?

MW: I love to teach writing, because it keeps me in mind of the fundamentals and reminds me what I know—and don't know—about craft. Just this morning I was struggling with a scene in a new novel, not getting what the scene was about, but stubbornly writing and writing, all this lyrical folderol. Then I asked myself how I'd advise a student in my situation. I ended up doing one of my favorite exercises: rewriting a scene using words of only one syllable. Once I dispensed with the fancy stuff, I got to the heart of something that had been bugging me for weeks. Teaching prevents me from getting overconfident about my abilities just because I'm experienced. Probably the opposite is true: The more experience you have the less you can rely on your past tricks.

Reading Group Questions and Topics for Discussion

1. When Faith remembers her wedding, she believes "that if she had only been able to warm herself, if she had only stayed inside her body as she pledged forever and true, she might have learned to live with a man like Joe, a man who loved her." What is Faith acknowledging about herself here? Does it seem like a fair self-assessment?

2. Why is it so hard for Faith to be part of her husband's family? After Joe confesses his affair, Faith speaks of an "unpleasant but strangely welcome feeling: her old, frozen self, finally delivered from the terrible trouble of love." Why is the feeling unpleasant? Why welcome? What has been troubling, for her, about the love that Joe—and the Fullers—seem to offer and, perhaps, demand?

3. What kind of mother is Faith? What kind of sister? What kind of wife? What kinds of love is she adept at? What kinds of love mystify her?

4. What characters seem to speak a "secret language" in this book?

5. Russian novelist Leo Tolstoy holds that art is the means of transferring feeling from one man's heart to another. Where does Wood best convey the feelings of her characters?

6. A pleasure of fiction: We can understand another person's version of the world, even if it isn't our own version of the world. When did you trust a character's version of the world, even if you didn't agree with it? Did you ever fail to trust a character's version of the world when you disagreed with it?

7. What does Isadora James mean to Connie? To Faith? How do you interpret Isadora's interest in finding her half-sisters and maintaining a relationship with them?

8. Faith and Connie are clearly damaged by their past. What, exactly, is it that they can't seem to escape about their past? Are they doomed to re-enact the past forever, or does the story suggest a way to move beyond childhood damage?

9. How would you describe Connie and Stewart's relationship?

10. Connie and Faith are very different people, yet Connie, too, struggles with love. What is hard for her about love? Faith, we know, fears love, as if it might kill her. Does Connie have a similar fear?

11. When Connie is in the hospital, Isadora whispers to Faith, "I wish I *had* to be here, Faith. Some burdens are good." Given Isadora's later behavior, it is hard to take this sentence at face value. Is Isadora in earnest? Does she seem to be speaking the truth, whether or not she means it?

12. *Secret Language* circles back to memories of Grammy (memories of Grammy's home start the book and memories of Grammy seem to resolve the sisters' altercation in Part VI) and to significant performances. (Part I ends with the line, "It is opening night," and Part VIII is titled "Opening Night.") Why does the novel circle back this way? What does the novel seem to be suggesting about memory and the influence of the past?

© Dan Abbott

About the Author

Monica Wood is the author of two other works of fiction, *Ernie's Ark* and *My Only Story*. Her short stories, some of which have been nominated for the National Magazine Awards, read on public radio, and awarded a Pushcart Prize, have been widely published and anthologized, most recently in *Glimmer Train*, *Confrontation*, *Manoa*, and *Best American Mystery Stories*. She is also the author of two books for writers, *The Pocket Muse* and *Description*. She can be reached at her Web site, www.monicawood.com.